Items should be returned on or before the last date
shown below. Items not already requested by oth
borrowers may be renewed in person, in wri[...]
telephone. To renew, please quote the [...]
barcode label. To renew online a P[...]
This can be requested at your [...]
Renew online @ **www.dublin[...]**
Fines charged for overdue items [...] ...ge
incurred in recovery. Damage to [...] ...ns will
be charged to the borrower.

Leabharlanna Poiblí Chathair Bhaile Átha Cliath
Dublin City Public Libraries

Baile Átha Cliath
Dublin City

Date Due	Date Due	Date Due
05. NOV 14.	28. MAR 15.	
3 0 MAR 2016		

Also by David Logan

Lost Christmas

The League of Sharks

THE NINE EMPERORS

DAVID LOGAN

Quercus

First published in Great Britain in 2014 by

Quercus Editions Ltd
55 Baker Street
7th Floor, South Block
London W1U 8EW

A CIP catalogue reference for this book is available
from the British Library

PAPERBACK ISBN 978 1 78087 579 8
EBOOK ISBN 978 1 78087 580 4

10 9 8 7 6 5 4 3 2 1

Printed and bound in Great Britain by Clays Ltd, St Ives plc.

In memory of
Veronica Leonie Mary Parr,
my lovely mum, who passed away
while I was writing this.

1

Junk Doyle watched as his hands disconnected from his wrists and flumped on to the table in front of him.

There was no blood. It was reasonable to expect blood but there was none. His hands lay there looking like a pair of dead spiders with an insufficient number of crooked legs sticking up in the air. Junk felt light-headed. Then one of his hands, the right one, twitched. A moment later, it jerked. Shortly after that it spasmed. Then suddenly it jumped up and stood upright. The index finger and the middle finger were acting as substitute legs. The thumb and little finger were arms hanging loosely by its sides. The third finger hid itself from view as best it could to aid Junk's hand in its effort to look like a little person standing there in front of him.

A small slit about a centimetre in length appeared about two-thirds of the way up the back of the hand. As Junk watched, it stretched, tore and repaired itself, taking on the aspects of a tiny mouth. It grinned and flexed and Junk saw two rows of crooked teeth. A tongue slithered out like a little pink maggot trying to feel the warmth of the sun. It moistened the newly created lips before darting back inside. Above it something small and spherical moved beneath the skin. Then another similar object appeared next to the first and the two small bumps pushed their way to the surface. They blinked. Eyes. They looked up at Junk. Junk looked back.

'You're probably thinking this is a bit odd,' said the mouth on the back of Junk's hand.

'Yeah,' said Junk. 'Odd sort of covers it.'

'Well, hold on to your hat. You ain't seen nothing yet,' said the small man that his hand had now become. He spoke with a curious accent. A slight Scots brogue with a sh sound on the s. Junk thought he recognized it.

'Are you doing a Sean Connery impression?' he asked. Junk was a big fan of James Bond. Had seen all the films numerous times and read the books at least three or four times each. *Moonraker* was his favourite book but his least favourite film.

'Maybe, maybe not. We'll see as we go.' It wasn't a good Sean Connery impression, but then, thought Junk, it was just a disembodied hand who had only had a mouth for less than a minute so he shouldn't be too critical.

'Simon, my dear boy, if you'd be so kind,' said the hand.

'Who's Simon?' asked Junk.

In answer, the other hand, the left one, Simon apparently, came to life, flipped over and scuttled, crab-like, over to the right hand where it flipped itself over once more and froze into a sort of throne-shaped pose. The hand-man settled himself down on it, crossing his index-finger leg over his middle-finger leg.

'Now then,' said the hand-man, 'I suppose you have questions.'

'Only a hundred or so,' said Junk. He looked around, only now taking time to study his surroundings. He was in a very dark room. There was light coming from above but he couldn't make out the source. It stayed obstinately just on the edge of his peripheral vision. The room felt small and restrictive though it was so dark he couldn't see the walls, ceiling or floor. The legs of the table, chair and his own feet dissolved into blackness. It felt as if the walls were within reach, but when he held out a stump, the tip was swallowed by watery shadow and didn't touch anything. He pulled his arm back and cradled the stump in his lap with the other stump. He focused his mind. 'Why are my hands talking to me?' he asked.

'Smart question,' said the hand-man, 'clever boy. Let me answer your question with a question: tell me, what do you remember?'

Junk closed his eyes and tried to think, tried to corral the many wild thoughts galloping across the open plains of his memory. But it was like the thoughts were made of smoke, and as he tried to gather them to him he only managed to waft them further away. He tried again, harder this time. He latched on to one thought as it passed. He remembered Lasel on the balcony of the hotel in Arrapia. He could remember the smell of her, and the

3

smell of her triggered more memories. He concentrated on her face and she became more solid and focused. Other memories surged towards him now, taking on substance as they approached. Garvan. First his jailor, then his friend. A Goliath of a man. His ancestors had been elephants in the same way that Junk's had been apes. Garvan stood four metres tall and almost as wide but not fat. Strong. Muscular. Powerful. Junk remembered the attack of the birdmen. Creatures that were an evolutionary midpoint between bird and man. Scrawny. Feral. He heard the guttural cries they made as they came for them, sounding like a didgeridoo:

*IwannagetinthereIwannariphimapart
IwannagetinthereIwannariphimapart.*

He remembered Dr Otravinicus. The little man. Devious. Self-serving. Had tried to steal the box from Junk. Got thrown through a portal for his duplicity. Spoke with a southern American accent straight out of *Huckleberry Finn*. An accent he picked up from a man calling himself Han Solo. Someone from Junk's time. A mystery to be solved.

He remembered the *Casabia*; a ship that runs on land and sea, with blood-red sails. Her disparate crew. Her captain, Hundrig. Larger than life. Hands the size of shovels. A round jelly belly like an inflated Santa.

He remembered the Brotherhood of the One True God, Pire. Monks. Holy men. Zealots. He remembered

4

the intense, torturous pain they inflicted upon him and he remembered the copper-coloured box they guarded so carefully and that he and Lasel stole.

He remembered Jacid Mestrowe and the League of Sharks. The stark, dusty compound they called home. He remembered the Twrisks. He remembered the physically superior Pallatans being overcome by their much smaller parasitical opponents. He remembered the screams and the fat little bodies, hollow and discarded.

And finally he remembered Ambeline. His sister. He remembered her face. All her faces. From squalling infant to feisty toddler to terrified six-year-old being carried away over Mestrowe's shoulder, screaming, reaching out to Junk to save her. For a long time he thought he had failed and that she was dead. Now he knew otherwise. Mestrowe had not murdered her but abducted her on the orders of the unknown Nine Emperors. Why? What did they want with her? Who were they? And where was she now? More mysteries to be solved. He needed answers. Direction. Help.

He remembered now. Remembered why he was here, in this room. Remembered what this room was. *Where* this room was.

They had left Cul Sita where the League of Sharks compound was, the four of them, five if one was to count Mestrowe and Payo as separate individuals, but of course they weren't. Not any more. Now they were something else. A new creature, more than the sum of each. Payo the parasite and Mestrowe the host. Payo the pilot and

Mestrowe the vehicle. Every day there was a noticeable change in them. Payo's sweet, happily inquisitive disposition was seeping into and infecting Mestrowe's suspicious, aggressive, ornery personality. The image of the big, angry Pallatan stopping to smell a flower or climb a tree was always a little amusing to Junk. Even if the idea of seeing his enemy in a more charitable light was difficult when he stopped to think about it. So he decided that the easiest thing to do was not to think too much.

The Nine Emperors had taken Ambeline. 'Fatoocha mammacoola charla,' Mestrowe had said to Junk the night he ripped Ambeline from her bed and changed the course of Junk's life forever. 'Fatoocha mammacoola charla – The Nine Emperors send their regards.'

The key to finding Ambeline was finding the Nine Emperors, so they had travelled through the Room of Doors to a pinprick of an island in the middle of the Glarn Arka Sea (what in Junk's day was the North Atlantic). Little more than a volcanic burp, the island was so small it had no name, which made getting there courtesy of the Gatekeeper a nerve-jangling business as they had to trust Mestrowe to guide them honestly. He did. Mestrowe explained that whenever he had worked for the Nine Emperors in the past he had been instructed by an intermediary. A man called Tolfke, whose face he had never seen. Tolfke always wore a mask, and Mestrowe understood that he had been horribly disfigured somehow.

In the past whenever he had been summoned to meet with Tolfke, he received instructions on where to find the entrance to the Room of Doors. He would go through and his course would already be mapped out for him. He would merely follow the illuminated path, step through the door at the other end and find the masked man waiting for him on this little island. He would be sitting in the shade of a clump of trees that were bent over severely, a casualty of their exposure to the harsh ocean winds. The only man-made structure on the island was here: a rickety old lean-to that housed two chairs and a table, all constructed in an exceedingly slapdash fashion. From the lean-to they could see nearly all of the island. Tolfke spoke H'rtu (the language of Mestrowe's people) fluently, though it was clear from his slight build that he wasn't Pallatan. He would give Mestrowe detailed instructions on what the Nine Emperors required him to do, his payment (the Nine Emperors always paid well) and then Mestrowe would leave. He would travel back the way he came, through the Room of Doors, and would follow another pre-decided (by Tolfke or someone else) route and carry out whatever task was required of him, without the slightest intentional deviation. Then, once done, he would follow the set path back home and wait until he was needed again.

That meant of course that once they all got to the tiny island the trail went cold. In the past Tolfke had always been there when Mestrowe arrived and would still be sitting at the lean-to when Mestrowe left. He knew nothing about the masked man or how to find him.

They would have been stumped then had it not been

7

for Lasel's keen powers of observation and her rather fortunate knowledge of nasal leeches. In certain parts of the world some people enjoy inserting small slug-like creatures, called flatoushes, into their nostrils, where the flatoush will crawl up deep into the nasal cavity, attach itself and feed off its host's blood. In return, they emit an intoxicating odour directly into the olfactory system. Flatoushes being greedy little parasites, they will gorge themselves over a period of several days until they burst from overindulgence. This leads to a sudden and rather dramatic outpouring of blood from the host's nose, and shortly after the carcass of the dead flatoush will slither out encased in mucus and yet more blood.

As Lasel described this practice, Junk was revolted but thought it was probably no more disgusting than certain practices in his time. He remembered seeing his paternal grandfather, Eugene, coughing up a yellow-brown ball of phlegm the size of a walnut, the result of smoking three packets of cigarettes a day. Grandpa Eugene died when Junk was eight and had lived the last four years of his life without a voice box of his own and instead had to rely on a strange electronic substitute that he pushed against his throat any time he wanted to speak.

Lasel had found several dried husks of flatoushes in various stages of dessication. Assuming Tolfke was the only person to come to this island regularly, then it was a safe bet that he was the one who liked to floushe, as the practice was known, and as a flatoush could be traced to its origin point easily enough by anyone who knew their markings, Lasel collected several of the curled dried balls that were once the blood-sucking nose-dwellers and they went back through the Room of Doors to Corraway, the Bartayan coastal town where Junk and Garvan had first met Lasel. There she knew a flatoush dealer who identified the dead leeches as being Cul Jjenian. It was a reasonable assumption then that Tolfke came from Cul Jjen, what in Junk's time had been the more southerly regions of the Arctic. A little voice in the far reaches of Junk's head was hollering for attention right about now, but Junk wasn't sure why. He knew there was something relevant that he was missing but he couldn't say what. He figured it would come to him in time.

While in Corraway, Garvan had spotted a stall in the marketplace that sold dried nolic petals. These were the same petals that Garvan had used to brew the hallucinogenic tea that had mapped out his journey from his home in Cantibea to the island where he netted Junk and from there to the Room of Doors, Cul Sita and beyond. It was unusual to find nolic petals in this part of the world so Garvan bought a small sachet.

Lasel had friends in Corraway and knew a place on the fringes of the town where they could spend the night. Her friends, musicians called Yartik and Huppa, were warm and hospitable. They cooked them all a hearty meal and played music around an open fire in the walled courtyard of their home. Garvan and Junk snuck off quietly together, leaving Payo–Mestrowe singing most enthusiastically of all, and Garvan brewed up a pot of tea from the nolic petals he had bought. As soon as he told Junk he had them, Junk was eager to try them. He wanted to see what would happen next. He wanted to know what the journey ahead had in store for him.

Garvan had steeped the dried petals in a small amount of water and then squeezed out as much of the liquid as he could before transferring the petals to a pot. Then he added boiling water, put on the lid and allowed it to sit for ten minutes. Junk and Garvan sat staring at the pot as it brewed, neither of them speaking, which made ten minutes seem like an interminably long time. Finally Garvan took the lid off the pot and inhaled deeply. The aroma made him jerk and cough and his eyelids fluttered. Then he poured out a small amount, no more than two mouthfuls, into a warm cup and passed it to Junk. Junk sniffed it. The smell was powerful, a mixture of rancid vegetables and rotten eggs, and he could feel almost every muscle in his body contracting for a split second and a wave of dizziness passed over him.

'Drink it back quickly,' said Garvan. 'Oh, and try not to throw up,' he added. Junk took a deep breath, held his nose and knocked back the hot, pungent liquid.

It had coated his tongue and throat in what felt like a carpet of tiny barbs and he could feel the heat flooding down to his belly. Very quickly he then started to feel drowsy. He closed his eyes briefly and when he opened them he was sitting in the small dark room watching his hands disconnect from his wrists and drop on to the deep-grained table in front of him.

2

Junk looked down at his hands. One with two small eyes and a mouth on the back sitting on the other, Simon, which was pretending to be a throne.

'This is a vision-quest dream thingy,' said Junk. That explained the hands. Bit of a relief really. 'Garvan never said my hands would talk to me.'

'He wouldn't necessarily know. The experience is different for everybody. Each person brings their own uniqueness with them.'

'Is that why you sound like Sean Connery?' asked Junk. 'Because it's something I know, something I'm bringing in?'

'Precisely.'

'I see. So how does this work?' asked Junk. 'Do I ask questions and you tell me the answers?'

'No. Nothing so unimaginative. The answers you seek are already here. There're all around you.'

Junk looked around once more and still he saw nothing but darkness. 'I can't see anything,' he said.

'That's as may be,' said the hand-man, 'but they're

there nonetheless. You just need to relax. Open your mind.'

Junk frowned, then closed his eyes. Took a deep breath. Tried to breathe in a steady rhythm. He opened his eyes again and absolutely nothing had changed. He was still surrounded by thick, dripping darkness. 'How do I go about opening my mind?'

'You don't. It's not something you can force. Think about something else, let your mind wander, sing a song, count backwards from a hundred. Relax and you'll see.'

Junk considered the hand-man's words. It was hard to relax when someone told you to, because you were thinking about relaxing and therefore not relaxing. It was like being told not to think of the colour green. All you could do then was think of the colour green. Junk closed his eyes and let his mind wander as suggested. This he could do. A mnemonic Mrs Trethewey had taught them at school to remember the eight planets (post Pluto being demoted) popped into his head: Mary's Violet Eyes Make Johnny Stay Up Nights. He said it over and over in his head. Mary's Violet Eyes Make Johnny Stay Up Nights. Mercury Venus Earth Mars Jupiter Saturn Uranus Neptune. Mary's Violet Eyes Make Johnny Stay Up Nights. Mercury Venus Earth Mars Jupiter Saturn Uranus Neptune. Mary's Violet Eyes –

He opened his eyes and the room was gone. He was in space, moving considerably faster than the speed of light (which was 186,000 miles per second; he had learned that in the same class). He passed Mercury, Venus, Earth,

Mars, Jupiter, Saturn, Uranus and Neptune, saw Pluto in the distance and then swung back around, his speed increasing as he went. The planets became blurs of colour as they shot past him until he was on a collision course with Earth.

He went faster and faster now. Passing through the layers of the atmosphere, the names of which flitted through his mind ever so briefly from the very same lesson. Then he saw the names written in front of him as if on a screen: 'Exosphere . . . Thermosphere . . . Mesosphere . . . Stratosphere . . . Troposphere'. He was passing through clouds now. They parted and there were green fields beneath. The ground hurtled towards him and he towards it. He braced himself for an impact that never happened. Instead he came to an abrupt but gentle stop a few centimetres above the ground and then his feet were touching land. There wasn't so much as a jolt.

He turned and looked all around, rotating three hundred and sixty degrees. There was nothing but green fields in any direction. He stopped for a moment and something, instinct, a feeling, told him to look again. He glanced slowly over his right shoulder. Everything was accelerated, his feelings, his thoughts. His heart thumped . . . ba-ba-ba-ba-ba-ba-bum-ba-ba-ba-ba-ba-ba-bum . . . with either anticipation or trepidation, Junk couldn't tell which. A huge building was behind him now, having appeared out of nowhere, as if it had sprung from the ground fully built. A skyscraper, a palace. As broad at the base as it was tall. It appeared to be made

13

of chrome or some similar reflective metal. A cloud must have moved, uncovering the sun, because at that moment the metal palace was hit by the sun's rays and it bloomed, bright orange. An explosion of light pulsed out from it. Junk turned away, closing his stinging eyes tightly. When he looked again, the palace was gone. Or possibly he was the one who had gone.

He was no longer standing in an open field. Now he was inside a cavernous room. The floor beneath his feet was copper-coloured and covered in lines and squiggles. He recognized it immediately. It was the box, the key to the Room of Doors. But a thousand times its normal size. Almost immediately it started to change shape. The edges were vanishing before his very eyes, moving inwards towards where he was standing. The box was shrinking. It made a sound like a million beetles scuttling over glass and each other. The cube was separating into smaller cubes; the smaller cubes were sinking into one another as if the whole thing was consuming itself. The box continued to dissolve until what he was standing on wasn't big enough to hold Junk and he fell. He tumbled down and down through impenetrable blackness, falling, screaming.

And then suddenly he was back in the small dark room, sitting in the chair in front of the table with the deep grain. And there in front of him, on the table, was the box. He reached out to it. Paused for a moment as he realized that his hands had returned to his wrists, which was nice. He picked up the box and felt its familiar solid weight in his grasp. As if independently to the rest of him, his hands started to move over the surface of the box, tracing out seemingly random patterns, tracing the bumps and indentations. Then, all of a sudden, the smaller box started to collapse in on itself just as the giant version had. And just as the giant one had done, it broke down into smaller cubes. Three-dimensional pixels making the complete object. Junk tried to catch the falling mini-blocks, but soon realized they weren't dropping. They were transforming. The cube was changing shape. As if it was melting, it changed from a cube to a band and looped around Junk's wrist, becoming a bracelet. The bracelet thinned out and stretched up his forearm, covering it like a layer of armour. The armour spread out over his entire body, encasing him completely. Then just as swiftly, as if it was a living creature, the armour swirled around him briefly in a serpentine sort of way and curled around his neck like a chain. Suddenly the chain shot off and turned into a pole some two metres long, which Junk caught in his hand. Then both ends shot towards the middle, disappearing from view entirely. When Junk opened his hand there was a much smaller cube sitting in his palm. It was the size of a die. Then it started to grow. More and more tiny cubes vomiting out impossibly from within. And as he watched it dance and transform, it took on the shape of a bird, which became a cat, which became a mouse, which became a flower and the flower bloomed. Its copper petals spread out, opening themselves up until a tiny vibrant emerald-green core was revealed. Junk saw an image engraved on it. The image was of a tree, the trunk broad and ancient, the lower leaves young and sprightly and the upper leaves strands of fire from a blazing sun. Then just as quickly it closed up again and vanished.

Junk glanced around him, searching for it. Where had it gone? He became aware that he was standing in a vast shadow and the shadow was moving. He forgot about the box as he looked up and up and up some more and saw the silhouette of a giant. An easy thirty metres high. Backlit by the sun. He could make out no details but he could tell the giant was coming towards him and he knew he had to run, so he ran.

He entered a forest choked with blazing yellow leaves on the trees, on vines, on the forest floor, so that yellow filled his entire field of vision. He could hear the giant coming after him, crushing the trees in his path. Junk ran faster.

As he ran he became aware of someone or something running parallel to him. Maybe whatever it was was running away from the giant as well. He caught brief flashes of red, standing out against all the yellow, flitting between shadows and trees, moving fast with sure-footed agility. An animal? His curiosity was guiding him towards it rather than away.

Suddenly the ground gave way beneath him and he was falling, sliding, screaming. His feet were scrambling against the collapsing earth, kicking up a cloud of yellow leaves that danced and swirled around him. The floor disappeared completely and he now faced a dizzyingly high drop. The forest had simply gone. Far below there was nothing but white. Was it snow? Cloud? He couldn't tell. All he knew was that he was about to find out. His panicked scrabbling for purchase was failing. He was about to drop.

Then suddenly a hand clamped around his wrist. Junk looked up and saw a small wiry figure dressed all in red, its face hidden by a mask. All Junk could see was a pair of huge merry blue eyes. Eyes that for a moment he thought he recognized, but before he could say anything the owner of the blue eyes spoke:

'Sometimes down is better than up.' The voice was husky. Almost certainly that of a young girl, a young Irish girl, but before Junk had time to think or speak the red figure spoke again: 'Find Pirestus,' she said, and then released her grip.

'AMBELINE!' Junk cried out as he fell. He was looking up at the red figure, watching it watch him fall, and then the white clouds wrapped their ghostly tentacles around him, enveloping him, and his vision started to fade until he could see nothing at all.

He woke with a start and he was back by the stove in the kitchen of the house on the outskirts of Corraway, with Garvan sitting nearby.

'Did it work?' asked Garvan. 'Did you see anything?'

Junk didn't reply. His breathing was heavy and his mind was racing.

17

3

The following morning Yartik and Huppa prepared a lavish breakfast and packed food for their guests' onward journey. Junk was unusually quiet and just pushed his food around his plate. There was so much to process and he worried that if he focused too much on one thing he had seen he might forget other things. So he played everything over and over in his head constructing a sequence of events: space, planets, Earth, skyscraper, changing box, shadowy giant, yellow forest and, finally, Ambeline. If that's who it had been. He asked Garvan if he knew who or what Pirestus was, but the word meant nothing to him.

He so wanted to believe it was an indicator of things to come, but how could it be? How could a foul-smelling cup of tea predict the future? Of course it couldn't. It was just his imagination running riot. He wasn't going to be flying through space any time soon, that was for sure.

'It might not be so literal,' said Garvan when he spoke to him about it later in the courtyard as they were preparing to leave. 'If you remember, in my one you were a rodent of some description. You're not a rodent,' he added unnecessarily. 'Maybe space doesn't mean space. Maybe it means somewhere wide open.' He waved a hand at the uncultivated expanse of fields that stretched out before them. The house where Yartik and Huppa lived was situated on the very edge of Corraway, where the town ended and there was nothing to see from here to the horizon apart from dusty fields with the land-ship track cutting through the middle of them.

'Maybe,' said Junk, 'but some of yours was literal. Like a prediction or whatever you call it. Us sitting on a ship next to a tree, for example. That's pretty damn specific.' Garvan thought back to the moment he and Junk had been sitting on the *Casabia* and he'd first told Junk about his vision-quest dream thingy, as they had taken to calling it.

'And maybe some of yours will be literal too. Only time will tell.'

'But it can't be,' said Junk. 'It's not possible.'

'Why not?' asked Garvan.

'Think about it. How could petals from a flower know the future? They couldn't. It's just our imagination, and then we read into it, see what we want to see.'

'Maybe,' said Garvan, 'or maybe it's not the petals that can see the future, it's you. The petals just let you.'

Junk screwed up his face as he played Garvan's words through his head a couple of times, trying to make sense of them and failing. 'What does that mean?'

Garvan considered how to answer. 'In Cantibean legend, folklore, there were people who could do magic. I don't know what they'd be called in your language. We called them nawgru. But it is said that such people died out long ago and their abilities were lost . . . forgotten. They became stories and nothing more.'

Junk nodded. 'We had the same sort of thing in my culture. They were called wizards or witches.'

'It's believed that a nawgru could see the future, among other things. Just say it was true and my, I don't know, great-great-great-great-great-great-great-great-great-great-grandfather was a nawgru who could see the future and somewhere deep down inside I have his abilities but I don't know how to access them. What if all the nolic tea does is make me forget that I don't know how to access them?'

Junk thought about that and nodded. 'Wow, that's kind of deep.'

'I thought so,' said Garvan.

Junk, Lasel, Garvan and Payo—Mestrowe bid farewell to Yartik and Huppa and set off for the land-ship station. At least that's what they told their hosts. Having access to something like the Room of Doors was not a fact they were keen to broadcast unnecessarily. Once a safe distance away, Junk withdrew the copper-coloured cube he and Lasel had stolen from the Brotherhood of the One True God, Pire, from a leather satchel he carried slung casually over his back. He manipulated its surface, placing his fingers precisely, and a doorway of green light materialized in front of them. One by one, they stepped through.

The Room of Doors was vast. A seemingly never-ending cavern full of thousands of portals of green, shimmering light stretching into the distance. There were no walls or ceiling they could see. Just a metallic green-black floor that reminded Junk of the wings of a scarab beetle. The only anomaly in the whole place was a single raised dais on top of which stood a column about a metre and a half high. On top of this was an indentation.

Junk stood on the dais and opened out the grapefruit-sized cube, unfolding its six solid faces and the six transparent, almost invisible, faces within. They slotted together again to form a dodecahedron. This he placed in the indentation on the top of the column, where it clicked into place with a satisfying snap. A projection surged outwards, filling the entire cavernous room, labelling every glistening green door within view and probably all the others that were too far away to see.

'Morning, Horace,' said Junk.

'I am the Gatekeeper,' said a booming disembodied voice, 'and I have asked you to stop calling me Horace.' The Gatekeeper was the Room of Doors' super-sophisticated operating system. It spoke every language under the sun and understood every calendar system that had ever existed. The Gatekeeper could send you anywhere to any time. It could deliver you to your chosen destination to within the specified second and to the millimetre if necessary.

'Gotta call you something.' Junk had decided to christen the Gatekeeper, and for some reason, unknown even to Junk, the name he chose was Horace. He'd never known a Horace, so wasn't entirely sure why he'd gone for that. It seemed to irritate the Gatekeeper, which made Junk all the more eager to keep it. Though it did make him wonder just who or what the Gatekeeper was. Could computer programmes get irritated? Junk liked the idea that this one was actually a little man behind a curtain somewhere, like in *The Wizard of Oz*, which had been Ambeline's favourite film. He corrected himself. Still is. Now that she's alive again. Three years was a long time. A lot could have happened and he still had no idea why the Nine Emperors had arranged for her to be abducted in the first place. Abduction was unlikely to be a good thing, but Junk pushed all such negative thoughts from his mind. His little sister was alive again until he found out differently.

'Horace, we need to go to Cul Jjen,' said Junk.

'Temporal information required,' came the Gate-keeper's baritone response. 'And don't call me Horace.'

Ignoring him, Junk turned to the others. 'What do you think? Do we go present day or past?'

'There's no way of knowing if this Tolfke person is still in those parts,' said Payo.

'How long do you think those slug thingies had been there?' Junk was looking at Lasel.

'Weeks, not months,' she said. 'They don't last too long after they're desiccated.'

22

Junk considered this and nodded. 'I say we go present, and if we don't have any luck finding him we can always go past later.' The others nodded. It was agreed. 'Horace, Cul Jjen, presen—' Junk stopped. Ever since they had visited the flatoush dealer the day before there had been a nagging voice at the back of his mind desperate to be heard. Junk knew he would work out why sooner or later, and now he had. Cul Jjen: a place Otravinicus had mentioned. He had taken the man from Junk's time, the man who called himself Han Solo, to Cul Jjen, to a town called Ollamah, where they collected a crate. Coincidence possibly. Probably. Maybe. 'Horace, Ollamah. Present day.'

A line in the projection flowed quickly out from where they were standing and made its way to a door ten levels up and twelve doors along. 'Location: Ollamah. Present day,' boomed the voice of the Gatekeeper. 'And don't call me Horace.'

Junk plucked the dodecahedron from the top of the column and stored it back in his leather satchel. He and the others followed the projected line through a door on the ground level that whisked them up to the tenth level. They hurried along the tiny metallic black ledge to the twelfth door along and one by one they stepped through.

They came out into a swirling, whirling torrent of snow. Each of them was shivering violently and crusted with ice in seconds.

'W-we really n-n-need to s-start p-p-p-planning ahead a little m-m-more,' said Junk through clattering teeth. Ollamah was the frozen north. Having travelled from balmy Cul Sita to sultry Corraway, all of them were decidedly underdressed for sub-zero temperatures. The blizzard that raged around them made the world appear to be blank and empty.

'W-w-w-we sh-sh-should p-p-p-probably g-g-g-g-go b-back,' said Mestrowe. It was so cold it was a job to speak and the others all nodded in agreement, but they were all shaking so much anyway that none of them could tell. Then just for a moment the storm paused as if the wind had changed its mind, and they saw a light about a hundred metres away.

'D-d-d-did y-you see th-th-that?' Junk managed to say. His arms were wrapped around him as he tried desperately to retain any residual body heat, but he was losing the battle rapidly. His black hair was completely white, and tiny icicles were starting to form on his eyebrows.

'S-s-s-see w-w-w-w-what?' chattered Lasel.

'L-l-light.' Junk made a decision. They had to do something. Back into the Room of Doors or forward. One or the other. He took Lasel by the hand. 'E-everyone hold on . . . to each other.' It took a lot of effort to keep his voice steady and shout over the wind that was screaming like a demented hag. He set off towards the light, pulling Lasel after him. In turn she grabbed hold of Garvan's hand and Garvan grabbed Mestrowe's hand. The Pallatan shook free as if holding hands was an insult to his masculinity. But the more sensible part of him, namely Payo, grabbed on to

Garvan's shoulder. The four of them formed a living train and they shuffled towards the light. The wind slapped them with a million tiny ice crystals and every gust felt like beaks pecking at their skin. Garvan and Mestrowe were considerably thicker-skinned than Junk and Lasel because of their ancestry and their size, but even they were suffering. All of them kept their eyes screwed half shut and shielded them as best they could, but the sharp snow found its way through, seemingly determined to seek out their faces.

Junk noticed that the snow and ice were clinging to the arm he held in front of him. It was turning white and blending into the background. He had lost sight of the light but was hopeful that they were still moving in the right direction.

'W-we're g-g-going the wr-wr-wrong way,' Mestrowe shouted, and his powerful voice was nearly obliterated by the wind so the words were weak by the time they reached the ears of the others. Garvan stopped and his stopping stopped Lasel and her stopping stopped Junk. He looked back to see what was wrong.

'Mestrowe s-s-says we're g-g-going the wrong w-way,' Garvan called to Junk.

'Th-there's the l-l-light!' Mestrowe pointed, and all their squinting eyes turned to catch a brief glimpse at a light even further away than before and in a completely different direction.

'M-m-maybe it's m-m-m-moving,' said Lasel. 'I th-th-think w-w-we should g-g-g-go b-back.'

25

Junk knew she was right. It was so cold he was finding it difficult to concentrate. He tried to pull the satchel around so he could get to the box, but his hands were now frozen. He couldn't move his fingers. Panic was starting to set in. If he couldn't move his fingers enough to open the bag, there was no way he could manage the digital dexterity required to activate the box. He rubbed his hands together to try to get the circulation going. 'M-m-my h-h-hands are f-f-frozen.'

Suddenly Lasel stumbled. Garvan caught her before she fell. As the smallest of the group she was the most vulnerable to the intense cold. Junk knew he wouldn't be far behind.

'W-we have t-t-to g-g-g-g-get back into the Room of D-D-D-Doors,' said Garvan, wrapping his arms around Lasel in an attempt to warm her up. Junk refocused himself, forcing his frozen fingers to move. It was agony. They were curled up into claw-like hooks. He tried to straighten them but they didn't want to respond. 'I c-c-can't d-d-do it!' His vision was almost gone now as the moisture of his eyeballs was freezing. Unless a miracle happened right now, thought Junk, they were dead.

And just then a great light shone down on them from directly above. It was so bright they now had to protect their eyes from it as well as the biting snow. Junk looked up, shading his eyes with his hand. It took him a moment to realize that the light was in the shape of a whale smoking what looked like a fat cheroot cigar. It wasn't neon but it was something similar. The light blinked out again. Then a door beneath, directly ahead of them, opened and an inverted triangle of warm orange light shone out, cutting a path through the blizzard. From within they could hear chattering voices. They saw a broad figure standing in the doorway.

'Arnk carg va doon ansnac hacal,' said the broad figure, and gestured for them to enter. The four of them raced inside.

4

The door slammed shut after them, locking the blizzard and the ruckus it was making firmly outside. There was a thunderous fire romping in a grate in the middle of the room and Junk and the others collapsed in front of it, letting its welcoming heat thaw their limbs. Two dozen pairs of eyes regarded them curiously, watching steam rise from their scantily clad bodies.

A buxom, healthy-hipped woman stepped forward, pulling animal skins from the backs of chairs. She draped the hides over each of them in turn.

'Nuck nu chik droonk corrncut,' she said, clearly addressing the four of them. Her language was coarse and flat. Emphasis was placed on the ends of words.

Junk was starting to feel his extremities again. He took his hands out from under the animal hide and flexed his fingers. Pins and needles shot through his entire body as his circulation returned. He looked around the room. They were in some sort of tavern. The customers were all tough, stocky and weather-worn. Their hair was the most colourful thing about them. They were mostly blonde or ginger and all, including the women, had facial hair. The men had impressively voluminous beards, while the women sported either a moustache or sideburns. Junk glanced at Garvan. 'Do you know what language she's speaking?'

Garvan shook his head. 'A northern language obviously, but not one I know. Payo?' Payo looked up at him through Mestrowe's one good eye and shook his head.

'It'll be Prusk,' said Lasel weakly. Her head was pounding from the cold and even the low level of lighting in this place was making it worse. 'Around these parts. I don't speak it either.'

'We maybe should have thought this through a little better,' said Junk. He looked up at their rescuer, who was regarding them with a frown. He was just trying to work out how they were going to communicate when the woman spoke in Jansian:

'We do speak Prusk. We speak many languages. Who are you? And how did you get out here wearing no clothes? There's a storm coming in. Another few minutes out there and you would have died.'

'Storm's *coming*?' said Junk. 'What do you call that outside?'

'That's no storm,' said the woman with a chuckle in her throat. 'That's just a grumble.' Many of the people around them chorused her chuckle and Junk realized most if not all of them spoke Jansian. He took a moment to look around now. He was starting to feel normal again. They

29

were indeed in a tavern. There was straw on the ground to soak up the melting snow everyone invariably brought in on their boots, and several long, heavy tables made of thick dark wood. There were benches and plenty of chairs scattered about though none of them matched. The place had a thrown-together feel about it as if everyone had just brought in whatever they could find or scavenge. The bar was just another long table that had a length of brightly coloured material pinned to the front side. The material had been patched many times and it was streaked with stains from years of having spilled drinks drip down it. Behind the bar were three square barrels side by side. Each had a window in them showing the contents. In one was a dirty light brown liquid that looked like dishwater, thin and sudsy. In the next was something black that didn't allow light through. And in the third a burgundy brew, like a rich wine. These appeared to be the only choices of beverage in the place. All the customers had small squat glasses in front of them containing one of the three drinks.

'I'm Tunka,' said the woman, 'and this is my husband, Grush.' She indicated the man who had let them in. He was short, almost as wide as he was tall, but solid and powerful-looking. He had broad facial features, a flat nose with flared nostrils and his large eyes were out of proportion to the rest of his cracked, weather-ravaged face. He sported a huge, impressively bushy blond beard. 'This is our place.'

'This is Ollamah?' asked Junk.

'That's right,' said Tunka. She shook her head as if the movement might help her to understand. 'How do you not know where you are? How did you get up here?' That was the second time she had asked the same question.

'Our airship developed a fault,' said Lasel. She was a great liar, which Junk assumed went hand in hand with being a thief. 'We had no choice but to bail out.'

'It crashed?' This was Grush. He sounded alarmed.

'That's right,' said Lasel. 'It was still going. We lost sight of it, so no idea where it eventually came down.'

'And you didn't have time to put on any decent clothes?' asked Tunka.

'We barely got out alive,' said Lasel with no hint of an untruth, but Grush and Tunka turned to look at one another, as if they didn't quite buy this story. 'I know what you're thinking,' Lasel said. 'We don't look like airship types.'

Tunka looked guilty then, and it was clear that was exactly what she was thinking.

'You're not catching us at our best,' said Lasel. 'This –' she gestured now to Garvan – 'is Prince Garvan of the clan Fiske of Cantibea.' A ripple of excitement ran through the patrons of the bar and all eyes turned to Garvan to scrutinize him. Junk could see he wasn't happy being the centre of attention.

Tunka suddenly bent at the knees and the waist in something that was part-curtsy, part-bow. The sudden movement thrust her voluminous bosom forward, where it threatened to escape the confines of her shirt. Then Grush and the other patrons all followed suit as Garvan cringed with embarrassment.

'Please stand up,' he said forcefully. 'That's not necessary.' The bar patrons all looked a little unsure now, as if maybe they were being tested. Tunka barked several commands in Prusk and there was a quick flurry of activity as four chairs were dragged forward to the fire and four glasses of the burgundy drink were poured. Garvan and the others were ushered into the chairs and the drinks were thrust into their hands. Tunka fussed around, tucking the animal hides in. She paid the most attention to Garvan.

Then one of the locals, who introduced himself as Drunb, leaned forward and thrust a small rusty tin towards Garvan.

'Do you floushe, Your Highness?' He smiled respectfully, showing off a mouth filled with crooked yellow teeth. Garvan stared down at the tin, which was crawling with greasy red-and-orange maggot-sized nasal leeches, and tried but failed to hide his revulsion. Drunb didn't seem to notice and he offered the tin to Junk, Payo–Mestrowe and Lasel but briefly, not really giving them time to accept, which none of them were going to do anyway. Then he plucked out one of the little syrupy, writhing creatures and perched it on his top lip. He snorted loudly once, and the maggoty leech disappeared up his right nostril. Never having seen this before, Junk and Garvan stared. They could see the creature moving about under the skin at the top of Drunb's bulbous purple nose. Then Drunb let out a snort from the back of his throat, a groan of deep-felt satisfaction, and slid down into his seat a little more.

Tunka bustled into the kitchen and came back with a large spread. There were about twenty separate dishes, but they all seemed to be variations of pickled fish that pretty much tasted alike. The one exception was a soup dish that Junk was enjoying greatly until he stirred it up and two dozen little fish eyes floated to the surface, seemed to blink at him and then sank back down. After that he lost his appetite.

'So what brings you to Ollamah?' asked Grush.

'We're looking for someone,' said Junk. Talking gave him an excuse not to eat any more. 'A man called Tolfke.' A ripple went around the room. A stiffening of shoulders. Hurried glances exchanged.

'He is a friend of yours?' asked Grush, clearly forcing a level tone into his voice.

'No,' said Junk, 'we've never met him. Apart from . . .' and he gestured towards Payo–Mestrowe, who had until now not really garnered any attention.

'Are you Prince Garvan's bodyguard?' asked Tunka.

'No!' growled Mestrowe. 'Yes,' said Payo in a more agreeable tone almost immediately after, both answers coming from the same mouth. It was very confusing for an onlooker. The Ollamuts (as the residents of Ollamah called themselves) didn't know what to make of his

33

response, so chose not to question him any further on the matter. He was far too scary-looking.

'We think he can direct us to a group who call themselves the Nine Emperors. Have you heard of them?' Junk asked hopefully. His question was met with a lot of blank faces and shaking of heads. Skipping over some of the more tricky-to-explain aspects of the story, such as the Room of Doors and the whole truth of Mestrowe's involvement, he went on to recount Ambeline's abduction and his quest to find her killer only to discover she might well still be alive. Halfway through his story Payo–Mestrowe burst into tears. Everyone turned to looked at him. Junk, Lasel and Garvan assumed this emotional outburst was down to Payo, but then they heard Payo's voice.

'It's not me,' he said.

'It's your fault though,' said Mestrowe, 'whatever you're doing up there!' And he punched himself viciously in the side of the head. After that Payo–Mestrowe took himself off to the toilet. No one commented on his behaviour. Junk carried on with his story. Lasel chipped in occasionally to add a lie here and there to make her earlier story about the airship more convincing and to reinforce Garvan as royalty.

When Junk was finished the Ollamuts agreed it was an astonishing story. 'There is someone around these parts called Tolfke, but it can't be who you're looking for. He's just a strange old hermit. Lives alone on an island in the bay. Never leaves. Never comes ashore. Food is sent to him on a boat. He pays well. We never see him. He never comes out. No one ever goes in. If he was to go anywhere he would have to come through here first.'

Junk, Garvan and Lasel exchanged a look. They of course knew he had another way to get off the island without ever stepping foot out of his house.

'That's not quite true,' said Tunka.

Her husband looked at her frowning. 'Which part?'

'That no one ever goes over to the island. There were those men, if you remember.'

'What men?' said Grush and Junk in unison.

'The little man with glasses and the man with the colourful shirt.'

'Oh yes,' said Grush, nodding. 'I had quite forgotten about them.'

'The little man with glasses,' said Junk, 'was he skinny with a long face?'

'Yes, that's right,' said Tunka. 'Do you know him?'

Junk nodded. She was describing Dr Otravinicus. The man with the colourful shirt must have been the one who called himself Han Solo. Dr Otravinicus had said they came here to Ollamah to collect a crate. He hadn't mentioned going to see Tolfke.

'And they went over to this island you're talking about?'

'Yes,' said Grush, 'I rowed them out myself. Went back for them later.'

Tunka insisted that they spend the night with them and as soon as the storm died down she turfed out all the regulars and made up beds in the bar. She had tried very hard to insist that Garvan take her and Grush's bed, but he had declined the offer. He had to turn her down a dozen times before she would admit defeat.

As they were lying in bed waiting for sleep to come, Junk told the others what Otravinicus had said about his visit here.

'He never mentioned going to see Tolfke,' said Junk. 'Why would he lie?'

'The best lies are always partly based in truth,' said Lasel.

'Like our airship, you mean,' said Junk with a grin.

'Exactly.' Lasel returned his grin. They held the look for several long moments until both realized they were staring at one another. They turned away. As they lay with their backs facing, Junk remembered Pirestus and asked Lasel if she knew what it meant. She didn't. They went off to sleep.

5

The next morning it was as if the storm of the previous night had never happened. The sky was a crisp, cerulean blue. Ollamah was built in a dip at the base of a shallow valley. The snow had all but blown away and there was only a very light dusting on the craggy, charcoal-grey ground. The town itself was made up of about twenty-five separate buildings. Nothing higher than two storeys and all built from the same dark stone as the landscape. The roofs were all steeply pitched, bottle-shaped, like an old pottery kiln, so snow had little chance of collecting. All were brightly painted and no two were the exact same colour. It gave the town a slightly magical quality, like something out of a fairy tale.

The townsfolk of Ollamah, most of whom they had met in the tavern the previous night, dressed plainly and uniformly in drab furs and brown animal hides, which made them look like stumpy Vikings. Tunka had presented Junk and the others with suitable clothing for the environment: bear-fur chaps and tunics and hooded leather greatcoats. It seemed unlikely that she just happened to have something in their sizes, particularly Mestrowe and Garvan who were at least twice the height of anyone in Ollamah, so they concluded that she must have been up all night making them. The quality of the craftsmanship was exceptional.

To the south was a wide-open bay looking out on icy clear water as smooth as glass. An undulating layer of early morning mist floated just above the surface of the sea like the ghosts of a thousand dead sailors reaching up out of their watery grave. In the distance was a small island. Tolfke's island. The middle man for the Nine Emperors. The man who hired Mestrowe and instructed him to abduct Ambeline. Tolfke was a direct link to the Nine Emperors, and Junk could feel he was getting closer to the answers he sought. The island appeared bare apart from one small single-storey building. Junk stood staring out at it. He sensed movement behind him and turned to see Grush approaching.

'Are you ready to go?' the man asked.

Grush's fishing boat was a sort of outrigger dhow. It was a large but shallow flat-bottomed boat with a float projecting out on either side. It cut through the water at a fair clip even with five people on board. There was a small jetty on the east side of the island, but no boat moored there.

'I know you said he never leaves, but what would he do,' asked Junk, 'if he ever did want to get off?'

'He has a bell. He would ring it and someone would

38

come over,' said Grush. 'That's never happened as long as I can remember and I've been here all my life.'

'How long's Tolfke been here?'

Grush thought about it and shrugged. 'Forever,' he said.

Junk, Garvan, Lasel and Payo–Mestrowe climbed up on to the jetty. Grush pointed out the bell he had mentioned, hung in an iron frame at the start of the jetty. He told them to ring it when they wanted him to come to collect them. With that, Grush headed back to the mainland and Junk and the others made their way to Tolfke's small house. Like the buildings in town it was made of local stone, but instead of the distinctive bottle-shaped roof it had a simple pitched roof with a chimney, and the snow of the night before was still heavy on one side. The windows were all shuttered. It didn't look inhabited.

They reached the door and Junk raised his hand to knock, but then stopped. He looked around at the others.

'What do we say?'

He was met with blank looks.

'Say you want to know where to find the Nine Emperors,' said Lasel. Simple was probably best. Junk knocked. They waited, but there was no reply. Junk knocked again. Again they waited, and with the same result. He looked at the others and shrugged, not sure what to do now. Lasel moved forward and tried the handle. The door was unlocked and opened silently inwards. They headed inside.

Had any of them looked back towards the mainland at that very moment they would not have failed to notice a huge dark dragon-shaped object hanging in the sky over Ollamah, shrouded behind a veil of flimsy clouds. Like a panther padding through morning mist, it was getting closer.

Junk and his friends found themselves in a long, dark, un-inviting passageway that stretched from the front of the house to the back. Papery flying insects spiralled through the mustard-brown air and the house exhaled an over-poweringly musty, damp smell from its gizzard. Garvan held Junk back and entered first. Payo–Mestrowe shoved Junk hard with one hand and steadied him with the other.

'Watch where you're going, boy,' said Mestrowe.

'Sorry about him,' said Payo.

Junk gestured for Lasel to follow Payo–Mestrowe, leaving him to bring up the rear. He found a rock just outside that he used to hold the door open. It was the only source of light.

The four of them walked cautiously and quietly along the passageway, listening for any signs of life. Apart from the front and back doors, there were only two doors leading off the passageway, in the middle, one on either side. Garvan took hold of the handle of the door on the left and Mestrowe the door on the right. They opened them in unison. Both stepped into almost identical, nearly empty rooms.

Black, oily darkness draped itself over three-quarters of each room, and the whisper of weak sunlight that was seeping in through the hallway via the front door was unable to penetrate very far. Just enough to illuminate a sliver of bare floorboards and a single chair in the middle of each room.

Lasel grabbed Junk by the hand and led him outside. She pointed to the shutters on the window of the room on the left.

'Open those up,' she said. Junk did as instructed while Lasel went around and opened the shutters on the windows of the room on the right.

Light sloshed into the two dank rooms. Payo–Mestrowe and Garvan blinked as their eyes adjusted to the sudden brightness. Lasel and Junk returned and hovered in the passageway between both rooms. They gasped at what they saw. The walls, floor and ceiling of each room were covered in words scrawled over and over again in various alphabets. Junk didn't recognize any of them.

'What does it all say?' he asked.

Garvan, Lasel and Payo–Mestrowe shared a cautious look. 'It all says the same thing, but in many different languages,' said Garvan.

'That's H'rtu,' said Mestrowe, running his fingers over a simplistic, repetitive alphabet of lines and dots that looked more like a child's secret code.

Garvan pointed: 'Jansian. Uomot. Nykil. Ingiste. Baak. That's Prusk, I think. Or something similar.'

'But what does it say?' asked Junk again.

41

Garvan paused for a moment before he answered, 'Nine Emperors.'

Junk looked around at all the different writing.

'Many languages but the same words,' said Garvan.

'Why?' asked Junk. 'Why would anyone do this?' Another more pertinent question occurred to him just then. 'And where is he, this Tolfke fella?'

'Not here, clearly,' said Lasel. 'No one lives here. There's no bed, no stove, no toilet.'

'But everyone back in Ollamah thinks he's here and never leaves. Why the charade?'

No one had the first clue.

The four of them floated from one room to the other staring at all the graffiti. Something was gnawing at Garvan. He felt as if he had spotted something but he wasn't sure what. He stood in the room on the left and turned in a slow, steady circle. Window. Door. Chair. He went into the other room and did the same thing. Window. Door. Chair. He went back to the first room. Window. Door. Chair. Second room. Window. Door. Chair. He was about to go back to the other room when he saw it. Saw what had been bugging him. This room was not as long as the room next door. Not by much. Maybe half a metre, if that. The difference was slight and could easily have been missed.

He moved to the back wall of the smaller room and spread his vast hands out over the end wall. It was tacky to the touch. He applied pressure little by little until he felt the wall shift. It was a false wall. Not stone like the others. He moved from left to right brushing the tips of his fingers across the graffiti. He stopped. He felt something. A groove. Invisible to the eye. He traced it up, along and down. It was door-shaped. He pressed the heel of his hand against it and felt it move in. He let go and a spring popped the hidden door open. A narrow set of steps descended into a cellar lit with mournful grey light.

'You should come and look at this,' he shouted to the others.

Garvan led the way down the steps. At the bottom they found themselves looking along a low, tight corridor carved into the rock. It stretched ahead for a dozen metres before splitting left and right. The passageway was too restrictive for either Garvan or Payo–Mestrowe to go any further. Even if they crawled on their bellies they would get stuck.

'We'll go,' said Lasel.

Garvan shook his head. 'We don't know what's down there, and we can't help you if something happens.'

'Then let's hope nothing happens,' said Junk, stepping forward with Lasel.

Junk led the way. Light came from reflective tubes embedded in the rock running up and out to the surface. Icy air crept in through the tubes too, making the passageway feel refrigerated but providing fresh air.

When they reached the fork, Lasel looked left and Junk right. Both saw shorter passageways that split two ways as well.

43

'This place is a maze,' said Junk. 'We stay together. No matter what, OK?'

Lasel nodded. 'Which way do you want to go?'

Junk shrugged. 'Left,' he said, saying the first thing that came to mind. 'We'll keep going left so we'll know how to get back.'

They went left and then left again. There was another longish corridor, which felt as if it was on a slight slope. They were descending further into the earth under the island. The passage carried on for two more turnings before they found a room. It was only a little bit wider than the corridor and no higher. It was full of jars, each about the size of a demijohn with a piece of rag secured under the lid. Each jar was full of liquid. Yellow liquid, which Junk thought might be urine. He didn't plan on opening a jar to find out.

The room was a dead end, so they went back the way they came, retracing their steps and trying different turnings. They found other similar rooms full of boxes, crates and more jars. It was like some sort of weird storage facility. One of the rooms had a hundred boxes full of pebbles. Just ordinary pebbles as far as they could tell.

They doubled back again and came to a three-way intersection that they hadn't seen before. Somehow their plan to stick left hadn't worked and neither was sure where they had gone wrong.

'Which way did we come?' asked Junk.

Lasel frowned. They were lost. She looked down

one turning and then the other. All looked identical. She shook her head.

'GARVAN?' Junk shouted and waited for a reply. They heard Junk's voice echoing away, quickly dissipating to nothing. Whatever the walls were made of clearly absorbed sound. No reply came. 'Arse,' said Junk. After a brief discussion of available options they decided there weren't many. They started walking and hoping for the best.

After half a dozen more turnings, they came to something new. A heavy wooden door. It had a U-shaped iron handle. They each debated silently whether or not to open it, then both put an ear up against the wood and listened. They heard nothing from within. They held one another's gaze as Junk took a hold of the handle and turned it slowly clockwise. He could feel the mechanism within shifting. It did so silently until just before it opened, when one heavy piece of metal inside clashed with another and it let out a sharp clang like a hammer hitting an anvil. Junk threw the door open and they stepped quickly into the largest room they had seen so far. It was three times as wide as the storerooms and almost twice as long. It looked lived in. There was a fireplace to one side, though no fire was burning. Junk remembered seeing a chimney as they approached but it only occurred to him now that there was no fireplace upstairs. In front of the fireplace was a single well-padded armchair and a small side table. There was an empty glass on the table that contained the dregs of a dark red drink, and a small wooden box that might have been a music box.

Junk and Lasel stepped further into the room. Behind the door was a robust armoire made from solid dark wood that stood almost three metres high and two metres wide. As Junk glanced around more he saw a table, chairs, a bookcase, jardinières, a grandfather clock ticking loudly. The room reminded him of his grandma's home back in Ireland. She had died when Junk was little, but until then had lived in a bungalow in County Limerick. The only thing missing here were the knick-knacks. His grandma had figurines and commemorative plates and candles she never lit, that were only for show, and lots and lots of photographs. There was nothing like that here.

Junk and Lasel moved further into the room. Lasel nudged Junk to direct his attention to a narrow table up against the wall beyond the fireplace. There was a row of porcelain busts, seven in total, and each wore a mask. Each mask was the same, smooth and featureless, no eyeholes, no mouth. The only thing that was different was the colour. Two were scarlet, two black, one white, one gold and one blue. Junk and Lasel stared at them.

'Would you mind handing me one of those?' said a gruff, distorted voice, taking them both by surprise. Junk and Lasel spun around. They saw a doorway that had been concealed by the bookcase. The room beyond was pitch black but they could just make out a figure standing in the shadows within. 'Please.' Junk glanced at Lasel, not sure what to do. She gave him a little shrug. Junk turned and picked up the nearest mask, one of the red ones. He stepped towards the darkened doorway, holding the mask out at arm's length. As the man reached out a gloved hand, Junk caught the merest glimpse of his face as a sliver of light fell across him. His skin was horribly burned and twisted. Junk heard himself utter an audible gasp of repugnance. The man pulled back sharply and slipped the mask over his face. He stepped out into the light.

He was not a big man. His frame was slight and Junk towered over him. However, he walked with a certain air of confidence and authority that made Junk and Lasel back away from him. He was dressed from the neck down in a long black coat that hung almost to the floor. The red mask was the only colour on him. He crossed to the chair in front of the fire and turned it slightly so when he sat down he was looking at his visitors.

'I don't get many callers,' he said. He spoke English. From the way he constructed his sentences it was apparent that he was educated, but his words were slurred as if he couldn't open his mouth fully. 'Would you like to sit?' He gestured to the table behind him.

Lasel shook her head. 'We're fine,' she said. 'Are you Tolfke?'

'I am,' said the man in the mask. 'What can I do for you?'

'We're looking for the Nine Emperors,' said Junk.

Tolfke's head twitched at Junk's words and he threw a brief glance over his left shoulder at a roll-top writing desk. Even though there were no eyeholes in the mask, it appeared that the man could see.

47

'Why do you think I can help you?'

'You have it written all over the walls upstairs,' said Lasel.

'Oh yes.' Tolfke chuckled. 'I rarely go up there any more.'

'And we're travelling with a Pallatan called Jacid Mestrowe,' said Junk. 'He's worked for you.'

'Yes. Yes, he has. Many times.' As he nodded his head, a tear of blood dripped down from behind the mask. Junk and Lasel saw it a moment before Tolfke became aware of it. He pulled a raggedy piece of cloth out of a pocket and held it up to his nose, under the mask. 'I'm sorry. Please forgive me.' He turned his head away to one side and angled the mask up. Lasel saw a slash of pink, scarred flesh. Tolfke held one nostril, though Lasel couldn't actually see the whole nose from her angle, and blew hard through the other. A small ball of blood-soaked mucus dropped out into the cloth, followed by more blood. Junk and Lasel didn't know where to look. They had no choice but to wait for Tolfke to finish. When the blood had stopped flowing, Tolfke fished the solid discharge out of his handkerchief. It was an eviscerated flatoush. He tossed it into the hearth where it landed on a soft bed of ash. He dabbed until the blood had stopped. Then he repositioned the mask and turned back to Lasel and Junk. 'You were saying . . .'

'The Nine Emperors,' said Junk. 'Where can we find them?'

'Why do you want to find them?' asked Tolfke.

'They took something from me, something that I would like back.'

'I see.' The mask didn't change of course, but Lasel and Junk could both tell Tolfke was considering his answer as well as if they had seen his furrowed brow. He reached out to the music box on the table next to him and laid it on his lap. He didn't look down at it as he flipped up the lid. It was crawling with live flatoushes, at least a dozen of them. He picked one up between gloved forefinger and thumb. The fat little maggot creature writhed fiercely as Tolfke pulled the mask forward and his hand briefly disappeared. He snorted once and then relaxed. Having seen flousheing in the tavern the previous night, Lasel and Junk understood what he was doing and were glad of the barrier offered by the mask. Tolfke gave a little shudder and relaxed back into his chair. He closed the lid of the box and slipped it into a deep pocket in his coat.

'I can't help you, I'm afraid. I have worked for the Nine Emperors in the past, and I hope I will again. They pay well. But I have no way of finding them. They find me when they require my services. I never know when that will be.'

'Is that right?' asked Junk. 'When I first mentioned them, you looked over at that desk. Mind if I take a look inside?'

'That's private,' said Tolfke with a flutter of concern in his voice.

Junk shrugged and crossed to the desk anyway. He lifted the lid and an avalanche of papers tipped forward.

Junk had to twist his body, pushing his hip against the edge of the desk to stop them spilling over.

Tolfke looked at Lasel and saw her attention was on Junk. The masked man suddenly leaped to his feet and grabbed hold of her. He had the advantage of surprise and he caught her off-balance. He threw her towards Junk and she stumbled forward, flailing her arms as she sought something to grab on to. Junk ignored the desk and the lip dropped forward as he moved to catch Lasel.

Tolfke ran to the armoire and pulled back the doors. Inside was a shimmering green rectangle of light, a portal to the Room of Doors. Tolfke threw himself through and vanished. A split second later the portal closed and the armoire became nothing but an empty piece of furniture.

It took Lasel and Junk another hour to find their way back to the staircase and Garvan and Payo–Mestrowe. On their way back to the jetty they told them what had happened and that they had searched through Tolfke's papers but couldn't find any clue that would help them. It seemed that Tolfke's glance at the bureau had been just a ruse to get Junk and Lasel out from his escape route in the armoire. They rang the bell and waited for Grush to return for them.

6

Junk and the others were all very quiet on the journey back to the mainland. All were trying to make sense of what they had seen. Had they not been so distracted, one of them might have noticed that Grush was acting strangely. He was twitching nervously and whistling poorly to try to hide the fact he was nervous.

When they came ashore, Grush avoided eye contact and told them to go on ahead as he had to secure his boat. Junk and the others didn't think twice about that as they trudged back up the beach towards the tavern.

'What now?' said Lasel.

'I don't know,' said Junk.

As they entered the town, Junk did notice that the place was strangely quiet. When they had left, it had been bustling with life as the townsfolk went about the chores of the day. Now it was empty and silent. However his mind was preoccupied and he didn't dwell on it. Once all four of them were within the confines of the town square, they were wrenched from their thoughts by a hundred thunderous clangs sounding simultaneously, as if heavy metal gates had been slammed shut all around them. And in a way they had.

In the blink of an eye the town of Ollamah had been surrounded by soldiers clad from head to toe in sleek black-and-orange armour. All were wearing ferocious full-face war-masks, like the *Somen* of the samurai. They formed a living, fortified fence enclosing the whole town. Each of the soldiers was the size of Garvan, making it a formidable wall. All were armed with a selection of weaponry unlike anything Junk had set eyes on before. Some held what appeared to be massive armoured fists, making their already gargantuan hands even bigger. Others held broadswords that had four blades set together in one hilt. Junk took a moment to wonder how they would work, but didn't have time to dwell on the question. Others held massive crossbows, the centre of which sported a huge barrel with multiple openings that looked like one of those ridiculous miniguns so beloved by macho action-movie heroes back in Junk's world.

Garvan pushed Junk and Lasel behind him to shield them and Payo made Mestrowe protect their rear. The four of them turned in a slow circle.

'What's happening?' asked Junk. 'Who are they?'

Before Garvan could answer the wall parted with a resounding metallic clank, creating a single opening. Through this stepped two men who looked just like Garvan. They too wore armour but theirs was black and gold, perhaps signifying a higher rank. They carried their helmets under their arms. As they walked through, the opening closed behind them. They stopped six paces from Junk and the others and looked straight at Garvan. The slightly taller of the two was darker. The other was blond and had shoulders even broader than Garvan's, which Junk hadn't thought was possible. The tall one's taciturn face suddenly broke into a broad smile.

'Teawunagun, Garvan, anee tratoodoo junchun narnpit, banchu.' Junk didn't recognize the language. The cadence was strange. It sounded as if he was speaking backwards. He spoke with a flat, level tone. It was not an expressive language.

Garvan answered him, 'Farges ay, Jadris. Meentra nurararay hup.' Then Garvan stepped forward and the two others did as well. The three of them met in the middle and threw their arms around one another. They hugged, embracing each other affectionately. Junk relaxed a little then. Garvan turned and spoke in Jansian. 'I want to introduce you to two of my little brothers. This is Jadris.' The taller, dark-haired one nodded politely and smiled at Junk, Lasel and Payo–Mestrowe in turn. 'And this is Kyril.'

He nodded too and spoke in accented Jansian: 'A pleasure to meet you.'

'These are my friends. Junk, Lasel and Payo,' Garvan said.

Junk smiled. 'That was scary for a moment there. I didn't know what was going on.' Just then he remembered something Garvan had said to him once and he frowned.

'Wait, didn't you say if your brothers ever found you they would—'

Garvan didn't let him finish the sentence. He didn't need to. 'Yes, they're here to kill me.' He said it in a very matter-of-fact sort of way and Junk wondered for a moment if he wasn't as proficient in Jansian as he thought he was. He must have misunderstood.

'They don't look like they're here to kill you.'

'Oh no, we are,' said Jadris. 'To try anyway.'

'No choice,' added Kyril, 'but Garvan was always the best fighter in the family, so he might kill us.' They spoke calmly, as if they were talking about the weather or what to have for dinner.

'Oh, I don't plan on defending myself,' said Garvan. 'I didn't want to hurt Father and I don't want to hurt either of you two. Tell me, how is everyone back home?'

'Everyone's missed you. Father's a bit annoyed still. You know what he's like about tradition. He's always getting under Mother's feet. And you want to see Cortree now. He's bigger than us.'

'No way,' said Garvan. He turned to Junk and the others. 'Cortree's our little brother. The baby of the family.'

'Wait a sec!' said Junk, sounding indignant. 'How are you having such a calm conversation? You're about to kill him, and you're about to let them.'

'Well, we don't really have any choice in the matter. Oh!' A thought occurred to Jadris and he looked at Garvan eagerly. 'Unless you've changed your mind, of course, and you want to come home and behead the old man.'

Garvan shook his head. "Fraid not.' Jadris and Kyril looked mildly irritated, as if Garvan had just refused to let them borrow a pen.

Junk couldn't get his head around any of this. 'This is nuts!'

'It's Cantibean tradition,' said Garvan with a shrug. He turned to his brothers. 'Listen, afterwards, do me a favour. Junk is on a mission. He's looking for his little sister. Will you help him? Send a legion with him or something.' Garvan gestured to the soldiers making up the wall around them.

'Of course we will. Anything else?'

'I don't think so. Tell everyone back home that I love them and miss them. Tell Father I'm sorry and I'll see him soon. You'll make a good king, Jadris.'

'Wait!' shouted Junk. 'This is insane. You can't just kill your own brother –' he spat his words at Jadris and then turned to Garvan – 'and you can't just let him!'

Garvan crouched down on one knee so he was closer to Junk's height, but he was still looking down at him. He put a weighty hand on his friend's shoulder and smiled. 'Look around you, Junk. There's nowhere left to run. I will not harm my brothers for the same reason that I would not kill my father. I told you once that it's my way of thinking that's unusual here, not theirs. This is the way things have been done in Cantibea for centuries.'

'But . . .' Junk didn't know what to say. Garvan was so calm and collected about all this that it was confusing.

It had come as a shock to Junk when he discovered that his big friend was in fact heir to the throne of a small but powerful country called Cantibea. He was the eldest son to King Cadrew and Queen Adilla of the clan Fiske. Cantibean tradition dictated that one king succeeded another only by defeating them in hand-to-hand combat. It was Garvan's duty to cut off his father's head and take his place on the throne. Garvan had chosen to leave home rather than murder his father, and King Cadrew had no choice but to remain king until either Garvan returned and decapitated him or his next eldest son, Jadris, found his brother and killed him, thus becoming the heir and then he could decapitate his father and everyone would be happy.

'But,' said Junk again, 'there were other things in your dream vision thingy. You know, raining snakes and volcanoes and stuff.'

Garvan frowned as he thought about his nolic-tea-induced dream. He nodded. 'That's true, but like you said, maybe it's just our imagination and we see what we want to see.'

Junk could think of nothing else to say.

'Goodbye, Junk. Jadris and Kyril will help you. When you find Ambeline, tell her I'm sorry I didn't get to meet her.'

Tears were coursing down Junk's cheeks now. He couldn't believe this was happening.

'You should go. I don't want you to see this.'

Junk threw his arms around Garvan's mammoth neck and hugged him. Lasel and Payo joined the embrace.

Mestrowe's face switched between his dislike of all this hugging and Payo's sadness. It was an odd sight for an onlooker who didn't understand the arrangement. Lasel kissed Garvan on the cheek and then she took Junk by the hand and led him away. The Cantibean soldiers parted to let them through and then closed ranks again behind them. The sound of their armour crashing together sent a jolt through Junk and he broke into a run. Lasel and Payo–Mestrowe hurried after him.

Garvan gave his brothers one last hug and then got down on his knees. He bent his head forward, exposing the nape of his neck. One of the soldiers broke rank from the wall and approached Jadris and Kyril. He held out his four-bladed broadsword to Jadris, who took it, and the soldier retreated. Jadris held the hilt in both hands and raised it above his head.

Beyond the town, Junk, Lasel and Payo–Mestrowe saw Jadris and Kyril's airship. It was vast. Twice the size of the largest land-ship Junk had seen in Corraway. It looked like a huge jet-black dragon with a hull in the shape of a hammerhead shark. The robust fuselage stretched outwards and in the air it would resemble the wings of a manta ray. Unlike most vessels, it didn't look as if it was made of components that had been joined together. Instead it looked like something carved from a single enormous black diamond. There were no seams or visible joins. Its landing struts were part of the undercarriage. The windows that dotted the main body looked like scales glistening in the sunlight. It had two wings that were locked in a vertical position. Inscribed on the underside of the wings was the airship's name: *Xcsso*. There didn't seem to be any obvious power source. No jet engines or propellers or rotors.

'What the hell is that?' asked Junk.

'That's an airship,' said Lasel. 'Cantibea has one of the greatest armies on the planet. There are only about twelve airships in the entire world. Cantibea has eight of them.'

Junk stared at it in awe. Then he remembered what he was about to do and pulled himself away.

'Come on, we haven't got much time.' He carried on running.

'Time for what?' Lasel called after him.

'To save Garvan, of course.' As Junk ran, he reached into his satchel and pulled out the box.

'How are we supposed to save Garvan?'

Junk didn't answer. He had already opened a portal ahead of them and one by one they all jumped through.

Once inside the Room of Doors, they approached the dais, pulling off their furs and winter clothes as they went. Junk quickly transformed the box into its dodecahedron formation and planted it on top of the column.

'Gatekeeper,' he called, 'I need a door.'

'I have lots,' said the Gatekeeper's disembodied voice.

'Can you open a door anywhere?'

'Locational information required.'

'How do I position it?'

*

Out in Ollamah's town square, Garvan was bowing his head. Jadris raised the broadsword above his neck. Kyril closed his eyes, not wanting to have to watch what was about to happen. Jadris twisted his two hands in opposite directions on the hilt and it turned. The four blades fanned out. Jadris took a deep breath and then heaved the sword to one side. Slicing through the air, using his upper body to manoeuvre it, he brought it down on to Garvan's neck. About a tenth of a second before the first blade was about to make contact, a green door opened up beneath Garvan and he vanished from view as he dropped into it. The door was only open for a flash and Jadris was left stumbling forward as the weight of the sword and the lack of meaty neck to cut through meant he lost his balance. Kyril opened his eyes as Jadris hit the ground. There was no sign of Garvan.

'Twantan farnip?' said Kyril. Jadris was open-mouthed with shock as he lay on the dusty ground. All he could do was shake his head. He had no idea what had just happened.

In the Room of Doors, Garvan looked up from a prone position on the cold metallic floor. Junk, Lasel and Payo–Mestrowe stood over him, all smiling.

'I figured there was another place left to run,' said Junk with a grin.

Garvan sat up and nodded. 'I guess so. It was nice to see my brothers again.'

7

'So I've been thinking,' said Junk. 'We're kind of back to square one. Where do we go from here? I've got an idea.' The others waited. 'Otravinicus.'

'What about him?' said Lasel.

'We know he was with this guy who called himself Han Solo, and we now know Han Solo is connected to the Nine Emperors through Tolfke. Otravinicus never told me what happened after they went to Ollamah, and he never worked out Han Solo's connection to the Nine Emperors. He could know something he doesn't realize is relevant.'

'You're suggesting we go and find him?' asked Garvan. Junk nodded.

'How?' asked Lasel.

'We go through the same door he went through – the Gatekeeper will know which one – and see if we can pick up his trail.'

A green rectangle of light hovered a little above a dusty, cracked road. Garvan stepped through. The force pushed him and he stumbled a little but kept his balance. He turned and waited. Junk was next, and Garvan caught him as the door spat him out. Then Lasel came through and finally Payo–Mestrowe. The door closed behind them and they started walking, turning in small circles as they went, studying their surroundings.

They were in a city built on an enormous scale. The buildings towered over them, reaching five hundred storeys into the air and disappearing into the clouds. Upper floors of buildings were connected by a web of transparent tubes. There were buildings that defied logic and physics, born of architectural genius and imagination. As they looked down endless straight roads they could see single buildings that covered a dozen blocks. All the street signs and writing on the front of the buildings appeared to be written in some sort of Scandinavian language. Although Junk had learned a little Swedish, Finnish and Danish, he couldn't read any of it. He only recognized it by the liberal use of umlauts, carets and rings on many of the letters. There were lots of blank billboards. He assumed that once they would have been powered and advertisements would have played across their faces, but now all were lifeless. There were all sorts of rusting vehicles lying around too. Some had wheels and some had wings. All were abandoned. Junk and the others knew immediately that the city was deserted. There was a silence, unnatural in its totality. There were none of the sounds of life one would expect in a city: no engines, no car horns, no people, nothing. A strong wind whipped up the rubbish littering the roads. This was a ghost town.

'What's happened to all the people?' asked Payo.

'I've never seen anywhere like this,' said Junk.

'I think it's the past,' said Garvan. 'There used to be stories about cities that were as high as the sky. Never really believed it. Guess I was wrong.'

'Well, it's not my past,' said Junk. 'Nowhere on Earth was like this when I was alive. And all the writing's in Swedish or something.' He was looking at a shop sign that read 'ÅNGSTRÖM' in grubby brown letters. 'I guess we're in Sweden.'

'Sweden?' asked Lasel.

'Further north than Arrapia,' said Junk, picturing the map Garvan had drawn in the sand back in Corraway. The oceans had consumed most of northern Europe. 'It's not there any more.'

'Can you read any of it?' asked Garvan.

Junk shook his head. 'I speak a little, but reading it's a different thing. This could be Stockholm maybe.'

Just then they turned a corner and Junk stuttered to a stop. The others stopped too and looked at him. He was frowning as if he couldn't believe what he was looking at.

'What's wrong?' asked Lasel. Ahead of them was an inland bay and a rusting orange suspension bridge. Junk had seen that bridge many times. He knew it immediately. It was the Golden Gate Bridge. He recognized the land around it. The shape of the bay.

'This isn't Sweden. This is San Francisco. America.'

He pictured Garvan's map. 'Mallia.' He turned and looked back at the city. 'But why's everything in Swedish? That doesn't make any sense.'

They turned back the way they had come and headed back into the city, walking four abreast down a wide and eerily empty road.

'So how do we find Otravinicus then?' asked Junk.

'Well, if we're all agreed this is the past, then he must have found a way out. A way to get back to our present,' said Garvan. 'Which means we won't find him here.'

'We could try to find how he got back.'

'The Nine Emperors,' said Mestrowe. 'Must be.' The others looked at him for explanation. 'Well, the only way back is through the Room of Doors, and the only other people we know with access to it are the Nine Emperors.'

'Makes sense,' said Junk. 'So if we find Otravinicus, we find the Nine Emperors.' Then a thought occurred to him. 'How would they know?'

'Know what?'

'Where he was? How could Otravinicus let them know that he was in San Francisco in whatever year this is for them to come and save him?'

At that, brows furrowed with thought. As they were thinking they gradually became aware of a noise. It sounded like rumbling thunder and it was drawing nearer rapidly. They looked up and the sliver of sky they could see above the buildings was a deep and rich rose. A tranquil dusk, not a thunderstorm sky.

'That's no storm,' said Garvan.

The ground started to shake.

'Is it an earthquake?' asked Junk, but before any of the others could respond a herd of twenty zebras came rampaging around the corner. Junk and the others leaped behind a decaying red car and watched them pass.

'Stripy horses,' said Garvan once they had gone by.

'Zebras,' said Junk. 'They're called zebras.' From the blank look on Garvan's face it was clear that zebras were extinct in Garvan's time. He had never seen their like.

'Why would there be a herd of zebras in San Francisco?' said Junk. 'Maybe they're from a zoo.'

'Wonder what made them run,' said Lasel.

No sooner had the words left her lips than a pride of lions appeared in pursuit of the zebras. Payo–Mestrowe, Lasel, Garvan and Junk froze, waiting for them to pass. Evidently lions did still exist in Garvan's time, and he knew to be afraid of them. Either that or he noticed the huge teeth and claws and put two and two together.

The zebras turned a corner at the end of the street and vanished from sight. The lions were close behind them. In a few seconds they had gone too. Junk and the others breathed a sigh of relief and stepped out from behind the car.

'Something's very weird here,' said Junk. 'Those were African lions. They didn't roam the streets of America ever.'

'What's a zoo?' asked Lasel. 'You said the stripy horses might have come from a zoo. Could the lions be from this zoo place too?'

64

'Maybe. I think –' Junk froze mid-sentence as he saw that one of the lions had padded back around the corner and was staring right at them. She tilted her head from side to side, perhaps trying to work out if they were more or less tasty than a zebra and easier or harder to catch. She must have decided on tastier and/or easier because suddenly she roared over her shoulder and very quickly she was joined by the rest of her pride. The alpha male pushed his way through to the front and roared at the top of his lungs, just to set the mood.

'What do we do? What do we do?' asked Junk, trying hard not to panic but failing. His heart was beating so fast he could feel it in his throat.

'We have lions in Cantibea. They're called ranucks but they're much the same. The only thing I know is you're not supposed to run,' said Garvan. 'Least I think that's right.'

The alpha male padded closer.

'He's coming closer,' said Lasel unnecessarily. 'What do we do?'

'I think we should run,' said Garvan.

'You just said not to run.' The alpha male lowered his head until it was level with his shoulder blades and exposed his jaws in a display of aggression. He was getting ready to attack. Garvan looked to see what was behind them. There was the entrance to a department store, but it was a hundred metres away and there was no guarantee that the door was unlocked. However standing still wasn't an option.

'RUN!' shouted Garvan. He turned and started running, grabbing Junk, who in turn grabbed Lasel. Payo–Mestrowe brought up the rear. The lions, led by the male, set off in pursuit.

As they drew closer to the entrance to the department store they could see that the door was open. It moved back and forth in the breeze. This gave them a boost and Garvan sped up. By this point, Junk and Lasel were completely off the ground and Garvan was just carrying them under his arm. It meant that Junk was looking back and had a unenviable view of their pursuers. They were catching up.

'FASTER! FASTER!' he yelled. Garvan found another burst of acceleration and they reached the door. They hurled themselves through and then Garvan scrambled backwards and put all his weight against the door. Payo–Mestrowe joined him. The lead lion jumped at the door and bounced off it when it didn't move.

Junk looked around and saw some metal poles, parts of a clothes rail. He fed them through the handles of the door, stopping it from opening. Outside, the lions were throwing themselves at the doors in an attempt to get in.

'Come on,' said Junk. 'There must be a back door somewhere.'

Junk and the others started to walk away. They hadn't got more than a dozen steps when the lions' ceaseless assault on the door ceased. Junk and Garvan turned and saw the lions lined up outside, watching them, observing but not trying to break in any more.

'Why've they stopped?' asked Junk.

'Don't know,' said Lasel. Then one of the lionesses nudged the door softly with her head. The metal poles stopping it from opening jiggled and bounced a little to the left. The lioness did it again and the same thing happened. One more time and the metal poles were shaken free. They dropped to the floor with a clatter and the doors slowly opened inwards as the pride entered.

'Have lions got much smarter?' asked Junk.

No one answered. They all just turned and started running. The lions fanned out in pursuit.

The ground floor of the department store was full of clothing hanging from hundreds of free-standing racks. Junk and the others split up and weaved in and out of these racks, trying to throw the lions off their scent.

They came together again at the foot of a wide staircase and started up it. There was a massive chandelier hanging above them and as Junk ascended he looked up and saw that the chandelier was home to a nest of writhing snakes. Scores of them dripped from it like strands of tar, falling on to the steps below when they lost their purchase. This didn't hurt them. It just seemed to irritate them and they would hiss and snap at the air around them.

On the first landing Junk stopped and looked back. The lions had reached the bottom of the staircase. The alpha male locked eyes with Junk and growled deep in his throat.

Further up, Lasel realized Junk was no longer with them and turned. She looked down and saw him staring at the lions. 'Junk,' she said, but quietly in a panicked whisper.

'It's OK,' said Junk in a subdued tone so as not to startle the pride. 'I'm right behind you.' Keeping his movements to a minimum, Junk reached behind him and curled his hand around the greasy shaft of a lamp that was part of a display gathering dust. The lions started to pad up the stairs, advancing slowly as if they could sense a trap. With each step the lions took, the bolder they became. They started to crouch, getting ready to pounce. Junk whipped his arm around and launched the lamp at the chandelier with all his might. It hit, jarring loose at least fifty of the snakes. They rained down on to the steps between Junk and the lions. Being dislodged like that really ticked the snakes off and they were hissing and snapping at each other and at anything else. The lions studied the outraged reptiles carpeting the stairs between them and their dinner. You could almost see them thinking, Is it worth the risk?

Junk didn't wait around to find out. He hurried up the stairs and rejoined the others.

'Clever,' said Garvan.

'Did you notice something?' said Junk. Garvan shrugged. 'It was raining snakes.'

The reference was to Garvan's nolic-tea-induced vision. Garvan thought about it and slowly smiled.

8

'Let's get out of here,' said Lasel.

'Where do we go?' asked Junk.

'Anywhere. Just not here,' said Lasel. 'There's something about this place I really don't like.'

Junk understood. He took the box out of his satchel and opened a doorway in front of them. Lasel entered first and then Payo–Mestrowe. Junk gestured for Garvan to go ahead and his big friend was pulled into the green door. Then, just as Junk was about to follow, he heard something. It sounded like someone shouting, and for a moment he was sure he had heard his name. He listened again. He didn't hear anything and decided he must have imagined it. He turned back to the door, but just as he was about to enter, he heard it again. It was closer this time.

'JUNK!' It was coming from the street. Junk stepped away from the door and moved to the windows, where he looked out. There in the middle of the desolate road was Dr Otravinicus. He was running, turning, looking, searching and crying out.

'PLEASE, JUNK! WHERE ARE YOU?'

Junk tried to open the window but it wasn't designed to open. He banged on the glass, but Otravinicus was still too far away. Then something caught Junk's eye and he looked straight down to see some of the lions coming out of the store. Evidently they had been attracted by all the noise Otravinicus was making.

Out in the street, Otravinicus hadn't yet spotted the lions. He was panting hard, having been running. Sweat was pouring down his face. He was coughing and wheezing and seemed on the verge of tears.

'JUNK! DON'T GO! I'M HERE! I'm here.' His voice gave out on him then and he couldn't shout any more. He fell to his knees and put his head in his hands. The tears came. His scrawny body juddered as he wept. His bony shoulders moved up and down like a pair of pistons. Then he heard a growl. A deep, sonorous growl. He stopped mid-sob and tilted his head up to see what was left of the pride standing a dozen metres in front of him. He got to his feet ever so slowly and looked around for a way to escape. There was nowhere to go. The big cats would be on him before he could get to the nearest doorway. They were lowering themselves, getting ready to attack. This time they were not going to be denied their dinner. Accepting that his death was inevitable, the doctor closed his eyes and spread his arms, ready for the end. The lions pounced, powering off the ground, using the incredible muscles in their hind legs to propel themselves forward. Otravinicus could hear their approach, sense their closeness. Curiosity tempted him to look and see, but he denied it and strained to keep his eyes closed. He screamed at the top of his lungs.

The first lion took hold of him and Otravinicus could feel its teeth sinking into him. The pain crescendoed and unconsciousness quickly overtook him. For an instant, just before he blacked out, Dr Otravinicus thought he could hear the lions crying out in distress. He half opened one eye and saw a huge figure standing over him. He looked sort of like a Pallatan and he was holding one of the lions by its throat. But that was impossible. Then he passed out.

In the Room of Doors, they laid the unconscious Otravinicus on the floor and Garvan tended to his wounds with some buchelous grass, the same foul-smelling concoction they had used on Junk when he had been burned by Brother Antor in the monastery. The doctor would sleep for several hours, so they wouldn't be able to question him till later.

They all sat on the floor around the raised dais, their backs leaning against it, but the metallic floor was hard and uncompromising. No one could get comfortable.

'Hey, Horace, old fella, is there anywhere in here we can sit?' Junk called out.

'I am the Gatekeeper,' replied the booming disembodied voice.

'OK, is there anywhere in here where we can sit, Gatekeeper?' The Horace joke was getting stale anyway, thought Junk. 'Somewhere not so hard.'

Before their very eyes the floor started to grow upwards as if it was made of a million tiny pixel-sized cubes. The cubes moved and blistered and multiplied, like a colony of ants coming together. The way they moved triggered a memory for Junk but he couldn't place it. When the cubes stopped growing they were in the shape of a shiny black curved seat, big enough for Garvan to stretch out on. Despite the curvature, it still looked rock hard, but when Junk ran his hand along the surface it felt softer than the fur-lined bed he slept on in Garvan's cabin.

'Feel that,' he said to the others. All of them gasped as they touched the seat. It didn't feel like they expected it to. Junk sat on it and couldn't help but let out a long 'Aaaaahhhhhhh', an expression of relaxation. He turned and the chaise-longue-like chair adapted its shape so as to compensate for the change in his posture. 'Look at that,' he said. It was one of the coolest things he had ever seen.

Four more identical seats grew up from the floor, and as each of the others sat they all let out a long 'Aaaaahhhh', just as Junk had. One by one they all closed their eyes and drifted off to sleep.

Junk was the first to wake. His eyes blinked open. A thought had woken him. He had remembered why the movement of the cubes had seemed familiar. It was from the nolic-tea vision. The cubes that grew from nothing into the chair he was now lying on had moved in the same way that the box had changed shape. He sat up, and

72

silently the seat beneath him adapted to his new position. He looked at the others. They were all still sleeping soundly.

He reached for the satchel, which he had kept on because of Otravinicus. Even though the doctor was still out cold, Junk didn't trust him not to wake up and try to steal the box again. He opened the bag and took out the box. He held it in one hand, close to his face, and turned it slowly, studying it intently. Then he held it firmly in two hands, remembering how he'd held it in the tea-induced trance. He moved his fingers over the surface in random patterns, feeling the bumps and indentations on its otherwise smooth exterior. Nothing happened. Somehow, without even thinking about it, he knew why. It was because he was trying to make it change. The same rules applied as when his disconnected hand told him how to trigger the dreamscape: he had to clear his mind, think of nothing, distract himself. Part of him could recall how his brain felt when he was reciting the solar system mnemonic. This time it was easier to skip straight to that same mindset, as if he had left imaginary breadcrumbs in the corridors of his subconscious.

In his hand the box exploded, making no more sound than a feather bumping against a buttercup, and a million tiny cubes shot out and then, faster than could be seen, reversed their trajectory and headed back to Junk's hand. However, instead of reverting to their original master-cube shape, the minion cubes enveloped his whole hand, taking on the shape of an iron glove.

Junk looked at his hand from all angles. What was once the box now covered his hand perfectly. It was form-fitting, as if it was a liquid metal that could change consistency at will from solid to fluid and back again.

As Junk stared at the glove, he wondered if it could change colour. Immediately it went from copper to blue to green to black, then it matched his skin tone to perfection, rendering it practically invisible, before it became mirrored and Junk smiled at his reflection. There was a connection. It knew what he was thinking. But there was more. The connection worked both ways. It wasn't a living, breathing, sentient thing, but it possessed something that could be described as consciousness and suddenly it had a name, and Junk knew what it was. It was called an Antricle. It was good to have something to call it, Junk thought, as they couldn't call it 'the box' any more on account of it not being a box. He understood, without knowing how, that their opening it out and turning it into a dodecahedron had all been terribly unnecessary. It had become that shape because Junk had jumped to the conclusion that it was that shape.

He got up then and crossed to the column on the raised dais. He remembered thinking that the hexagonal indentation on the top of the column was perfect for the dodecahedron, so that must have been correct. Junk saw the familiar indentation and let his hand hover over it. It changed shape, mimicking the dimensions of his hand exactly. Junk knew then that it would become whatever it needed to be to fit the Antricle.

'Junk?' He turned to see Lasel propping herself up on one arm, looking at him from under heavy eyelids. She wasn't fully awake and had a look on her face as if she was questioning whether or not she was dreaming. Junk smiled at her, ready to show off. He spread his arms, and the Antricle glove dissolved from his left hand and travelled up his arm in a line like a serpent, across his chest and down the other arm to his right hand. There it became a glove again, returned to its copper colouring and spread up that arm, encasing it.

By this point Lasel was wide awake and punching Garvan in the butt to wake him up. Garvan woke, as did Payo–Mestrowe. All were fully alert within seconds as they saw what Junk was doing. As they watched, the Antricle receded until it was a broad bangle clamped around Junk's wrist.

'How long were we asleep?' asked Garvan. 'Is that the box? What did you do to it?'

'It's called an Antricle,' said Junk. 'We weren't using it right, but I think I've figured it out now.'

'I'm confused,' said Payo. 'Where's the box gone?'

'This is the box,' said Junk. 'Except it was only box-shaped because someone, somewhere had decided it should be box-shaped. If they had decided it should be round . . .' The Antricle morphed into a perfect sphere sitting in the palm of Junk's hand. '. . . or a pyramid . . .' It became a pyramid. '. . . or a bottle . . .' It took on the proportions of a bottle. '. . . it would have been that.'

'How are you doing that?' asked Garvan, the astonishment in his voice clear.

'This is what it's built to do. I didn't understand before but I do now. I know what it's thinking; it knows what I'm thinking,' said Junk.

'It's thinking?' Lasel sounded incredulous.

'In a roundabout sort of way,' said Junk. 'It's not alive exactly, but it's intelligent.'

Lasel threw a questioning frown at Garvan. He added a hint of disbelief and threw it straight back. They were subtle so Junk wouldn't notice, but they needn't have worried. He was far too engrossed in his new toy.

'Its purpose is to help the wearer, keep them safe as they go through the doors into the unknown.'

Faster than a hummingbird could wink, the Antricle spread over Junk's body, encasing him completely from head to toe in a solid coppery husk. It was so quick and unexpected that it made all the others jump. Payo–Mestrowe let out a short strangled cry of surprise. After a few seconds the Antricle snapped back to being a bangle wrapped around Junk's wrist. It let out a whistling *thup* sound as it changed.

'You're doing that?' asked Lasel.

'Yeah,' said Junk with a grin.

'Where am I?'

Junk turned from the Antricle to see Otravinicus was awake.

'Am I dead? I remember . . .' A pained expression crossed his features as he thought back. He saw the buchelous grass on his skin. He moved to investigate but Garvan stayed his hand.

'You're going to be fine, Doctor.'

Otravinicus looked around. He saw Junk, Garvan, Lasel and a Pallatan he didn't recognize staring back at him. He started to weep tears of joy.

'I knew you would come back for me.' He was laughing and crying at the same time. 'I knew you wouldn't abandon me. Not after everything I had done for you.'

'Like trying to steal the box, you mean?' said Lasel.

The doctor let out a long, hyperactive 'mmmmmm- mmmm' and waved his hands over his face as if warding off a cloud of invisible wasps. 'A moment of madness. Nothing else. I would have turned right round and come back to y'all if it hadn't been for that –' choosing his words carefully – 'woman.' He meant Cascér. The last time they had seen Otravinicus he had tried to steal the Antricle and make his escape. He would have succeeded had Cascér not snatched the box from him and pushed him through the portal that took him to an unpopulated San Francisco.

Otravinicus looked around. 'Where is Cascér?'

'Gone,' said Garvan.

'Not . . . ?' Otravinicus couldn't quite bring himself to say the word 'dead'.

'No, just gone,' said Garvan. Otravinicus looked genuinely relieved.

'Where did you just come from, Doctor? How did you find us?' asked Junk.

'Well, like I said, I knew you'd be back for me so I stayed close to where the doorway was. I took up residence in the apartment building adjacent. Foolishly I chose the most aesthetically pleasing apartment, which was on the ninth floor. I kept watch morning, noon and night, waiting for your return. I must say I did expect it to be a little sooner.' He frowned to make sure no one missed his displeasure, but was met by such stony facades that he didn't push the point. 'But I knew you'd come eventually. I hadn't slept for a while, and when you arrived fatigue had got the better of me briefly. Fortunately I woke in time to see you walking off down the street. I ran after you but thought I'd lost you.'

'You almost had,' said Junk. 'Another few seconds and we'd have been gone. Where was that, Doctor? *When* was it? It looked like San Francisco, but everything was in Swedish.'

'That was the mid-forty-fourth century on your calendar, Junk. Remember I told you once that ape-descended humans died out. That was about fifty or so years after the final humans perished, close as I could figure. And it wasn't Swedish, it was Finnish. America had been owned by Finland for centuries by that point. Finland controlled pretty much the entire planet by the end. Not that it did them any good.'

'Finland?' said Junk, his incredulity apparent. 'Finland?' He said it again, wondering if the doctor had made a mistake or if he meant a different Finland.

'As as I understand it,' said Otravinicus, 'even in

your time, Finland had one of the best education systems in the world. While other countries were ploughing all their resources into industry and finance and what-have-you, Finland had a one-hundred-per-cent literacy rate. Turned out education was important. In the end they took over the world.' Otravinicus turned his attention to Payo–Mestrowe.

'Now if I am not very much mistaken,' he said, examining the Pallatan and in particular his scarred eye, 'this would be the person you were looking for. I must say I'm surprised that he seems to be one of your party. Isn't he the enemy?' He looked at Payo–Mestrowe and added, 'No offence.'

'None taken,' said Payo's light, cheery voice. Then Mestrowe added a particularly unpleasant curse in his deep, growling H'rtu, which Otravinicus spoke fluently and was clearly shocked by.

'It's a long story, Doctor,' said Junk. 'We'll tell you later. First we need to talk about Han Solo.'

9

Dr Otravinicus was feeling much better, but hungry, so they went to a colourful, noisy, bustling bazaar in the Varransea district of Huungun, a small country in central Payana, for breakfast. There were many street entertainers performing all around them. There were jugglers and acrobats and magicians and a man who danced alongside a fat chicken. The chicken was, by far, the better dancer of the two. The four acrobats seemingly defied gravity as they turned a dozen cartwheels in a row and flung themselves back and forth, somersaulting and flipping. Their signature move was a series of synchronized backflips that involved them running against one another's feet while in mid-flight. It was so jaw-droppingly spectacular that Junk and the others forgot why they were there while they watched. When the acrobats moved on to something less distracting, Junk turned his attention to Otravinicus.

'So, Doctor, we need to know what you did after Ollamah with the fella that called himself Han Solo. He has some connection to the Nine Emperors through the man in the mask, Tolfke.'

'What connection?' asked Otravinicus, and Junk studied his face, looking for any indication of a lie and making no attempt to hide his suspicion.

'I was hoping you could tell me. Tolfke lived on the island off Ollamah that you and this Han Solo visited.' Otravinicus started to speak but Junk cut him off. 'The townsfolk there remembered the two of you well.' Otravinicus closed his mouth again. He considered what to say next.

'I did go to the island but I didn't go inside his little house. I wasn't invited. I never saw this Tolfke. Why does he wear a mask?' No one answered so Otravinicus continued. 'Han went in alone, stayed for a short time and came back out again. After that we left.' There was a bubble of silence. No one believed Otravinicus, and he knew it. 'So who was this Tolfke?'

'Tolfke was or is a middle man for the Nine Emperors. He's the one who engaged Mestrowe to take my sister.'

Otravinicus glanced at Payo–Mestrowe, who seemed to smile and snarl at him simultaneously.

'Why?' asked Otravinicus.

'We don't know that yet,' said Junk.

'He doesn't . . . ?' Otravinicus looked with distaste at Payo–Mestrowe.

'No,' said Junk, 'he was just hired to get her. Doesn't know why. So where did you go after Ollamah?'

'Well, let's see, after Ollamah, we headed west by land-ship.'

'For what purpose?' asked Garvan.

'He was looking for somewhere to live, but he was always a little cagey about exactly what he wanted. He kept saying an island, somewhere remote, private, but he would never look at any of the ones I found. I always got the impression he was more interested in something bigger. We travelled over the Glarn Arka Sea, which took several days. He had a lot of books, which he gave to me to read. That's how I learned so much about your time, Junk. And we spent much time on the crossing talking, which is how I learned your language –' he was looking at Junk – 'and I taught him some of what I know. We talked about history and the state of the world today. He asked a thousand and one questions. He wanted to know everything. He asked a lot about Mallia. There's a lot of open, unpopulated land there. Hundreds of square miles. Great huge pockets of emptiness, which is why I thought he was more interested in something like that.

'Occasionally I got the feeling that he wasn't always on the ship with us. He came on board with a small bag but had all these books and clothes and whatever else he needed. I was never able to confirm my suspicions and I didn't know at the time about the box . . . or what do you call it now?' Otravinicus gestured to the bangle on Junk's wrist.

Junk touched it protectively. 'An Antricle.'

'Right. In hindsight I think I was right. Maybe.'

'So, Mallia . . . That's North and South America in my time. Where did you go when you got there?' asked Junk.

'Mallia isn't very heavily populated. There's only

a handful of tracks for land-ships. We continued west, stopping now and then and he would go off on his own. I offered to accompany him, but he wasn't interested. He would be gone for a day or sometimes two. Then he would come back and we'd carry on. That went on for about a week and then he came back from one of his excursions and announced we were done. We turned around and went home. He quizzed me even more about the world on the way back.'

'What happened when you got back?'

'The last time I saw him was when we reached the land-ship station in Turanay. The same one we departed from on board the *Casabia* all those weeks ago. He and I had an agreement that when we were done he would show me the Room of Doors. He said he had an urgent engagement and he would return to fulfil his side of the deal in a few hours. I never saw him again.'

Junk and the others pondered what Otravinicus had said. Junk was the first to speak. 'So, what if Han Solo was one of the Nine Emperors, or at least working for them, and he was looking for somewhere they could all live? It makes sense that the last place they visited met the criteria.'

'Yes,' said Otravinicus, 'but there's no way of knowing exactly where he went. Our last stop was a small land-ship station called Bullurgh. From there he set off north, but he could have gone anywhere once he was out of sight. He was gone for almost two days.'

'Well, two days away from the Nine Emperors is

closer than we've been before. Hopefully we can pick up their trail.'

Everyone agreed it was worth a shot. Garvan threw some money on the table for breakfast as Junk pressed simultaneously on several points of the Antricle on his wrist. A green doorway opened in front of them. He and Lasel were pulled into the doorway. The others followed.

No one around them noticed their departure except for one of the four acrobats. Unfortunately he was balancing upside down on one hand, on the right foot of one of his fellow performers, who in turn was balancing upside down on one hand on the left foot of another of their fellow performers, who in turn was doing a handstand on a chair which he was balancing atop a ball. Just as Junk and the others stepped through the doorway, the fourth acrobat was midway through a sprinting run-up, which ended in a jump on to a small springboard that shot high him up into the air so he could land upside down on one hand balancing on the top of the tower of his fellow tumblers. Now was not the time for any of them to become distracted.

The town of Bullurgh in the country of Mallia was little more than a dusty pit stop. It had one bar, one general store and a land-ship station. The nearest town was three hundred miles away. Bullurgh was a pimple on an otherwise featureless expanse of rust-coloured land topped with the bluest of big blue skies. The shade of blue reminded Garvan of the water around his island.

He hadn't thought about his island for a while. Right now it was sitting on the other side of the world to him and he wondered if he would ever see it again. Of course he knew he could see it whenever he wanted with the help of the Antricle. He could visit it at this moment in time or go back to the first day he found it or go forward and see what it would look like in a hundred years' time. He knew he could, but at the same time he knew he probably wouldn't. His focus needed to be on the here and now. He did consider that keeping track of where exactly the here and the now was wasn't that straightforward for a time traveller. It still created a butterfly flutter in his stomach to think about the fact he was a time traveller. Except he wasn't right now. Right now it was the same day of the year on his island as it was in Bullurgh. Right now he was just a traveller, but what a journey it had been so far.

Land-ships came through Bullough twice a week and brought with them a brief flurry of excitement and activity. For the rest of the time, very little happened. It was possibly the most boring place on the planet. This meant that Junk and the others were met with a lot of suspicious looks when they walked into town. The locals knew the only way in or out was by land-ship and the next one wasn't due for three days, so how had they got there? Lasel regurgitated her crashed air-ship story and everyone bought it.

They asked about new arrivals to the area and heard rumours of a mysterious invisible building a hundred miles north near a nameless lake. It turned out that a hundred miles was another country to the residents of Bullurgh so no one had bothered to go and investigate. They couldn't explain how or why it was invisible. That was just the way it had been described by other travellers (merchants, trappers and the like) who had passed through.

Junk and the others promptly vanished and were the talk of the town for the next few weeks until a family of hauk tines, small, ugly, muscular climbing lizards, took up residence in the water tower.

A circle of green light appeared in a lush, still forest. Garvan stepped through and his feet sank into a thick layer of spongy moss carpeting the ground. He stopped and listened. Birds chuckled high up in the treetops. Insects chirruped invisibly in the undergrowth around him. He walked on a few steps, feeling the bounce underfoot. Poles of fizzing sunlight snuck in through the canopy here and there. Garvan felt a pleasing coolness on his skin. This place reminded him of his island. Lots of things did. He missed it.

He turned back to the doorway and surprise made him catch his breath. The doorway was round. Every other time they had been rectangular. Why was this one different? As Garvan was contemplating this conundrum Junk appeared. He staggered a little as the door spat him forth and Garvan steadied him.

'Door's round,' said Garvan, pointing.

Junk turned and looked. 'Hhhmmm,' he said. 'I sort of half had a thought about the door being round as we were opening it. I was thinking how come they're always the same shape. Wondered if they could be any other shape.'

'Looks like the answer's yes,' said Garvan, just as Lasel stepped through. Junk steadied her and nodded his head to make her look at the door.

'Door's round,' she said.

'Junk can make them change shape just by thinking about it,' Garvan said.

'Cool,' said Lasel. 'Can you do it again? Make it something else.'

Junk shrugged. He looked at the door, closed his eyes, tried to clear his mind and then pictured a triangle. He opened his eyes again and the door was still round. He frowned. He tried again. Deep breath, closed his eyes and this time he imagined the round door turning into a square. He opened his eyes and the door still hadn't changed. He shrugged. 'I don't know. Maybe I have to do it from the other side.'

Just then Otravinicus came through. He stumbled and no one moved to steady him so he felt flat on his face. The moss made for a soft landing, however. He turned as he sat up and spotted the door.

'Door's round,' he said.

Once Payo–Mestrowe was through, the five of them walked towards the edge of the forest where the trees started to thin out. Soon they heard the sound of waves lapping against a shoreline and they knew they were close to a lake. The sound drifted towards them, weaving between the trees. They walked on. Junk asked Dr Otravinicus if he had ever heard of Pirestus. Like Garvan and Lasel, he hadn't. Junk was wondering if he had misheard.

They soon came to a body of water that was longer than it was wide. Tall coniferous trees covered the banks on all sides. As they left the shelter of the trees behind and walked out on to a band of shingle they could see nothing that resembled a building. Not unless it was a building that looked like a tree. Junk's heart sank. Every time he thought he was close to the end, his journey found a way to carry on.

'They did say it was invisible,' said Garvan.

'What does that mean though?' asked Junk. 'It can't actually be invisible.'

Just then Junk felt a hand on his arm and he looked at Lasel, who was staring intently at the north end of the lake, her head tilted to the right. She switched over to the left and then back again. 'Do the trees look strange to you?' she asked.

Junk looked where she was staring and saw only trees that looked like trees, but when he tilted his head and mimicked Lasel's strange side-to-side motion he suddenly saw what she meant. The trees rippled like a mirage. The five travellers stood at the water's edge tilting their heads from left to right. Had anyone seen them, they would have thought them very odd.

They made their way around the shoreline to the shimmering patch of forest. As they drew closer they were astounded to discover that there was indeed a building there. It was a mirrored cube. Two storeys high and just as wide. It sat among the trees, hidden in plain sight. To all intents and purposes, invisible.

'Is this it? Have we found them?' asked Junk with an excited, breathless tone to his voice. Was this the end of his journey? Was this where the Nine Emperors were? Was Ambeline here?

They set off around the mirrored structure. At the rear, they discovered there was more to it than just a single cuboid. That was good, thought Junk. The cube was too small to house nine people. There needed to be more. The cube connected to a corridor – also mirrored – that stretched off into the trees. It was hard to gauge just how far it went as they needed to be within a few metres to see it at all. They walked along, brushing a hand against the reflective glass as they went. Five pairs of identical twins traipsing side by side, hand in hand, through the woods.

After walking for the best part of a minute, they saw themselves ahead, coming towards them, and realized that the building broadened out. They looked up and saw that the structure rose dramatically from this point. It was an incredible, soaring tower. The cirrocumulus cloud mottling the sky was reflected on the upper reaches of its surface like a slowly moving rash. It was impossible to tell how tall the tower stood, but it appeared to reach higher than the trees around it, and they would dwarf the giant tree that Junk had climbed back on Garvan's island. The trees here were easily two hundred metres high.

'How do we get in?' asked Otravinicus.

'I haven't seen any doors,' said Garvan.

'I can smash it!' Everyone turned to see Payo–Mestrowe brandishing a chunky piece of mossy rock he'd found on the ground. He drew his arm back ready to hurl it, but Junk jumped up in front of him and put his hand in the way.

'Whoa, whoa! Wait! We don't need to do that,' shouted Junk. He put his right hand on the Antricle, which was still on his left wrist, positioned his fingers in a certain way and started to move them in gentle clockwise circles. He placed the palm of his left hand on the section of mirrored wall directly in front of them, and an opening appeared as a section of the wall dematerialized.

Beyond was a long thin passageway that dissolved into darkness once the muted light from the forest faded away after about twenty metres.

'How did you know how to do that?' asked Lasel.

Junk shrugged. 'I don't know. I guess the Antricle told me.'

Lasel glanced at Garvan. Both wore a look of concern.

Otravinicus was the first to step forward. He stared into the dark. 'This must head inwards from this point. It's very dark. That thing –' he indicated the Antricle – 'doesn't have a light on it, does it?'

In response, Junk stroked the pad of his thumb in a figure eight on the underside of the Antricle and it started to glow green. One by one, they stepped through the opening Junk had made. He followed them through, and the moment he took his hand away from the glass the opening vanished to be replaced with the complete mirrored wall.

10

The only light now came from Junk's wrist. He held it out in front of him as he led the way.

'Stay close,' he told the others.

The dark passageway appeared to be some sort of service corridor. It continued on for about a hundred and fifty metres until they came to a door. A real door this time. Junk opened it and light flooded in. It took a moment for their eyesight to adjust. They saw a narrow stairway ahead of them. The glow on the Antricle extinguished itself without Junk doing anything and he started up the stairs. The wall to their left was the mirrored outer wall, but unlike the passageway they had just left they could see through to the forest outside. From this side it just looked like a wall of glass.

After they had gone up one flight, they found themselves facing another door.

'Wait,' said Lasel, and the others turned to look at her. 'Do we have any sort of plan? The Nine Emperors stole Ambeline, remember. They don't sound particularly friendly. Are we just going to walk right in?' It was only then that she noticed Junk wasn't with them any more. 'Where's Junk?'

In answer to her question the door at the top of the stairs opened and Junk appeared. Evidently he hadn't waited around to hear Lasel's note of caution.

'You guys should come and look,' he said, and disappeared through the door again.

They stepped out on to a wide internal glass veranda and walked to the balustrade, where they looked down on the sprawling ground level of the tower and up to the tapered roof two hundred and fifty metres above them. The interior of the tower was pyramidal. As had been the case in the small stairway, the walls of the entire building, both outer walls and internal ones, were transparent. A building of glass. They were on the first floor looking down on a vast open space that looked like the world's largest shopping mall, although there were no shops. It was deserted and eerily silent.

'HELLO!' shouted Garvan without warning, making everyone jump. Payo let out a little involuntary yelp. Garvan's voice echoed around them, soaring upwards and swooping down and past them. The acoustics in this place were incredible. In the middle of the ground floor sat a grand piano (also made of glass), so maybe the acoustics were no accident. No reply came. 'I don't think anyone's here,' said Garvan.

'No,' said Junk, clearly disappointed. Another dead end. No Han Solo. No Nine Emperors. No Ambeline.

They walked around the veranda. It had the feel

of a place that was just finished and about to be opened to the public. Everything was clean. Sterile even. They descended a flight of glass stairs to the ground level. There they found a great glass elevator.

'How very *Charlie and the Chocolate Factory*,' remarked Junk.

'Very what?' asked Garvan.

'It's a story from my time,' said Junk. 'One of my favourites from when I was a kid.' He reached out and pressed the call button. Instantly the doors of the glass lift opened. Junk hesitated for a moment and then stepped inside.

'I'm not sure it looks safe,' said Otravinicus, clearly nervous.

'Then stay here,' said Junk with an unconcerned shrug. 'I want to see what's at the top.'

'It might not work,' said Otravinicus.

'Doors opened,' Junk said. Garvan, Lasel and Payo–Mestrowe stepped inside. There was more than enough room for all of them.

'Can it take the weight of all of us, do you think?' Otravinicus really didn't want to get in almost as much as he didn't want to be left behind.

Something caught Junk's eye and he saw a small plaque that read: 'This lift can carry weight equivalent to two metric tonnes'. He nodded. 'It's fine, Doctor,' he said.

Otravinicus poked his head around the door, but only for several staccato glimpses, each time pulling back sharply.

'It says the lift can take us all, so make a choice. Are you coming or staying?'

Otravinicus screwed up his face as he considered his options. 'I think I'll stay,' he said. Junk nodded and reached out to press the button for the top floor. 'Or actually . . .' said Otravinicus, and Junk pulled his finger back. Again Otravinicus hesitated. 'No, no, I'll stay.' Junk started to reach for the button again. 'No, I'll come.' Junk paused. 'No, I'll stay.' This time Junk stabbed the button quickly before Otravinicus could change his mind. As the doors started to close, the doctor changed his mind one last time and jumped inside. The elevator started to rise. Slowly for the first dozen metres, and then it shot into the air as if it was a fairground ride. The ascent was surprisingly smooth. Unaware of what he was doing, Otravinicus grabbed hold of Payo–Mestrowe's sleeve and closed his eyes. As they climbed, he let out a low, choked whine.

Junk, Garvan, Lasel and Payo–Mestrowe looked out, one on each side of the lift. Every wall in the whole building seemed to be made of glass, and as they rose they could see that the place was indeed deserted.

The elevator reached the top floor and Otravinicus scrambled to be the first one out, shoving the others aside. He stumbled as he exited and fell, face-planting on the floor. The floor, as it turned out, was made of glass too and the doctor found himself staring at the ground a hundred storeys below. He let out a strangled squeal like a dormouse being trodden on and curled up into a protective ball with his eyes squeezed as tightly shut as possible. Garvan picked him up as he passed and carried him like a suitcase.

It was only the floors of the walkways around the elevator that were see-through and they soon reached normal, non-transparent floors and Otravinicus recovered.

'I'm not keen on heights,' he said, somewhat redundantly.

As they wandered from room to room, they drifted off in separate directions. Junk entered a room with a huge, luxurious, square sofa in the centre. He noticed a control panel fixed to the wall by the door. It looked similar to an iPad but thinner and lighter, and when he touched it, it came away from the wall. It wasn't obvious how it had been attached to begin with. Junk touched the screen and it came to life with a *zzzzmmmmm* sound. Several boxes appeared on the display, labelled: 'Lights', 'Entertainment', 'Walls', 'Seating' and 'Food'. Junk pressed 'Walls'. The picture on the screen changed to a plan view of the room they were standing in. Each of the four walls was highlighted. Nothing else happened so Junk touched one of the walls in the diagram and the corresponding wall in the actual room became opaque.

'Cool!' said Junk. He tapped the other three walls on the display and they all turned opaque too. He was suddenly plunged into darkness, the only light coming from the tablet in his hands and the open door.

He pressed 'Lights' now, and an array of concealed floor and ceiling lights blazed to life in the room. He played with the on-screen controls to vary their brightness and colour. He grew bored of that quickly and tried 'Entertainment'.

The entirety of one wall became a giant high-definition screen. A crystal-clear logo, a sleek sports car speeding towards the camera, filled the screen. Music played from hidden speakers and the clarity was bewitching. The sound brought the others. They all watched open-mouthed. They had never seen anything like this.

'What is that?' asked Garvan.

'It's a car,' said Junk. 'Don't know what make.' On screen, the car skidded to a stop, making everyone but Junk flinch, and a hunky male model type with glinting eyes got out, winked and tossed a coin towards them. The spinning coin filled the screen, finally coming to a stop as the legend 'EveryFilm Entertainment' filled their vision.

When the logo faded away, the image on the screen changed to mirror the room they were standing in, doubling its size. A slim, beautiful blonde woman appeared from a door in the distance and walked towards them. Her high heels click-clacked on the hard floor. They could hear the swish-swish of her silk dress. When she reached the foreground of the picture, she stepped out of the screen and a three-dimensional, photo-real hologram of her appeared among them. Everyone tittered with surprise.

'Hi,' she said in a cheery American voice, 'I'm Jenny and I'll be your guide through the set-up and use of your

EveryFilm Entertainment System. Let's start. Would you like me to read through the Terms and Conditions or would you like to skip?'

'Skip,' said Junk without hesitation.

'We can come back to that any time you like,' she said, smiling and showing her perfect white teeth. 'Next, would you like to customize your interface?'

Junk looked at the others and they all shrugged. 'I don't know,' he said to Jenny. 'What does that mean?'

Jenny laughed girlishly. 'I mean me, silly. You can change the way I look . . .' Instantly Jenny became a small Oriental boy, then a lanky basketball player, then Abraham Lincoln, then a blue-furred tiger, then a mermaid, before reverting back to her original form. She continued: '. . . the way I speak . . .' Her neutral West Coast American accent changed to something from the Deep South: '. . . I can speak like this if y'all prefer . . .' All eyes turned to Otravinicus. She sounded just like him. Then her accent became that of a sultry French woman: '. . . or more like zis if you like.' She started speaking in different languages: Japanese, then German, then Spanish.

'That's OK,' said Junk, cutting her off. 'Just how you were is fine.'

'That's super,' said Jenny. 'We can come back to that any time you like. Now would you like to choose something to watch?'

'Sure,' said Junk, 'what have you got?'

Jenny threw her head back and laughed as if he'd said something adorable. 'Why, everything, silly.'

Junk frowned. 'You can't have everything.'

'Try me,' said Jenny.

Junk thought for a moment and remembered the great glass elevator. '*Charlie and the Chocolate Factory.*'

'Which version would you like to watch? I have twelve . . .'

'Twelve?' Junk frowned.

Jenny continued: 'Starting with the American version, from the year 1971, called *Willy Wonka and the Chocolate Factory*, all the way through to the Uzbekistani version, from the year 3644, entitled *Artem Niyazi and the Glorious Candy Empire*. Would you like me to list all twelve titles?'

'No, that's OK,' said Junk. He thought some more. He wanted to test this and see if she really did have *everything*. 'Do you have TV shows too?'

'We have everything,' said Jenny.

'News shows?'

'Everything.'

'Sporting events?'

'Everything.'

'Everything? OK, show me the local weather report for Malmö, Sweden, on –' he picked a date at random – '24 June 2063.' The screen on the wall switched to a handsome man in a tailored suit standing in front of a map showing the south-west corner of Sweden. He spoke enthusiastically, in Swedish naturally, while pointing to different parts of the map. He froze mid-sentence.

'This is how the original item was transmitted, but I can translate it into any language of your choice and show it in 3D, 4D or as a hologram.'

'I like a hologram best,' said a reedy voice with a distinct Edinburgh brogue. Everyone turned. Standing next to Dr Otravinicus was a small, odd-looking man in his early twenties. He had long, lank, unwashed hair that fell across his eyes. He brushed it aside but it fell back almost immediately. He wore several layers of mismatched clothes, and the buttons of his shirt were out of alignment, which meant one side of his collar stuck up from under the neck of the thick-knit green jumper he was wearing. What looked at first glance like a pair of spectacles turned out to be drawn on his face with felt-tip pen.

The moment it registered with Dr Otravinicus that he was standing next to a complete stranger who had seemingly materialized out of nowhere, he let out a cry of surprise and jumped back. This had the effect of making everyone cry out and jump, including the scruffy Scottish interloper. Suddenly the expression on his face changed. The benign interest of a moment before was replaced with real fear, as if he had just realized he was standing in the middle of a cave of bears. His reaction was extreme. He grabbed clumps of his hair and howled in distress. This made everyone back away from him some more.

'Who are you?' he cried, as if their presence had only just registered with him. 'Are ye demons?' With that he waved his hands wildly in front of his face, then let out a *fump* sound as he froze on the spot with his fingers spread in front of his face as if he could hide behind them. No one said a word. They all exchanged anxious glances while keeping one eye on the strange new arrival. He let his breathing level out and then he looked up, slowly peeking through the lattice of his fingers.

Lasel stepped forward and put out a hand. 'Who are you?' she asked gently.

'Oh God,' said the Scottish stranger. 'I think they can see through my power barrier.'

'We don't mean you any harm,' said Lasel.

The man closed his eyes and practised deep breathing. He started counting quietly. 'OK, one . . . two . . . three!' With that he sprang into a sprint and shot out of the room.

'Wait!' shouted Junk, running after him.

'Where are you going?' called Garvan.

'He's the only person we've seen. We need to talk to him.' Junk ran out of the room and one by one the others followed.

The small frantic Scotsman sprinted along the corridor, back towards the lift, with Junk and the others in pursuit.

'Please! Wait!' cried Junk. 'We just want to talk to you.'

The Scotsman was too panicked to listen. He slipped on the glossy glass floor as he took a corner too quickly, but was on his feet again almost immediately and heading for a door marked 'PRIVATE' in large, aggressive red letters.

He got to the door just ahead of Junk and the others and went through, locking it behind him. Payo–Mestrowe didn't even slow down. He hurled his head at the door, shattering the thick frosted glass and reaching through to unlock it.

They went through into a tight stairway. There was a door at the top of the steps that they could hear the stranger locking. Payo–Mestrowe this time threw his shoulder into the door, following it up with the rest of his considerable bulk, knocking the door off its hinges.

The five of them dashed into the next room and immediately stuttered to a stop, shocked by what they discovered. The room was small and round, like a bell tower. The stranger was nowhere to be seen. There was only one thing in the room: a rectangle of shimmering green light: a doorway to the Room of Doors.

11

It was just like the one they had seen in Tolfke's armoire, except this one didn't vanish. As far as Junk knew, only he and the Nine Emperors had access to the Room of Doors, so maybe the Scotsman was one of them or was at least connected to the Nine Emperors in some way, like Tolfke. Either way he was a definite step in the right direction. It made Junk even more eager to find him.

They each stepped through without hesitation but the doorway didn't take them to the Room of Doors as they had expected. They came out in another small, though high-ceilinged, and this time square, windowless room. It seemed that this particular portal had only one task: connecting two points. They were all immediately aware that they were moving, rocking rhythmically from side to side. Junk recognized the familiar drumming noise that filled the air.

'We're on a train,' said Junk.

'A what?' asked Lasel.

'It's like a land-ship,' said Junk, 'but smaller and doesn't go on water.'

'Doesn't go on water?' said Garvan. 'What's the point of that?'

Junk shrugged.

'How can we be on a train?' asked Otravinicus. 'We were just in a tower.'

'The doorway,' said Junk, 'it doesn't go to the Room of Doors. It must be linked to this place. Fixing two points in space.'

'So we're not in the tower any more?' asked Mestrowe.

'We could be anywhere,' said Junk.

'I think we should go back,' said Otravinicus, sounding nervous. This was more discombobulating than he liked.

'You can,' said Junk. 'I don't know who that guy was, but he's the only person we've seen. I want to find out who he is.'

Ahead of them was a sliding door that shimmied a little from side to side with the motion of the train. Junk slid it open and he and Lasel stepped out into a narrow, empty corridor. They were indeed on a train, and what a train it was. It looked like something from the 1930s. All art deco, sleek and refined. Plush, monochromatic patterned carpeting lay underfoot.

In front of them the exterior wall sported eight floor-to-ceiling windows from end to end, but frosted so they couldn't see out. They could tell that it was extremely sunny outside, but the frosting muted the sun's brilliance. However each window had a small circle of clear glass in the middle of the frosting and eight distinct beams of sunlight shone in at a shallow angle along the length of the carriage. Junk stepped towards the nearest and put his eye to the clear circle to see what was outside. Lasel did the same at the neighbouring window.

They were travelling through a mountainous landscape that couldn't have been more different from the wooded area that surrounded the mirrored tower. They had definitely gone somewhere else. But where? At that very moment they were on a massive curve in the tracks and Junk could see that the train was immense. They were somewhere around the middle carriage of about twenty-five.

Far out at the front, the locomotive was splendid. It looked like a steampunk version of an art-deco idea of an electric train. The iron child of Leonardo da Vinci and Raymond Loewy. It was a deep burgundy-red colour. Its nose was torpedo-shaped and the pilot or cow-catcher spread out beneath it like the rigid skirt of a ball gown. The locomotive flowed back from the nose in gentle, upwardly flowing strata, each just a little higher than the one before. It was so high at its vertex that it would dwarf Garvan if he was standing alongside it.

The adjoining tender was lower, but then the carriages were of equal height with the locomotive. All were the same burgundy colour. All sported the same floor-to-ceiling frosted windows.

Junk and Lasel turned back to the others. They almost filled the little room containing the green doorway. It looked faintly comical to see three people of vastly differing sizes crammed into such a tiny space. Junk and Lasel caught one another's eye and did their best to hide their smiles.

'It's a big train,' said Junk, 'and we're about in the middle of it, so I say we split up. Some of us go forward, some of us go back, see if we can find this guy. Good thing about trains is there aren't a lot of places to hide. We'll meet back here.'

'I'll go with you,' said Otravinicus, and he pushed his way between Garvan and Payo–Mestrowe and popped out into the corridor. Junk wasn't thrilled at the idea, but he didn't argue.

Payo–Mestrowe stepped out next. He had to duck and contort himself, to make himself as narrow as possible to fit through the door. Then Garvan tried to get out, but no matter how he turned and twisted his big body he found it impossible to squeeze through. Junk looked at the corridor he was standing in and realized it wasn't much wider.

'Maybe you should stay here, Garvan, and guard the doorway. Otravinicus and me'll go this way –' he pointed forward – 'and Lasel and Payo go that way.' He pointed back. 'We go as far as we can and come straight back. OK?' All nodded and they set off. Payo–Mestrowe wasn't as big as Garvan, but he was big enough, and the only way he could move along the corridor was to shuffle sideways like a hunched crab.

Junk and Otravinicus entered the next carriage and discovered it wasn't divided into compartments. It was one large empty space. They carried on. The next few carriages were the same. They had just about given up hope of finding anything different when they entered the next carriage and were surprised to discover it had a corridor running down the side of it like the first one but with only one compartment that took up the entire length of the carriage. They entered and found it was a bedroom. There were clothes scattered everywhere: all over the floor, all over the circular bed, spilling out of hidden cupboards and drawers and dripping off an easy chair sitting in a corner and a light fixture hanging from the ceiling. Junk and Otravinicus searched the room. There was no one hidden in the cupboards, and the base of the bed was solid and fixed to the floor. They carried on.

The next carriage had the same layout again. This time the end-to-end compartment was home to a screening room. The far end of the room was one giant screen. Not quite as big as the one in the mirrored tower, but a close second. Junk and Otravinicus started to search the room, but there weren't a lot of places to hide. Junk turned to the doctor and was about to suggest they carry on to the next carriage when he saw something that made him freeze with fear. 'Doctor,' he said, his voice barely above a whisper, 'don't move.'

Otravinicus knew from Junk's expression and tone of voice that something was very wrong and whatever was causing his consternation was directly behind Otravinicus.

'What is it?' Otravinicus whispered, the words

coming out on the tip of a panicked breath. He turned his head ever so slowly and looked over his shoulder. At the end of the room there stood, on all fours, a fully grown grizzly bear. Its thick fur was dark chocolate brown, becoming almost black around its ears and underbelly and lighter on its snout. The in and out of its breathing made its fur bristle. It had small but soulful, almost human eyes. It was looking directly at Otravinicus and Junk, swaying a little from side to side, and a throaty grumble reverberated up from its belly. 'How did that get in here? It wasn't here when we came in.' They kept their voices low.

'Yeah, think we might have noticed,' said Junk. 'Maybe it's house-trained. Like a pet or something. Tame, you know.' Just then the bear let out an almighty roar. It was deafening. Elastic strands of spittle flipped through the air. Junk was certain he was about to be pebble-dashed, but the spray didn't reach him. The bear reared up, standing on its hind legs and it bumped its head on the ceiling. It put its paws up on its head and let out a giggle.

'Did you see that?' said the bear, laughing. 'I hit my head. I feel silly now. Let's pretend that never happened, shall we?' The bear dropped back down on to all fours. 'I'm Steve – Steve the bear – and I'll be your guide to your EveryFilm Entertainment System.'

Junk and Otravinicus realized then that this was another hologram, like Jenny. They breathed a joint sigh of relief.

'As this system has been passcode protected,' said Steve the bear, 'please say your security phrase now.' The bear waited. Junk and Otravinicus looked to one another, wondering what to do.

'We don't know the security phrase,' said Junk to Steve the bear.

'That is incorrect. Please try again,' said Steve.

'Never mind,' said Junk. 'Switch off.' It wasn't like they were actually going to watch something.

'That is incorrect. One final try, but please be warned, if you enter the wrong passcode a third time I will have to alert the primary user.'

Junk rolled his eyes. What did it matter if they got it wrong? He said the first thing that came into his head: 'Donkey badgers!'

'That is incorrect,' said Steve. 'The EveryFilm Entertainment System has now been frozen and the primary user will be notified of an unauthorized breach.' A view of the room they were standing in appeared on the big screen. It showed Junk, Otravinicus and Steve the bear in situ. Then the point of view pulled back and out through the wall of the compartment. A computer-generated image of the train thundering along its tracks appeared on screen now and the next carriage along was highlighted in flashing red. Junk thought about it.

'That's the carriage we've just been through,' he said, 'the messy bedroom one. Why's that flashing?'

'Because the primary user has been notified of the unauthorized breach,' explained Steve the bear helpfully.

'So the primary user's next door?' said Junk. They turned and headed back the way they had come.

Junk and Otravinicus entered the messy bedroom just in time to see the scruffy Scotsman running out through the far door.

'Wait!' shouted Junk and, set off after him. He noticed the mattress had been pushed off the bed to reveal a hidey-hole in the centre of the otherwise solid base. That's where he had been all along.

The Scotsman ran into the adjacent empty carriage and through to the next and the next and the next. He was squawking to himself as he ran, talking nineteen to the dozen, but Junk, who was close behind, couldn't make out what he was saying.

Junk had almost caught up with the little man when they got back to the first carriage they'd been in. The Scotsman raced into the little compartment that housed the green doorway that would take him back to the glass tower. Junk was just a couple of seconds too late. The Scotsman disappeared from view as he entered the compartment, but just as Junk reached the room, the man came flailing out again. Junk glanced in and saw that the little man had run smack-bang into Garvan and bounced off. The Scotsman then bashed his head on the frosted glass window with enough force to knock him out cold. He slumped to the floor as Junk and Garvan (still trapped inside the compartment) stood over him.

12

When he came to, the Scotsman was lying in his bed with Junk, Lasel, Payo–Mestrowe, Otravinicus and Garvan standing over him. Junk had used the Antricle to create a corridor for Garvan to move about the train.

'What happened?' said the Scot, sitting up and rubbing his head where it had hit the window.

'You hit your head,' said Junk.

'Did I? Brilliant! Just what I needed.' With that he rolled off the bed and started walking around the room, inspecting and mostly discarding clothes. If he found something he liked the look of he'd give it a sniff, and if its aroma wasn't too objectionable he'd add it to a new pile he was putting together on the bed. As he went he started pulling off the clothes he already had on until he was quite naked, though he didn't appear to notice or care that there were five other people in the room. As he pulled off what he was wearing, he would toss it aside where it would join all the other sartorial flotsam. This meant that he ended up putting some things back on that he had only just taken off. Junk and the others chose not to comment.

'Are you . . . Scottish?' asked Junk.

'No,' said the Scotsman. 'Why d'ye say that?'

'Well . . . because you sound Scottish,' said Junk.

'Do I? So I'm no' French? I always thought I was French. Am I not speaking French?'

'No,' said Junk, wondering if that was a joke. It didn't appear to be. The question seemed genuine.

'What's your name, sir?' asked Otravinicus.

'Danny,' said the man. 'Danny Lambe. That's a French name, right?'

'No,' said Junk. 'Not really.'

'Things are a bit mixed up. In my head, like,' said Danny. 'Sometimes I remember things, but then they go away again.' He paused for a moment. 'I like coffee mugs and sea lions,' he said randomly.

No one knew how to respond to that, so they didn't. 'Where are we?' asked Junk. 'Do you know?'

'Oh aye, we're on the Fife Flyer. This is my train. I love trains, me.' There was undisguised joy in his voice.

'Fife,' said Junk. 'That's in Scotland.'

'Is it?' said Danny. 'I could've sworn it was in France. Just outside of Moscow.'

'Moscow's not in France,' said Junk.

'What?' This clearly came as a shock to Danny. 'Everything's so muddled.'

'Do you know where this is?' asked Garvan, speaking English and pointing out of the window at the craggy, imposing landscape beyond.

Danny flinched when he noticed Garvan. It was like

he hadn't seen him before, which was difficult as Garvan took up a large proportion of the room. 'You're a big fella,' he said, and then turned quickly to Junk: 'He is a big fella, right?' Junk nodded. 'Ah, good. France is Russia is Scotland. Big might be small. Shirts –' he said picking up a sock – 'might be undercrackers . . .' He picked up a jumper. 'Everything's changing.'

'So do you know where this is?' asked Garvan again, as Danny had clearly forgotten the question.

'Well, no' really. Far as we could tell, it's somewhere in America. I think.'

'Who's "we"?' asked Junk.

'Me and my friends,' said Danny with a smile. 'There's . . .' His face darkened and the smile faded. He scowled as he tried to remember, but nothing was coming. 'There was a bunch of us. I remember.' He struggled to navigate through his befuddled mind.

'How many?' asked Junk.

'Nine,' said Danny. He said it quickly, without stopping to think about it.

'Nine Emperors,' said Junk.

Danny grinned again as he looked up. That name meant something to him. 'Aye, that's us.' He paused and the smile faded. 'Least I think it is.'

'So you're one of the Nine Emperors?' asked Junk, feeling confident that his quest was nearing the finish line. 'Do you know about a little girl? Her name's Ambeline.'

'A little girl?' said Danny, his brow furrowed with thought.

113

'She had long blonde hair and blue eyes,' said Junk. 'Three years ago, the Nine Emperors paid for her to be taken from her family. She's my little sister and I need to find her.'

Danny's face darkened. 'Don't know anything about a little girl, but if someone took her it would have been *him*.' He twitched as if the mere act of remembering whoever *him* was hurt.

'Him?' repeated Junk. 'Who's him?'

'The Peacock.' Danny said the word quickly as if to distance himself from the name as fast as possible.

'Peacock?' said Junk, wondering if Danny was talking about an actual peacock. 'What's the Peacock?'

'The Peacock Emperor.'

'I don't understand,' said Junk. 'Who is that?'

'He was called Danny,' said Danny.

'You're Danny,' said Junk.

Danny frowned. 'Am I?'

'Who's the Peacock Emperor?' asked Junk again.

Danny shook his head. 'I don't remember,' he said. 'Shaun would know.'

'Who's Shaun?' Junk asked eagerly. 'Is he another of the emperors? Where's he?'

'Shaun Dunmore – he was my friend,' said Danny. 'He was clever. He was the owl – the Owl Emperor.'

'And where is he now?' asked Junk.

Danny clamped his hands on both sides of his head and squeezed roughly, as if he could force the memory out.

'I can't remember. Why can't I remember?'

'Don't think about it,' said Dr Otravinicus.

Junk looked at him. Danny looked at him. 'What?'

'I find the best way to remember something that's proving elusive is to not think about it at all. Think about something else. Put your mind in another place and then sneak up on the elusive memory. Take it by surprise.'

Danny stopped punishing his own head. He lowered his hands and laughed lightly, as if Otravinicus's idea amused him. 'Take it by surprise. I like that.'

Junk shot a frown at Otravinicus. He didn't want Danny not to think about it. Quite the opposite. He wanted answers and he wanted them now. He had waited long enough. Otravinicus saw the displeasure writ large on Junk's face and shrank back.

'Come on, Danny, you can remember,' encouraged Junk. 'What about the other emperors? Where are they now? Was there one back at the glass tower?'

Danny nodded. 'That was Tunde's tower, but he's not there any more.'

'Why? Where is he?' asked Junk.

Danny closed his eyes and concentrated. 'Something happened,' he said. After a moment he looked up and shook his head. 'But I can't remember what. Let's eat,' he said. 'I'm hungry. Is anyone hungry? I love to cook.' Danny was so infuriating that Junk was about ready to howl with frustration, but Lasel took his hand. He looked at her and she gave him a calming look. It worked. Junk was aware of the tension in his shoulders ebbing away as he relaxed.

'OK, sure, let's eat,' said Junk.

They passed through the screening room, where Steve the bear sat reading a book (this being his standby mode) and Danny revealed that the security phrase was 'I want to ride a whale called Jeff'. Beyond the screening room was the kitchen. It took up an entire carriage. One wall sported eight frosted windows, just like those in other carriages, but on the opposite wall was one long picture window that afforded a stunning view of the beautiful vistas without.

There was plenty of food, but much of it was mouldy and rotten. Danny forgot to throw anything away. He was as choosy about his food as he was his clothes, and Junk and the others watched with faces creased with mild disgust as Danny chopped off whatever fungus was growing on his ingredients and then forgot what he was doing and put everything into the same pot.

There was plenty of counter space and cupboards, but that meant there was little free room left and Garvan and Payo–Mestrowe sat squashed into the corner, looking miserable. They most definitely did not like trains.

'So who's driving this?' asked Otravinicus.

'No one,' said Danny.

'What do you mean, no one?' said Junk, slightly terrified all of a sudden.

'I mean no one. It's all automatic. It's a train set.'

'What?' Junk, Lasel and Otravinicus shared a frown.

'What's a train set?' asked Lasel.

'It's like a toy, for kids,' said Junk.

'Hey! *Not* for kids.' Danny looked genuinely insulted.

'OK,' said Junk, and he tried again. 'Back home, people would build little models of trains on tracks with stations and hills . . .' A thought occurred to him. 'Wait, are those mountains real?' he asked, pointing to the phenomenal-looking landscape passing by.

'Of course they're real,' said Danny. 'I can't make a mountain.' Junk wasn't so sure after everything he'd seen recently. 'I just mean the train doesn't go anywhere. No, I mean it goes somewhere. We're moving. But it just goes round and round a track I had built.'

'How long's the track?' asked Garvan.

'Eight hundred miles,' said Danny.

'That's some train set.'

Danny smiled proudly and nodded in agreement.

'So you're on here all alone?' asked Lasel. She and Payo–Mestrowe had made it all the way to the end of the train earlier. Every carriage they had passed through had been empty apart from the last one, which was like an old-fashioned smoking car. There was a fully stocked bar, a walk-in humidor, card tables, a jukebox and a pool table. None of the bottles had been opened, none of the cigars had been smoked. The chalk for the pool table was still in its wrapper, as were the decks of cards. It was a place to be enjoyed with friends. It didn't appear Danny had any of those.

Danny nodded. 'Aye, all alone. No, wait.' He thought

117

of something suddenly. 'There were some people here earlier.' He had a brief moment of enlightenment and his shoulders sagged. 'Oh. No, that was you.' He sighed. 'Yeah, all alone.' He shook off the look of melancholy and smiled. 'But that's how I like it, you know. I've got my train and I go round and round and round. Got everything I need.' He floated away into his thoughts.

'But what about the other emperors?' asked Junk, pulling him back.

'Who?' asked Danny.

'The Nine Emperors.'

'Oh aye, good times.' Then, in the blink of an eye, his face drained of colour as if he had remembered something horrendous. 'No, bad times,' he said, staring into mid-space. 'Bad, bad times.' Junk, Lasel and Otravinicus said nothing for a few moments, hoping the Scotsman would continue, but then a timer started to beep on his cooker and the moment passed. Danny turned off the timer and lifted a pan from a burner, his sadness forgotten. 'Pass the yarud, will you?' He nodded at a bowl of blue gunk sitting in front of Junk. As he picked it up, Junk saw a skin of furry mould peppering the top of it. An army of white-and-green spores standing to attention.

'Think that might have gone off,' said Junk. Danny looked in the bowl and gave it a big sniff. He recoiled violently at the odour that caught in the back of his throat. He put the bowl down and wiped his watering eyes on his sleeve. Junk tried again. 'So where are the other emperors now?'

'Gone,' said Danny.

'What?' Junk looked panicked. 'Gone where?'

'I don't like to talk about it,' said Danny. Junk sighed. Talking to Danny involved one step forward, two steps back.

'So how did you get here, Danny?' asked Lasel.

'I've always been here,' said Danny. 'The train goes round and round and I go round and round with it. I don't go anywhere and we never stop.' He glanced out of the window as they were passing a broad lake surrounded by jagged mountains wearing snow-white hoods. As well as pointing up, the peaks pointed down in their reflection in the clear aquamarine water. The view was a marvel of nature framed in the kitchen carriage's picture window. 'I'll see that exact same view in four days, nine hours and twelve minutes.'

'That's not exactly true about you never going anywhere,' said Junk. 'You went to the mirrored tower.'

'Oh, yeah, sometimes I go there, but I don't have to leave my train to get there so I never really think it counts.'

'You said before it was Tunde's tower. Who's Tunde? Is he one of the Nine Emperors?'

'That's right. He was the Firefinch Emperor.'

'And where's Tunde now?'

'Gone,' said Danny, shaking his head. '*He* didn't like him.'

'He?' said Junk. 'The Peacock Emperor?'

Danny nodded. 'Tunde argued with him, you see.

119

The Peacock didn't like people arguing with him. Disagreeing.'

'So we've got the Peacock, the Firefinch and the Owl,' said Otravinicus. 'What are you?'

'I was the Pigeon Emperor. I wanted to be the Crane Emperor, but *he* said no.'

'Who were the others?'

'Well . . . there was the Seagull Emperor, the Magpie Emperor, the Penguin Emperor, the Falcon Emperor and the Swallow Emperor.'

'Why call yourselves after birds?'

Danny thought about Otravinicus's question. He shook his head. 'There was a reason. I know there was, but I can't remember it now.'

'Of course you can't,' muttered Junk.

'Shaun would remember,' Danny said again.

'But Shaun's gone,' said Otravinicus.

Danny nodded. 'Shaun's gone. I nip next door all the time hoping he'll be back, but he never is.'

'Next door?' said Junk. 'What do you mean?'

'Well, we're neighbours,' said Danny. 'Tunde one side of me, Shaun on the other.' He let out a braying sigh. 'But both gone now.'

Junk considered Danny's words, trying to read between the lines. 'Do you mean there's another doorway?'

'That's right,' said Danny. 'We all have two. Each emperor has two. We're all neighbours.'

'So where's the other door?' asked Junk.

'Tell you what,' said Danny, 'let's eat and then I'll

show you.' He spooned out some grey glop into a dirty bowl. Some of the more disgusting fungus had worked its way to the top and sat there like a hairy glaze. Danny set the bowl down in front of Junk.

'You know what? Let's take a look at the door first,' said Junk.

They made their way back to the first carriage they had entered. The one that housed the green doorway in the little room. Danny entered first and walked around to the other side of the doorway. As the doorways in the Room of Doors looked the same from both sides, it hadn't been apparent to the others that there were in fact two doorways here, back to back.

'So I go in that side,' said Danny, pointing to the front, 'and it takes me to Tunde's. I go in this side –' he pointed to the back – 'and I'm at Shaun's.'

'And Shaun's goes somewhere else?' asked Lasel.

'That's right. Shaun's connected to Ed, Ed's connected to Foster, Foster's connected to Ian, Ian's connected to Alan, Alan's connected to Paul, Paul's connected to Liam, Liam's connected to Tunde, Tunde's connected to me, I'm connected to Shaun, Shaun's connected—'

'I think we get it,' said Junk, cutting him off. There was a chance he might never have stopped. 'So that's . . .' Junk counted on his fingers, '. . . nine. The Nine Emperors. And we can get to all of them from right here.' They all turned to look at the doorway shimmering in front of them.

13

Garvan was only too eager to leave behind the cramped confines of the train. He was the first through the doorway. He found himself in an orchard of plum trees that stretched as far as the eye could see. He breathed in deeply, savouring the fresh air and sweet rousing aroma of ripe plums that hung in groups of three or four or five, blue or red or yellow skins vibrant against the green of the leaves.

The others came through after him. First Lasel, then Otravinicus, then Danny, Junk and Payo–Mestrowe. The sun sat low in a crisp cyan sky. All but Danny stopped to appreciate the beauty around them.

'I like it here,' said Lasel. Junk nodded in agreement. There was a hill nearby and Junk, Garvan and Lasel scrambled up to the top to see the view. On the other side of the hill was a vineyard stretching away from them. In the distance was what looked like a French chateau.

'Maybe we're in France now,' said Junk.

'France?' asked Lasel.

'It's what Jansia was called in my time.'

'I don't know,' said Lasel, and looked to Garvan for his opinion.

He shrugged. 'We could be anywhere, any time. I don't know how we tell.'

'No, we're still in America. It's called something different nowadays. Foster did tell me once but I can't remember. Before we all came here he went looking for places for us all. Where we could build what we wanted. A palace, a chateau, a tower, a train. Whatever we wanted. There was enough room for all of us here.'

'This Foster, was he from America originally?' asked Junk, pieces of the puzzle falling into place for him.

'That's right,' said Danny.

'Was he a big fan of *Star Wars*, by any chance?'

'He sure was. Everyone loves *Star Wars* but he was a total geek for it. That's why he called himself the Falcon Emperor. You know, after Han Solo's spaceship in it, the *Millennium Falcon*.'

Junk looked meaningfully at Otravinicus. 'Think we might have worked out who your Han Solo guy was.' Otravinicus hadn't understood much of the conversation Junk and Danny had had but he got the gist of it.

'So this is Shaun's place?' said Junk. Danny nodded. 'And he's definitely not here?'

Danny looked sad. He shook his head. 'Gone,' was all he said.

They wandered back down to the flickering green doorway. They walked around to the opposite side and Garvan stepped through first.

Garvan came out in a vast ballroom. The high ceiling was painted in the style of Michelangelo. Every centimetre of the walls was covered with paintings hanging in fat, gaudy gilt frames. Around the periphery there were free-standing sculptures, books in glass cases, pieces of jewellery on display stands and another dozen more obscure items. This palace couldn't have been more different from Danny's art-deco train or the minimalist glass tower belonging to the emperor called Tunde.

The others came through now. They paused to glance around at the grandeur of the room and all the treasures on display.

'Who lived here?' Junk asked Danny.

'This was Ed's place. He was a collector. He really liked pictures and things.'

'Clearly.' Something caught Junk's eye. 'Oh my God!' he said. 'Is that real?' He approached one of the paintings. It was the *Mona Lisa*. Junk didn't know a lot about art, but he knew that painting. Everyone knew that painting. His eye wandered to the neighbouring piece. He recognized that too. It was the famous bedroom scene painted by Vincent van Gogh. As he looked from painting to painting, Junk realized he recognized lots of them. He wouldn't be able to name the artist of some, but he knew the works. There were pieces by Gauguin, Monet, Picasso, Renoir, Vermeer, Rembrandt, Miró, Rothko, Cézanne, Degas and Dali, among others.

'How did he get all these?' asked Junk.

'Stole them mostly.' Danny said it in a very casual sort of way.

Lasel walked over to one wall that was covered in pictures all of the same person. He was a man with shaggy straw-coloured hair and sometimes a handlebar moustache, sometimes not. The portraits were in a variety of styles, all familiar and all signed. Picasso had painted one. Dali another. Francis Bacon, Marc Chagall, Toulouse-Lautrec. There was a series of sketches by da Vinci.

'That's Ed,' said Danny.

'Are these all originals?' asked Junk.

'Aye. Ed would take his turn and go back in time to have famous artists paint him. It was his thing.'

'How? I mean how did he persuade them to do it?'

'He'd pay them. Offer them a ridiculous amount of money. No one ever turned him down. When you can go anywhere, getting money's not a problem.'

'What did you mean when you said he would take his turn?' asked Garvan.

'Well, we only had the one box. Nine people, one box. We had to take it in turns, didn't we? Lot of disagreement about that.'

'Is Ed here so we can talk to him?' asked Junk.

Danny looked at his hands and shook his head. 'No, Ed's gone.' Then he looked up suddenly. 'No, wait, has he?' He frowned. 'Yes.' His frown turned to a look of bemusement. 'No.' Frown. 'Yes.'

Junk looked cross. He whispered angrily to Otravinicus. 'Shaun's gone, Ed's gone, Tunde's gone. This fella's marbles have gone.' He shot a glance at Danny. 'We're not getting any closer to finding Ambeline.'

'Patience, young Junk, patience.'

'I've waited more than three years, Doctor. I think that's long enough, don't you?' Otravinicus didn't reply. Junk turned and called to Danny, 'So who hasn't gone, Danny?'

Danny furrowed his brow and then rubbed it vigorously. 'I can't remember.'

'Your memory there seems to come and go a little,' said Junk. 'You can remember all about Ed's art collection –' he waved his hands in a sweeping gesture, taking in the entirety of the room – 'but you can't remember where Ed is. Or Shaun. Or Tunde. Or anyone else.'

Otravinicus opened his mouth to add his opinion as usual, but Garvan stopped him with a solid hand on his shoulder. The weight of it pushed Otravinicus down some and he knew to hold his tongue.

Danny was shaking his head. 'I want to remember,' he was saying, though it was barely loud enough to be called a murmur, 'but I don't want to remember.'

'What?' said Junk. 'What does that even mean?'

'Something bad happened. I know it,' said Danny. 'Don't make me remember.' His voice was becoming strained and it was clear that this was upsetting him. His fingers were twitching and his eyes were blinking fast in his drawn-on spectacles. Junk looked at Garvan and Otravinicus. The latter was making subtle hand gestures, which Junk interpreted to mean 'Go easy'. Garvan gave

Junk a small nod to say he agreed. Clearly Danny was not well. Junk acquiesced.

'So tell us about your train then, Danny,' said Junk.

Instantly Danny's squirming fingers stopped moving. He looked up at Junk. 'What?'

'Tell us more about your train. How did you get it?'

'Ah, I thought it through very carefully. It wasn't easy, I can tell you.' All traces of Danny's distress of just a few seconds earlier were gone. He smiled when he talked about his train and his body language was large and effusive. 'I had a very clear idea of what it was I wanted, so I started with some drawings of my own, you know, and I knew exactly who I wanted to design it for me, and to find him I had to go back to the 1930s.'

Everyone let Danny talk without interruption but no one really listened. Payo–Mestrowe turned to look at a series of paintings hanging next to him. There were four paintings arranged side by side. All had been painted by Vincent van Gogh, though of course neither Payo nor Mestrowe knew that. They had never heard of Vincent van Gogh. Payo–Mestrowe stared at one of the paintings in particular. It was of a night sky. At least he thought it was. The sky was made up of different shades of blue, fierce roiling jabs of colour. There was a big yellow crescent moon shining down on a small town that consisted of a tall, spired building and a dozen or so smaller ones. Some had lights burning within. The foreground was dominated by a tall slender tree of dark green and brown that reached up and up into the angry sky. The way the tree was painted made Mestrowe think of fire. That's what the tree looked like: black fire. He looked closer and then closer still with his one good eye. He could see each brushstroke, the individual lines of the bristles of the brush, could see where the artist had pushed against the canvas and smeared the paint. He had never looked at art before. Never seen the point of it. Now he could feel a distinct emotional reaction welling up inside him. He found himself thinking it was one of the most beautiful things he had ever seen.

'What are you doing to me?' Mestrowe spoke in H'rtu in his head.

'I'm not doing anything,' Payo answered in his own language, Tremmel. The two of them understood one another's languages as if they had been speaking them their entire lives rather than for a few days. They didn't have to speak out loud in order to communicate. This conversation was just between the two of them. Their symbiosis was becoming stronger all the time.

'You're making me like art. Pictures are for infants,' objected Mestrowe.

'I've never looked at a picture like this before and I didn't look now,' said Payo. 'That was you.'

'No,' said Mestrowe, with a hint of sadness apparent in his voice, 'there is no me any more.'

'Me either. We're becoming something else.'

'I don't want to be something else. I was happy as I was.'

'No, you weren't,' said Payo.

Mestrowe turned away from the painting and folded his arms angrily. Of course Payo was right. He knew that, just as Mestrowe knew Payo hadn't been happy before. Payo had been living half a life. Now his real life was beginning and Mestrowe's was ending.

He saw Lasel looking at him. She was leaning against a fireplace that was taller than her. In fact, it was tall enough for Mestrowe to stand upright within it. Lasel glanced back to Danny, who was still talking animatedly about his train.

Mestrowe looked back to the painting. 'I'm scared,' said Mestrowe in his mind.

'It'll be all right,' said Payo in his. 'We've got each other.'

Some part of the irascible misanthrope Mestrowe used to be was still festering in a dark corner of his confused mind and he rankled at that last exchange. He let out a bark of frustration. The sudden interruption made Danny stop in mid-flow and all eyes turned to look at Mestrowe. The Pallatan could feel himself reddening for the first time in his life. He felt as if he had to say something.

'We should see if anyone else is here,' was all he could think of.

Junk nodded. 'I agree. Doing something's better than just standing here, and maybe we'll find some clue to where everyone's gone.' He shot a look at Danny. 'Seeing as someone can't remember.' He said the last bit under his breath.

The rest of the building was just as grand and gaudy as the ballroom. It really was a palace fit for an emperor. It was vast. Mind-bogglingly vast. Need-a-golf-cart-to-reach-the-toilet vast. Junk couldn't quite get his head around just how big this place was. It reminded him of a museum. Interminably long, high hallways stretched out ahead of them wherever they went. When they finally got to the end of one corridor there would be another even longer passage around the corner. And like the room they first entered, all the walls were lined with paintings. Every artist Junk could name was represented along with another hundred or so that he couldn't.

They came to the most astonishing hallway yet. It was close to a hundred metres in length and as wide as it was high. There were gigantic floor-to-ceiling mirrors set into arched alcoves running down one wall, opposite windows looking out over manicured gardens. There were more than forty crystal chandeliers running the entire length of the hall. To the sides stood tall gold carvings, each sporting smaller resplendent light fixtures on the top. The curved ceilings were covered with ornate frescos.

'This place is crazy-mad,' said Junk. 'It's like Versailles or something.'

'Aye, that's what it's called,' said Danny, clicking his fingers.

'What does that mean?' asked Junk. 'This is actually Versailles?'

'What's "*Ver-sigh*"?' asked Lasel.

'A palace in France. It was like a tourist attraction in my time,' said Junk, 'but it used to belong to the king before they chopped his head off.'

Garvan's ears pricked up at that one. 'You used to kill kings in your time too?'

'Well, it was a couple of hundred years before my time, but yeah. The French peasants rose up and got rid of their monarchy.' Garvan looked troubled by that thought, as if it had never occurred to him that such a thing could happen. 'I don't know that much about it, to be honest. I had to read a book on it once at school.' He turned back to Danny. 'Explain how this is actually Versailles. You mean, the actual Versailles that was sitting in Paris or wherever?'

'That's right. I don't know exactly how they did it. It was Ed who worked it out. Something to do with opening a really big doorway. The Gatekeeper did it all. It's something to do with connecting two points in space and opening one door into another and then closing the first door. I don't understand the science of it. All I know is you can take one thing from one place and put it in another place.'

'So this Ed, he stole the Palace of Versailles?' Junk tried not to sound impressed but he failed. 'So what was he? The what Emperor?'

'The Magpie Emperor,' said Danny distractedly, staring at his reflection in the mirrored wall.

Figures, thought Junk.

They spent the next hour walking through the corridors and rooms of Versailles, but they barely searched a quarter of the whole place. There were no signs of life anywhere. The palace felt abandoned. Cold and deserted. They let their guard down.

They grew tired and hungry and when they came to the kitchen they found it fully stocked. Nothing fresh, but a walk-in pantry full of twenty-first-century tinned food. They couldn't be sure how long it had been here. Mestrowe pointed out that they hadn't eaten since breakfast in the bazaar. That had been almost twelve hours ago. They dined on baked beans with mini-sausages, alphabetti spaghetti, tomato soup and pears in syrup.

It was getting dark outside once they had eaten so they decided that they'd stay the night. There were a hundred bedrooms to choose from and all were made up. Though they also all smelled stale and airless as if they had not been used for a very long time.

Junk hadn't realized how exhausted he was until his head hit the pillow and sleep took him in seconds. He probably would have slept for a whole day if he hadn't been dragged awake by the sound of weeping. At first it sounded like a child crying – a young girl – and in that brief overlap between sleep and waking Junk thought he could recognize the sound. The blurred thought sent a spike of adrenalin barrelling through him and he was wide awake and on his feet in an instant.

'Ambeline?' He froze and strained to listen. Everything was silent now. There was no crying any more and Junk assumed he had been dreaming. His heart was *thump-thumping* in his chest. He lay back down on the bed, staring up at a threadbare canopy overhead. He closed his eyes and was trying to clear his mind, using a relaxation technique he had learned from a deck-hand on an Indonesian seiner fishing boat, when he heard the crying again. It was brief and this time it was muffled and sounded less like a child. He lay still and listened until he heard it again.

Junk came out into the corridor. Lasel was in the room to his left and Danny in the room to his right. Junk went to the right and pushed his ear against Danny's door. He heard whimpering from within and tried the handle. It wasn't locked.

Danny was asleep in a broad bed, no canopy, but with an elaborately carved headboard. Moonlight shone as brightly as a spotlight through the window, illuminating the Scotsman. He was squirming and frowning, his face contorting and relaxing alternately. He was breathing heavily through his nose and Junk could hear him grinding his teeth. He let out another pathetic, fearful cry and Junk reached out to shake him. He put his hand on his shoulder and gave him one sharp push.

'Danny?'

Danny's eyes were open in a second and he sat bolt upright. He grabbed hold of Junk roughly, his fierceness taking Junk by surprise. Danny froze, still holding on to Junk. His breathing rattled in his throat.

'I remembered,' he said, his voice high with terror.

'Remembered what?'

'I remembered what I was trying to forget. Oh God, I wish I could forget again.' He covered his face and breathed deeply, trying to control the horrors he was recalling. 'I remember what happened to Shaun. I know where he is.'

14

A doorway of green light opened on a dusty paved road and Junk stepped out. He was alone. No Danny. The sound of cicadas filled the air. It was evening but the sun hadn't yet set. Soon though. It was pleasantly warm and Junk took off his jacket.

He stood at the bottom of a hill, looking up at a road that curved away to the left. Behind him was the remains of a little village comprised of a handful of shops and restaurants. All were empty. Deserted. Their doors were open but there were no people. A small dog stepped out from behind some bins. He stopped to look at Junk with what passed for canine curiosity. It didn't last and he turned and trotted away. Junk started up the hill.

A whispering breeze gambolled through the olive groves that flanked the road on both sides, stirring up a blanket of dry leaves. There used to be houses here once upon a time. Junk could see the remnants of old stone walls just visible under the mulch, moss and other foliage. They had long ago fallen into disrepair, and disrepair had eventually become ruin and they were forgotten about and nature moved back in as it always does.

The road was steep and snaked up the hillside. After Junk had been walking for a short while he came to a fork in the road. To his right was the beginning of a small enclave of buildings that were still mostly intact. There weren't many of them. There was one large building with a bell tower. Clearly this had once been a church. Its buttercup-yellow facade had faded with age. An extended family of stray cats appeared to have moved in. There were dozens of them. On the doorstep and on all the windowsills. There were several tall, narrow stained-glass windows adorning each side of the building. The ones Junk could see were unbroken and the late sun was just at the right point in the sky to send beams of light through the windows at the back and out at the front where Junk was. A patchwork of muted colours fanned out over the building's courtyard before him.

The road grew steeper and narrower from that point on. Junk carried on walking. The hillside dropped away sharply to his right before gently plateauing out. He looked down to see a well-tended allotment that continued all the way to the top of the hill. Someone had taken much time and effort to grow their own food. There were plump, fire-engine-red tomatoes growing out from a chaotic lattice of interconnected vines. Elsewhere there were bulbous cucumbers so dark green that they looked almost black. Though still somehow appetizing. Fat juicy aubergine-coloured figs pimpled a stocky tree whose twisting, turning limbs canopied the road. As he passed beneath it Junk eyed one particularly tempting-looking fruit that oozed a few drops of sweet-scented succulence and he reached up to pick it. Suddenly there was movement and the head of a dozing snake shot out from the leafy branch and snapped. Junk whipped his hand back just in time to avoid a bite. The snake was about two metres in length with a glistening brown back and cream-coloured belly. It hissed to make sure its annoyance was clear to everyone involved. Then all the branches of the tree stretched as dozens of snakes shifted above Junk's head. He kept low and moved out from under the tree as fast as he could. He looked back to see the drowsy reptiles dripping down from the boughs. Some fell to the ground unceremoniously and slithered quickly away into the undergrowth. Others hung down like scaly decorations. As he hurried on he was reminded of the department store in Finnish San Francisco (*was that only yesterday?*) and the snakes hanging from the chandelier. It was raining snakes again, he thought.

He was almost at the top of the hill now and he saw a stone wall rising straight up for eight metres ahead of him. At the top of it was a vine-covered canopy. Even from down on the road below he could see it was pearled with bunches of tubby little grapes. Some green, some black, some in between. There was a high wrought iron gate at the end of the wall. Junk rattled it and noticed several chunky padlocks on the inside. The top ended in pointed spikes, the tips of which looked pin-sharp. As he looked closer he saw that there were razor blades embedded in the top metre of each spike.

'HELLO?' he called. He listened for a few moments but heard nothing apart from the cicadas and the dry leaves crackling as they tumbleweeded over the dusty road. He tried again: 'SHAUN DUNMORE?' Still nothing, so he put his hand on the gate and started to use the Antricle to create his own way in. Before he could, he heard the sound of a gun being cocked. It was a sound he had heard before, on more than one occasion. He had spent much of the previous three years in the roughest and most dangerous bars and dives the old world had to offer while searching for his sister's abductor. However, this was the first time a gun had been cocked for him. He froze on the spot and looked slowly upwards to see a tall, naked black man aiming a bolt-action rifle at his head.

'Who are you?' said the man with the rifle. His voice was rough and strained as if from lack of use. He was lean. Gangly even. His head was bald but he had a thick Quaker beard that was equal parts silver and black. 'What are you doing on my planet?'

'Shaun Dunmore?' asked Junk. The man with the rifle didn't respond. 'Danny Lambe told me where to find you.'

'Danny's still alive, huh?' He lowered the gun.

'So you're Shaun?' asked Junk.

'That's right.' Shaun sized Junk up, deciding what to do with him. 'Danny with you?'

Junk shook his head. 'He's back on his train now.'

'Wait there,' said Shaun. 'I'll come and let you in.'

Junk nodded and Shaun disappeared from view. A thought occurred to Junk and he called up, 'No rush. Feel free to get dressed first.'

A moment later, Shaun peered over the lip of the terrace and smirked. 'Don't count on it. It's naked Wednesday.' He vanished from sight again.

A short time later and Junk was standing on the terrace looking out over the olive groves to the old yellow church and beyond to the sea. The sun was close to disappearing over a range of mountains to the north. Junk looked around at the terrace. It was about as long as a tennis court and twice as wide. There were ten brick columns around the outside holding up a rusty iron trellis, which supported the ancient grape vines. All the grapes came from just two base vines, the trunks of which were ancient and gnarled. The floor of the terrace was paved with irregular slabs, and right in the centre was an old well covered with a metal grille. There was a long handmade table and just one chair.

Junk heard movement and turned to see Shaun step up on to the terrace carrying a plastic demijohn of wine and two stubby tumblers. Thankfully he was now wearing a pair of faded old shorts, though that was his only concession to 'naked Wednesday'.

'You take the chair,' he said. 'Don't have a lot of furniture. Don't get many guests.' Shaun was a Londoner, Hackney born and bred and had lost none of his accent.

Junk took the chair as instructed and watched as Shaun poured three fingers of thick black wine into each glass. He went to pass one to Junk but stopped and took it back. 'You old enough to drink?' he asked.

'No,' said Junk, surprised by the question. He couldn't remember the last time anyone had asked him that. He had spent so long in the world of adults that he sometimes forgot he was still only fifteen. Shaun thought about it for a moment, shrugged and handed the glass to Junk anyway. He took a sip from his own and then moved about the terrace lighting several lanterns that hung from the iron trellis or sat on the low surrounding wall. It didn't make a lot of difference, but it would soon as the sun vanished altogether. Darkness would come quickly.

'So,' said Shaun when he finally sat down on the wall and put his feet up. He lit a cigarette. He offered the packet to Junk, but Junk shook his head. 'What brings you here?'

'My sister. Her name's Ambeline. Ambeline Doyle. She'll be nine now. Almost ten. Pretty. Blonde. Blue eyes. You took her.'

'I didn't take anyone,' said Shaun with a defensive grumble to his tone.

'The Nine Emperors did. One of you, some of you, I don't know. Danny says it'd be the Peacock Emperor.'

'Danny's confused,' said Shaun.

'You're not wrong,' said Junk.

'I don't know what to tell you,' said Shaun. 'I don't know anything about your sister.'

Junk started to explain about Ambeline and the home he had left behind. He described working his way around the world on different boats for three years until he came across the green door when diving the wreck of the *Pegasus*. He told him about meeting Garvan, Lasel and Otravinicus, which led to Hundrig Shunt, captain of the land-ship *Casabia* and meeting the Brotherhood of the One True God, Pire. He told Shaun how he and Lasel, mostly Lasel, stole the Antricle from the Brotherhood, how that got them into the Room of Doors again, which took them to Cul Sita and the League of Sharks. He described Twrisks and the battle between the Twrisks and Pallatans. He recounted Payo–Mestrowe and his admission that Ambeline was still alive and in the hands of the Nine Emperors. He described their journey from Cul Sita to Ollamah and Tolfke. From there to San Francisco, from San Francisco to the mirrored tower, from the mirrored tower to Danny's train, from Danny's train to Ed's palace. He explained what had happened with Danny.

'So why come to me?' asked Shaun, emptying his glass and refilling it immediately. 'I've never heard of the League of Sharks. I've never hired anyone to do my dirty work. I don't have dirty work needs doing.'

'I need help.'

Shaun let out an empty laugh. 'I ain't got any to give. I'm the last man on Earth, me. Well, one of the last two now you're here.'

Junk rephrased his request. 'I need answers. Danny's mind is butter. No real help there.'

'Yeah,' said Shaun.

'Tell me who the Nine Emperors are,' said Junk. 'Tell me what happened.'

'Mate, I wouldn't know where to begin,' said Shaun. He downed his drink and refilled his glass again.

'Please,' said Junk, and the desperation in his voice was easy to hear. 'I need to understand. You're not what I was expecting. Out of the nine, there only seem to be you and Danny left. I need to understand who you were, who the Nine Emperors were, so I can find my sister. In return I'll take you wherever you want to go. Take you back to Danny or I can take you back home or anywhere.'

Shaun didn't answer immediately. He sipped his drink and looked at Junk, considering his response. 'Why would I want to go anywhere? Look around you. I own a whole planet. I go back to where I started from and do what? Rejoin the rat race? To what end? To earn money, to buy a house, put down some roots, get a bit of land?' He swung his hand out gracefully, gesturing to all Junk could see. 'I have land already. All of it.' He meant it. 'I used to fret. I was a fretter. I used to fret about forms and whether they were filled in properly or not. Forms! Can you believe that? I was particularly partial to the J4-11. Do you know what the J4-11 was?' Junk shook his head. He didn't know. How could he? Shaun wasn't expecting him to. 'A stationery requisition form. Nary a paper clip should leave the supply closet without a J4-11 being filed.' Shaun smiled a genuinely amused grin and shook his head.

'Being here, being alone, it puts things in perspective, you know. We're a blip. Our importance – humans, I mean – or our perceived importance, is meaningless in the greater scheme of things. Our arrogance made us believe this was our planet. Like fleas thinking they own the dog. But worse. Fleas who drill into the dog and suck out its innards, shave off its fur, set fire to it and blow things up on it. Churn out so many toxins that the dog withers and almost dies but it doesn't. It's stronger than that. Stronger than the fleas. The dog will long outlive the fleas and once they're gone it'll recover. It'll be a bonny, bouncing pup again, chasing its tail and sniffing its bum.'

There was a distinct lull once Shaun had finished his rant. Junk didn't know how to respond. He wasn't quite sure what the tail chasing and bum sniffing was referring to in planetary terms but chose not to question it.

'Plus I voted myself first president of the planet. I'm not sure I could keep that post if I went back to the twenty-first century.' Shaun chuckled to himself.

'So you won't help me?' said Junk after a few moments.

'Well, I didn't say that,' said Shaun. 'What is it you want to know?' He seemed somehow more congenial now, as if he had been itching to say all that to someone but hadn't had anyone to listen. Until now.

'Who are the Nine Emperors? How did you get here? And what happened to you?' One last thing: 'And what does my sister have to do with you all?'

Shaun let out a long sigh. 'You don't want to know much, do you?' He considered Junk's request. 'OK,' he said finally, 'are you sitting comfortably? Then we'll begin . . .'

'The Nine Emperors'

Dramatis Personae

Ian 'Evie' Vincent
'The Eagle Emperor'. Born in Hackney, east London.

Foster 'Pecker' Peck
'The Falcon Emperor'. Born in Mud Bay, South Carolina.
Star Wars fanatic.

Ed 'Ed-Head' Cresswell
'The Magpie Emperor'. Born in Frome, Somerset. Art
lover. Thief. Lives in the Palace of Versailles.

Shaun 'Dunny' Dunmore
'The Owl Emperor'. Born in Hackney, east London. Lived
in a French chateau. Now lives in a villa in Corfu.

Danny 'Larry' Lambe
'The Pigeon/Peacock Emperor'. Born in Fife, Scotland.
Lives on a train.

Alan 'Alfonso' Lynch
'The Seagull Emperor'. Born in Brighton, East Sussex.
Loves Brighton & Hove Albion football club. Oldest of
the group. Lives in a replica of the Royal Pavilion.

Tunde 'Boo' Buhari
'The Firefinch Emperor'. Born in Port Harcourt,
Nigeria. Lives in a mirrored tower.

Liam 'Emu' Rodericks
'The Penguin Emperor'. Born in Brockley, south London.
The youngest of the group. Lives in an amusement park.

Paul 'Bacon' Whittaker
'The Swallow Emperor'. Born in Grays, Essex. Mum died
when he was young. Ex-member of the Territorial Army.
Lives in a replica English village.

Nine Have an Adventure

How did this start? Where did this start? Where to begin? I guess to make sense of it we have to go back to before the beginning. To Horseshoe Financial Services Ltd. It's where we all worked. How we all knew each other. Boring job, as you can probably tell from the name. We didn't do anything. We didn't build anything or make anything. Couldn't really tell at the end of the day what we'd spent the time doing. We moved money around from A to B to C to J, back to B, off to P. We never actually saw any of the money. It was all electronic. Theoretical.

We were based in Horsham in Sussex. A modern building on an industrial estate. We shared the building with an IT consultancy firm, who had the top floor while we had the lower two, and we shared the estate with a branch of Halfords, a carpet warehouse and a Homebase DIY store. Our department was on the ground floor. We were the D'Artagnan Team. There were four teams, so some bright spark thought it'd be a clever idea to name us all after the Four Musketeers: Athos, Porthos, Aramis and D'Artagnan. This was a bad idea for two reasons. First, most people didn't know how to pronounce 'D'Artagnan' and when they phoned up they'd usually end up asking for 'Darkacanang' or something. And second, and far more annoying, were those who did know how to pronounce it and recognized the reference, who would invariably want to point out that there were only three Musketeers. They always sounded very pleased with themselves when they said it, like they were scoring major intellectual points because they knew something about a book. Then we'd have to explain that D'Artagnan was a Musketeer in the other books that Alexandre Dumas wrote – Twenty Years After and The Vicomte de Bragelonne – but as no one had heard of those they didn't believe us and were adamant that we were wrong and they were right. A dirty great chunk of every week was wasted having the same stupid discussion. I've never read any of them, though I did like Dogtanian and the Three Muskehounds when I was a kid.

Our boss was a man called Horseshoe. Lionel Horseshoe. An unlikely name, I know, but it was his and he had copies of his birth certificate that he would always carry around with him to prove it to anyone who had the misfortune to say something innocuous along the lines of, 'Oh, that's an unusual name.' Lionel would whip out the photocopied birth certificate and point out that it was an official document or at least a facsimile of one, and there in black and white for all to see was the moniker 'Lionel Albert Edmond Horseshoe'. He would then explain the history of his unusual family name. I won't repeat it. It was never interesting.

Lionel was little more than a fleeting presence in the office and left the day-to-day running of the company to the department heads. All four, without exception, were total and utter prats. They rarely socialized with the staff and each spent most of their time trying to think up new ways to sabotage the other departments so they would earn the bi-yearly bonus paid to the best team leader.

The real team leaders were the department supervisors.

Ours was Ian Vincent, who also happened to be my best friend from the age of eleven when we met at the Cardinal Pole Roman Catholic School in Hackney. Ian was a great man, great supervisor, a real motivator who'd get down and dirty with the rest of us and do as much work as anyone. He was one of the lads and he was a good friend.

We started there almost at the same time. I got the job first. Only by two months, so that didn't really mean anything by the time he was promoted over me eight years later. Nothing changed. Yeah, he got a pay increase, but he took a lot on his shoulders. Earned that extra money. And yeah, I would have taken it if I'd been offered it, but I wasn't so no matter. Didn't cause any sort of bad feeling between me and Ian/Evie. You know, E from Ian and V for Vincent obviously. 'All right, E-V?' became 'All right, Evie, yes, Evie, fancy a quick half, Evie?' No one was called by their actual name. I was Dunny, Alan Lynch was Alfonso, Liam Rodericks was Emu (Rodericks, Rod, Rod Hull, Emu), Foster Peck was Pecker or the Peckster, Danny Lambe was Larry (cos of Larry the Lamb), Paul Whittaker was Bacon (you have to pay attention for this one: Whittaker, Whitney, Whitney Houston, Houston, we have a problem, Apollo 13, Kevin Bacon, Bacon), Tunde Buhari was Boo, and Ed was Ed-Head but that got shortened to Ed so Ed was Ed.

We were a tight little team. The nine of us. So when Lionel, Mr Horseshoe to you, suggested a team-building weekend in Yorkshire, D'Artagnan Team were determined to be the victors. Lionel explained that it was about building trust and camaraderie between all the different teams, but there was going to be paint-balling so we planned to win.

On the Friday of the following week D'Artagnan Team, along with Athos Team, Porthos Team, Aramis team, the four department heads and Mr Horseshoe accompanied by Mrs Horseshoe, all boarded a coach bound for Ilkley in Yorkshire. Mrs Horseshoe was a game old bird and a keen advocate of liquor on long journeys, so the beers were handed out and it was a fun and rowdy trip. Mr Horseshoe popped in some headphones and listened to an audiobook of legendary cricket umpire Dickie Bird's autobiography for the duration, while the four sour-faced department heads were forced to endure six hours on a coach with us. Ha! Mrs Horseshoe was singing Lady Gaga songs by the time we reached the M25 and was asleep and snoring loudly on the back seat by Leeds.

Nine Go Out on a Windy Moor

The next day, Saturday, we all had a full English at the Best Western Hotel where we were staying, and then the coach was waiting to take us up to Ilkley Moor so we could start building trust or, as we liked to call it, kicking the arse of the other teams. It was absolutely twigging it down with rain and the moor was just grey wherever you looked. Great walls of grey wet greyness.

As an exercise to generate trust and camaraderie between all the employees we started, oddly enough, with a competition, which surely would defeat the purpose of the trip as the purpose of a competition is to defeat the opposition, namely the other teams. Only later did they remember that what they meant to do was mix up the teams so we would all have to rely on members of other departments. As it was, D'Artagnan, Porthos, Athos and Aramis were pitched against one another in a cross-country treasure hunt, all organized by a local firm who did this sort of thing on a regular basis. Funny really – if they had mixed us up like they meant to, then we probably wouldn't be sitting here.

The four department heads, Mr Prat, Mr Twat, Mr Twerp and Mr Butthead (not their real names), decided it was best if the exercise was for grunts only, meaning us, and they repaired to a nearby pub to get blathered. The four teams set off on a five-mile hike in the bucketing rain. We each had to find four flags and make it back to the coach. First team back was the winner.

Each team picked a different direction. We headed north-west. We walked for about half an hour before we found our first flag. It was halfway up a telegraph pole with no way of reaching it. Clever, you see – we had to all work together to find a way to get it down. Bacon had been in the Territorials and had done this sort of thing before. We built a pyramid. Me, Evie, Boo and Bacon on the bottom, cos we were the biggest. Emu and Pecker climbed on to us and hoisted Danny up so he could snag the flag. Teamwork that. We were quite proud of ourselves.

I remember the rain eased off a bit then and there were little bits of blue sky poking out. We came to a cave. There was a marker outside. The company that set it up left helpful arrows here and there so we didn't get too lost. We all filed inside. The cave was quite wide at the opening but it became much narrower very quickly. We couldn't see any sign of a flag and no one had thought to bring a torch. All we had were our mobiles. It was only later we discovered there was no flag. Porthos Team had moved the marker from elsewhere and pointed us into the cave for a laugh. Removed the 'Danger – cave is prone to collapse. Do

151

not enter' sign. Hilarious. Again, if they hadn't tried that little bit of sabotage we wouldn't be here.

So we were just about to give up when Pecker finds this little gap right at the back. It's pretty small but he shined his phone in and could see something blue inside. Our flags were blue, you see. We all figured the cave must be safe. They wouldn't send us in here if it wasn't. Not knowing anything about Porthos Team's high jinks. So as he was the smallest, we made Danny squeeze in through this little hole. Makes me claustrophobic just thinking about it. But he was young. He was only about nineteen then, and he was the newest recruit to the team. Meant he was the usual target of pranks and what-have-you. Nothing cruel. Usual stuff. Sending him out to buy a left-handed screwdriver or tartan paint or a new bubble for the spirit level. That sort of thing. You've met him. You know what he's like. Even for a scrawny little guy like him it was a squeeze, but he didn't want to let us down or appear weak in front of us. We've all done things we know we shouldn't do just because we didn't want to lose face. He did it. He got through to the other side. Opened out a bit then. No flag though. There was just an old bag in there, that's all. He turns to come out and there's this noise. It was like a growl, and I remember thinking, for only like a second, that there was some sort of animal in there with him and it wasn't happy to see him. But then it got louder and it sounded less and less like an animal and more and more like rocks shifting. Suddenly there's this almighty roar like the Earth itself was breaking, and the ground beneath Danny disappears and him with it. We heard him screaming as he fell. It went on and on like he was falling into a bottomless pit. Turned out it wasn't so bottomless.

He only fell about ten feet. I guess panic and imagination are not the best combination. When the dust – and, believe me, there was an ocean of dust – when the dust settled, we were calling to him. We could hear him fine when he answered. He was in a room. It was high but not particularly wide, he said. The floor that he'd been on earlier wasn't a floor, it was just fragments of rocks that had fallen down from the ceiling at some point in the last million years and got stuck. Just waiting for some numpty to scramble over them and dislodge them. Danny was such a numpty.

Now we had the problem of getting him out. No one else was small enough to get through the opening, so we figured we'd have to go back to the coach, get some rope or something, come back and pass it through so we could pull him up. But then he goes, 'Hold up.' He's seen something. It's metal. That's weird. I mean, we all think that's weird. Why's there metal in this cave? And what sort of metal? Danny couldn't say. A big, fat, chunky bit of metal half buried under rocks and stones and dust. Jointed in the middle. It had rusted up so it was a bit worn out in places. It weighed an absolute ton, he said, but he managed to get his arm under it and he shifted it enough to balance it on his knee, which let him bend down enough to stick his shoulder under it and once he'd done all that he was able to push it upright. Little by little, he was able to lift it up and position it in such a way that he could balance it up against the wall. Now all he had to do was to climb up. Now you've got to remember we couldn't see him, couldn't see what he was seeing. We could only hear him. We were calling to him, encouraging him, and he starts to climb, and next thing we know there's this horrible noise.

Metal scraping against rock. It's this screech. Danny cries out as he's falling, and cos we can't see nothing it's even worse. Our imaginations take over. That scream sounded like him falling to his death. But it wasn't. He just banged his elbow a bit. The metal thing had toppled to the side is all. So he has to start the whole process again. Except this time the metal's fallen differently. The end of it that was hidden under rocks and shale and stuff before is now exposed. He can see what it is. And it's a hand. The whole thing is an arm. A great metal arm with this huge, disproportionately massive, hand at the end. I don't know if what he said was true, if it was really a hand, I never saw it. But that's what he said it was. And it was holding something. That's what he says: 'It's holding something.' And he goes quiet. We're calling out to him but he's not answering. He's trying to prise out whatever this thing is in this big metal hand. We can hear this creee-ak-creak-creee-ak-creak *noise coming from below. It's Danny working the fingers on this big hand back and forth to get a bit of slack. Finally he lets out this happy yelp of triumph and then he goes silent. 'What is it?' we all shout down. He says he doesn't know. All he says is it's beautiful. So he positions the metal arm, if that's what it is, back up against the wall and this time he makes sure it's good and secure. Then he shimmies up to the top until he's able to grab a hold of Emu's hand and we pull him through.*

He struggles to get out of the opening, but finally he slides free and he's lying there prostrate on the floor, staring up at the ceiling with all our faces looking down at him. He's coughing up great clouds of white dust. He reaches into his pocket and pulls out an object, a shape like a pyramid. Anyway Ian takes it from him gently like it could break. We're all standing there, or lying there in Danny's case, the nine of us, and Ian's got this pyramid thing sitting in his hand. We're all staring at it. It is beautiful. Some of its faces are solid and some are transparent. Like glass but unbreakable glass. Ian pinged it with his fingernail and it let off this really nice, really melodious ting note. 'What is it?' someone says. It's maybe Alan, I don't know. But it's the question we're all thinking and not one of us had an answer. Not even an idea. What is it? And what was it doing down in that cave?

Now the next bit was a total fluke. But that's life, isn't it? A series of total flukes all strung together. Ian's still holding the pyramid. It's about so big and he's got it in one hand and Foster reaches out. 'Let me take a look at that,' he says, and he puts his fingers on it. On the other side. Ian's fingers here, Foster's fingers there. Eight, ten, whatever different points and the chances must be astronomical that the pair of them would hold it in just the right way, but hold it in just the right way they did, cos all of a sudden it comes to life. Lines of brilliant light spread all over the surface. Across all the faces. The light's coming out from the tips of their fingers and spider-webbing all over this thing until the lines all start to meet up, and then suddenly, boom, there's this projection that fills the cave. They drop it instantly and it sits on the floor and there's all these little green circles – not spheres, circles, flat – floating in the air. We were just mesmerized by it. It was all around us. And, like being in the cinema when you're watching a 3D film and something looks like you can reach out and touch it so you do, I reached out and touched one of the green circles. A line burst out of it and zigzagged down to this other circle, which, if you can imagine, was right in the centre of everything. It was the sun to these thousands of circle-planets. They all revolved around it. Then Boo waved his hand through another one and same thing happened. Line came out and went to the one in the centre. We all tried. Lines always went to the same place. Someone, I can't remember who, maybe Evie, wondered what would happen if we touched that one. The one in the centre. We all looked at each other. A collective shiver. Then we laughed. Our imaginations were getting away from us. It was just a light show. So Pecker reaches out and pokes a finger through the circle in the middle. And beams of light start to ping out of it. All over. More and more and more and more. And they start joining up until right there in front of us is a doorway, an opening, a portal. A portal made of beams of green light criss-crossing over each other to make an entrance, but an entrance to what? I put my hand out towards it and I could feel something pulling at the tips of my fingers. Some invisible force trying to draw me in so I snatched my hand back. All of us agreed we should get out of there then, but what about the pyramid? No one wanted to touch it and we didn't know how to turn it off. We were all standing there debating it when the portal started to move, started to come towards us. Instinctively we all moved back. Wrong choice. It kept coming and we had nowhere to go. The cave narrowed and we were all squeezed together. We couldn't go back any further and we couldn't go forward and this portal kept coming and kept coming until it passed over us and we weren't in the cave any more.

Nine Frolic Through History

We were in this weird place. It wasn't like any room I'd ever seen. It was endless. No walls, no ceilings, not that you could see. Just doors. Doors made of green light. Thousands of them. Hundreds of thousands. They stretched on and on and on and up and up and everywhere.

All nine of us are there along with the thing, the object. It's just sitting there on the ground and the light show's gone now. Then we turn and see this raised bit. This stage or plinth sort of thing. It's the only thing that's different in the whole place. Doors, doors, doors, doors, doors, doors, doors, doors, doors, doors, doors, doors, doors, doors, doors, doors, plinth. And there's a column on it. Square, straight sides. Made from the same shiny black whatever as the floors and on top there's a— What's that? Oh, you've been there? Of course you've been there. Daft of me. I've not had anyone to tell this story to for a while. So you know how this goes. We put the thing on top of the column on the plinth and voosh *the light show's back, but like a million times bigger. It's incredible, right? We all stand there, necks craning, turning in little individual circles, mouths hanging open. We probably would have looked quite funny to anyone watching. Then Emu, cos he's a bit of a joker, says, 'I wanna go home,' in a little scared voice and we all crack up, just what was needed, all getting a bit intense, but then this great big deep voice comes out of nowhere and goes, 'Temporal information required,' and we all freak out like nobody's business. All looking around but there's no one there of course. It's the Gatekeeper. I assume you know about the Gatekeeper. Yeah, right. So, long story short, we work out that*

157

if you give him a time and place you can go there. Anywhere on Earth at any time, past, present or future. Emu saying, 'I want to go home,' was the place. So it takes us a little while, but between us we work it out. We've got a time machine. I mean, how? Why? Why does it exist? To this day we still don't know, but someone gives you a time machine you're going to try it out, right? Of course you are. Well, we're no different. We all argue about where and when to go. Alan wants to know how many trips we get. Is it like a magic-lamp scenario? Three wishes and you're done. But it seems there's no limit. Not according to the Gatekeeper. So where to go first? Boo suggests ancient Egypt. Not a bad shout. Emu says the Titanic. We all point out it sinks. Pecker wants to go and listen to Lincoln giving the Gettysburg Address. As he's the only septic, none of the rest of us cares. He suggests going and watching Kennedy getting shot. Again no one cares. I suggest the future. I want to see jet packs and hover boards and flying cars. That goes down better. Then Alan suggests Wembley for the 1966 World Cup final. That one wins. So we say to the Gatekeeper, '30 July 1966'. We even specify exactly where we want to be in the ground. Don't want the door opening up in the middle of the pitch now, do we? That could be a problem. We say the exact time of day we want to get there and a line zooms out from the plinth thing along the ground, in one door, out another, six . . . seven levels up and then along fourteen . . . fifteen doors and stops. That's the one. 'So are we going to do this?' we all say. And we are. We follow the line to the first door and Evie goes first, I go second. He steps into the door and, like, half a second later, bang, he's coming out of the door up top. He's fine, so I go. It's the weirdest feeling. You're, like, pulled in. Well, you know. Next thing I know I'm up on this tiny little ledge, Evie's got my arm and we're looking down at the others below.

One by one they all come up and we head along to the next door and again one at a time, we all step through. And we're in Wembley Stadium. And it's 1966. I mean, actual 1966. We're there. We can touch 1966. We can smell it, we can taste it, we can hear it. 'ENG-LAND! ENG-ER-LAND! ENG-LAND! ENG-ER-LAND!' The chants of the crowd are deafening. Like it's shaking your whole body. You can feel it in your teeth. It makes your heart vibrate in your chest. Me and Evie used to go to the old Wembley all the time with my Uncle Oscar when we were kids, so we knew it. We knew exactly where to go. We were there just in time for kick-off. And we were there when West Germany went one–nil up. We were there when Hurst equalized. We were there when Martin Peters made it England two, West Germany one. We were there when Weber made it two–all in the bloody eighty-ninth minute. And we were there when Hurst scored two more in extra time. We were there to see England win. Four–two. Final whistle. That's probably still the best day of my life, and a lot's happened since.

After that we were cream-crackered and went back through the doors to the cave. No time had passed. We went back to the exact moment we left. We made our way back to the coach. We only had one flag so we'd lost the treasure hunt, but none of us cared. We knew then, sitting on that damp bus, none of us saying anything, waiting for the other teams to get back, we knew that everything had changed. Life was never going to be the same again.

*

And it wasn't. We kept it secret. Didn't tell a soul. Not our wives, those who had them, or girlfriends or friends. We kept it within the group. We figured if it got out the government would come and take it away from us. At first we didn't know what to do with it. I lived alone and I had an old safe. It had belonged to my grandad. I never used it. Never had anything worth putting in it. It was floor-standing and absolutely solid. You could've stuck a bomb underneath it and it wouldn't have made a dent. So we kept it in there to begin with. We made a pact to only use it together, but getting nine people to agree on where we'd go wasn't always easy, so we started taking it in turns.

Then one day Bacon decided he wanted to go back to see his mum. He was only young – twenty-five, twenty-six, something like that – but his mum had died when he was nine. He went back to a day a few years before she died. A day he had always remembered. His mum and dad had taken him to London Zoo for the day. They'd gone on a train and the Tube. Bacon followed them all the way. They got out at Baker Street and walked up through Regent's Park. They stopped at the lake to look at the ducks and his mum and dad had a bit of a kiss and a cuddle. Thing is, seeing his mum and dad like that, seeing how in love they were, had been more emotional than he had expected and he got rather upset. Then little him noticed big him crying and being a sweet kid decided to go and ask him what was wrong and promptly stepped out in front of a cyclist. Broke his arm in two places. Bacon watched as this scar appeared on his wrist and grew up his forearm. The great memory of that day vanished. It had never happened. Now he remembered going to London and getting hit by a bike. We realized then what a chance we were taking by going back in time. If we've learned anything from Back to the Future *it's that time travel is a minefield. After that it was agreed that we'd only go to the future. If we had to go to the past for anything we'd plan it and try to keep the variables to a minimum.*

Nine Frolic in the Future

Ed came up with an idea to make money. We'd go just one day into the future and grab a newspaper and come back. It had all the sports results from the day after. We'd each pick something, a footie match, a horse race, whatever, and go and place a bet. Lot of betting shops around, and in a very short time we made a lot of money. Then there was a Euromillions draw that rolled over for weeks and weeks until it was a hundred and sixty million pounds. We figured we could only risk a lottery win once without raising suspicion, so we should make it count. We popped forward, got the numbers, said we were a syndicate. All co-workers. No lie. Said we wanted to remain anonymous, but it didn't work out like that. You can't win a hundred and sixty million pounds and keep it quiet. Word gets out. And believe it or not, being rich wasn't that much fun and there were some things you couldn't buy. There was a woman Foster had always been in love with, and when we had all the money he went to see her. She was married with kids by then. They'd been childhood sweethearts or something. He thought the money would make a difference, but it didn't. She loved her husband and kids and told him to take a hike. Something changed in him then. I don't know, maybe he'd been holding on to this idea that he could win her back one day and then when he got back from seeing her he knew that would never happen and hope was gone. It was his idea that we go somewhere. Somewhere where we could live like kings. Evie said kings wasn't ambitious enough. We had this incredible gift at our disposal. We should live like gods! But it was agreed that gods was a bit much so we settled on emperors. We would be the Nine Emperors.

We went exploring then. We each took a different point in time. A thousand years into the future. Ten thousand. A hundred thousand. A million. We saw the planet ruined. We saw it flourish. We saw it devoid of life. We saw it overflowing with life. We settled on a point three million years into our future. There was life on the planet again but not too much. There were whole continents that were ours for the taking. Foster had found this bloke and employed him as a guide and translator. They travelled around the world, but we didn't want him – Otravinicus was his name – knowing more than was necessary, so Foster never told him where we had chosen. And where we had chosen was what was once America, North, Central and South. A lot of the continent had been lost to the sea over time, but that still left plenty of wide open spaces. The Americas are called Mallia now. We split up the whole continent into nine – nine empires – and set about building palaces fit for emperors.

I was born and bred in Hackney, east London. We lived in a cramped little flat in a tower block full of cramped little flats, on an estate full of tower blocks. Me, my mum and my three sisters. I always longed for space. Fields, trees. I wanted to grow things. Nothing grows in Hackney, least not where

I lived. I had a fantasy about living in a French chateau with an orchard and vineyards. Well, when we became emperors it wasn't a fantasy any more. I could do just that. We could alter the size of the doors. We could take anything we wanted from any time. We were never stupid about it. Didn't do anything that would draw too much attention. I did some research and found a chateau in northern France that was bombed during the war. It was obliterated. A pile of rubble was all that was left. No one had died in it. They had all been evacuated so it was an empty building when it perished. I took it minutes before it was about to be annihilated. One moment it was sitting in France, the next it was in west Mallia. Good wine-growing country. It was literally picked up from one place, foundations and all, and deposited in another. There was a vase of flowers in the hallway. It hadn't fallen over or spilled water or even lost a petal. Flowers from 1942 moved three million years in a split second and didn't even notice the journey. I had my chateau and I started planting my orchards. Except I was impatient. I wanted fully grown orchards stretching as far as the eye could see. I wanted healthy fully grown vines of grapes. I didn't want to have to wait for them, but I was a time traveller so I didn't have to. I went back in time twenty-five years and laid out the plans for the orchards and vineyards. Then I hired a gardener. This is a complicated idea to get your head round, but I hired him in 1983. I knew him from the pub we'd go to after work. His name was Cliff. He liked to talk. I knew that he had an allotment and loved to grow things, but his allotment was tiny so he couldn't grow very much. He never married, never had children. Never lived much of a life. With my lottery money I bought a piece of land in

163

Sussex. I made sure there was only one way in or out and then I set up a permanent portal but made it invisible. Every day for the next twenty-five years, Cliff would go to work in Sussex and pass through the portal without knowing and spend the day in Mallia. I say he did it without knowing, but I'm not sure that's true. He must have suspected something. I mean, some days he would leave home in the peeing rain, but as soon as he passed through the entrance to my land the sun would be shining. In winter there would be two feet of snow outside his house, but soon as he got to work there'd be bright clear skies and lush green fields. He'd have to be a fool not to know something was weird, but for whatever reason he never asked, never said anything. Probably because he knew he was on to a good thing. It paid well and it was what he loved doing. Because of the job, his life changed. He met a woman, got married, had kids. Four of them.

I created a legend for myself. Cliff never knew who he was working for. I hired a lawyer to act as a front. As far as Cliff was concerned his employer was an eccentric adventurer, off exploring the oceans but one day I would return home and until that day he would tend to the vines and the orchards. So I hired Cliff in the morning and set him to work. In the afternoon I rescued the chateau and plonked it on my land. And that evening I was drinking a glass of Pinot Noir in the garden of my chateau, looking out over my fully grown orchards and vineyards.

We all set about building our palaces then. Danny used the same invisible door trick to send builders and train designers into the future to lay his track. Ed did one better than me and picked the Palace of Versailles. He transported the whole thing, gardens and all. He took it in the early part of the twenty-second century. A hundred years to the day that we first found the box. It was an unsolved mystery to the people of that time. How can a building just vanish?

We had to be careful about paradoxes. Foster was a bit of a film buff. Well, total film geek actually. Knew all about the hazards. Like, Ed chose Versailles because he'd been there as a kid on a school field trip. Went to a posher school than I did. As a kid he thought it was the most amazing place he'd ever seen. Foster said that if he took Versailles from before that point in time, then he would never have been able to go there on a school trip so would never have fallen in love with the place so would never have chosen to steal it to begin with. Paradox, you see.

So we all built our empires and we connected them so we could move freely between them. Then we had to populate them. What's the point of being an emperor without people to lord over? Some of us didn't want that. Danny just wanted his train. I didn't want my chateau crowded, but I needed people to work the land. Evie and I came from a place where people struggled to make something of themselves. When we were exploring the different eras in Earth's history, looking for our new home, we saw that things get much, much worse. The planet becomes massively overpopulated. Bloated with humanity. Resources aren't able to sustain the masses. Society collapses. Crime rates soar. But we knew there were good people in among the gangs and the druggies. Good people who were stuck. That's where we recruited from, Evie and me. We walked through favelas that covered whole continents and handpicked people who we thought would appreciate the chance of a different life. I took thirty to begin with but there were so many more so we built a town too. After all, I would need people to buy my produce.

Evie did the same but took even more people than me. Even though we grew up in the same place, he didn't have the problem with overcrowding that I did. His empire was a city on the coast, dedicated to having fun. It was his version of Miami or Las Vegas or Blackpool.

We were all looking for different things. Some of us were more ambitious, some were less. Bacon called on lots of ex-soldiers he knew from his TA days and together they built a small quaint English village. I guess it represented the sort of place they felt was worth defending. Bacon said he wanted ex-soldiers because they were practical.

Emu was the youngest of all of us. A year younger than Danny even. He was a party animal. He lived to have fun. While we were at work, Monday mornings would always be exhausting, listening to the never-ending catalogue of things Liam had managed to squeeze in over the weekend. He was a young man who lived life to the full. He wanted every second to be filled with experiences. So his empire was bound to represent that sensibility. He built an amusement park. The greatest amusement park ever constructed. He included several extra portals that linked directly to the mountains for a morning spent snowboarding or to the ocean for an afternoon of surfing. He filled the place with his friends. He was of an age where he had a lot of friends.

Alan was married with three kids back when he worked for Horseshoe Financial Services, but he didn't want to bring any of his family with him. He left them his Euromillions winnings and said goodbye. He invited his footie mates to come with him. All men in their forties or fifties. Alan was from Brighton. He was a staunch supporter of Brighton & Hove Albion, also known as the Seagulls. Seeing Alan with his footie mates was a shock. It was a whole new side to him. At work he had always been fairly quiet and reserved, but with his friends he was completely different. They were loud, obnoxious thugs. Stereotypical football supporters. The rest of us all actively avoided Alan then. Maybe that was the first crack. There would soon be a lot more.

Nine Turn on Each Other Like Dogs

Evie was the first one to give himself a bird name. One day he unveiled a coat of arms he'd had designed by an artist in twenty-seventh century Tokyo. The main image was an eagle, and Evie said that he was going to be the Eagle Emperor. We all latched on to the idea. Straight away Alan announced he would be the Seagull Emperor, after his beloved football team. Liam, being a bit of a joker, liked the idea of being the Penguin Emperor. You know, emperor penguin – Penguin Emperor. No one laughed very much and we all wondered why he wasn't the Emu Emperor after his nickname, but he found it funny so stuck with it. Ed chose the magpie as his symbol because it represented the scoundrel he liked to think of himself as. Bacon chose the swallow as his late mum had a tattoo of a swallow behind her ear. Boo chose a bird native to Nigeria, where he was from, called himself the Firefinch Emperor. Always liked that one. Foster chose falcon because of its Star Wars connotations. I chose the owl as my symbol. And Danny chose . . . the peacock. What's that? Yeah, Danny was the Peacock Emperor. He was the Pigeon Emperor too. Later, when it all went bad, Danny would get very confused. But I'm getting to that.

Where was I? Oh yeah, the birds. Back then it was all fun and games. Ed had to outdo Evie by hiring Picasso to design his magpie coat of arms. Foster chose a guy called Drew Struzan, who did movie posters. Tunde chose some artist called Yinka Shonibare. Liam went to Salvador Dali.

And for a little while, everything was good. We thrived. Our individual communities grew and prospered. It was everything we'd hoped it would be. It was only later we discovered it was never that. There was already a cancer eating away at us. It was Bacon's village that caused the first problem. By bringing in ex-soldiers, Bacon was effectively creating an army. Least that's what Evie accused him of. He denied it. Said they were all ex-army. Comrades-in-arms, nothing more. But Evie looked at Bacon and saw a threat. So he secretly went and recruited his own army. He came to see me one day. We sat in my orchard drinking wine made from my grapes and he told me what he'd done. And not just him. Ed and Foster were with him. Evie and I had been best friends for almost thirty years. It hurt that he was only telling me now. Fourth on the list. They'd gathered their army from throughout history. Varangian mercenaries from Byzantium, Roman legionnaires, Cavaliers, Roundheads, Japanese rōnin searching for a master, elite twenty-third-century genetically modified super-soldiers, Tayanan Pallatan militia. The list went on.

'But Bacon's no threat,' I said. He didn't agree. Bacon had made a request to use the box. Some time earlier, Evie had

decided he wasn't happy any more with it staying in my old safe. He had a brand-new super-safe designed and built. One with nine locks, which meant all of us had to be present and in agreement when anyone wanted to open it. Evie was convinced that Bacon was about to try to overthrow the rest of us. I couldn't believe what I was hearing. This was crazy talk. Bacon? Evie said that the time had come to take sides and he wanted me on his. I told him I didn't agree with him. He said he was pretty sure that Liam, Alan and Tunde would side with Bacon. Foster and Ed were with him. Danny and myself, we were borderline. I told him I thought he was seeing enemies where there weren't any. Something had happened to him. This wasn't the person I'd known for thirty years, the person I'd grown up with. I guess the pyramid makes you question everything you've ever believed, everything you've ever known to be true. How could it not change you? I maybe could have done something different. Should *have done something different. Something to prevent it. I just didn't think it would get so bad.

You see, the army of mercenaries Ian, Foster and Ed had brung together continued to grow. It appeared that soldiers took such things as time travel in their stride. Though to be fair, they'd chosen a very specific breed of soldier. They weren't like twenty-first-century soldiers where the army was just a job, outside of which they were husbands and wives, fathers, mothers and other variations of normal human beings. No, the warriors Ian, Foster and Ed had chosen lived to fight. Everything else was secondary. They only cared about the battle to come. Never seemed that bothered about where and when they were. Only who the enemy was. And in this instance, it was us.

The army they had was big enough to attack us all at once. It turned out that the super-safe Ian had insisted on had a back door. He had sold us all on this idea that it would take all nine of us to open it, but it was all a lie. He could open it himself whenever he wanted. He opened it one beautiful crisp, clear morning. Then he opened twenty separate portals, allowing his soldiers to creep up on the rest of us, take us by surprise.

The first I knew of it was when I was woken up by a distant sound drifting up from the village to the south of my orchards. It was like this weird . . . discordant music. The volume rose and fell, rose and fell, rose and fell. I lay there in bed listening, trying to work out what it was. Thinking, Is it music? Is it an animal in distress? It was screaming. The screams of the villagers as the mercenary army cut through them. Sorry. I don't mean to get emotional, but it's hard, you know. I took those people from a living hell with the promise of something brighter and better. Ian's army slaughtered them all. Every man, woman and child. They were relentless.

At the same time they were attacking Alan and his footie mates, Bacon and his ex-squaddies, Tunde and his family and friends in their tower, Emu and his amusement park. Their orders were to leave no one alive. When they got to my chateau I tried to stop them, but there was nothing I could do. They didn't kill me, on Ian's orders. But his orders didn't stretch to Deni, my sister, or her girlfriend. They had been the only ones to come with me. My mum didn't understand any of it. It scared the willies out of her. She's a simple, church-going old lady. She never wanted to come here. Never wanted to see it for herself. She didn't want to believe it even existed. Probably told her

170

friends I'd gone to live in Scotland or gone to prison. Anything but entertain the idea that I could time-travel. The older two of my sisters chose to stay with her. My youngest sister, Deni – Denise – was more adventurous. She jumped at the chance. She and Polly, her girlfriend, were planning to head off to explore the new world. A week later and they would have been gone. As it was . . .

Sorry. I just need a moment.

I'm OK now. Sorry about that. Never used to be a crier. It's hard, you know. Where was I? The attacks lasted for less than an hour. When they came into the chateau I thought I was going to die too, but they knocked me unconscious. When I woke up it was all over. I was lying in a chair in Ian's throne room. He always called it an entertainment space, but it had a dirty great throne at one end that only he was allowed to sit in. It was a throne room. Ian was there, Foster and Ed too, and Danny. He looked ashen. He looked sick. He couldn't hold my eyes. He just stared at the ground. His fingers twitching, I remember. Couldn't hold them still. Alan, Tunde, Emu and Bacon were dead. We were the five emperors now.

'What have you done?' I asked Evie.

'What had to be done,' he said. He gave me a choice then: to join them or suffer the consequences. He said because I was his best friend he couldn't or he wouldn't kill me. He would just put me elsewhere. Out of the way. I told him he would need to do that and do it fast because I was going to kill him. Suddenly this blade, this long, thin blade, almost like glass, comes out of nowhere and stops right there, just under my chin. I freeze.

Can't even turn my head. I can feel its edge. It's like ice on my skin. I look with my eyes and there's one of his Japanese rōnin. You know what a rōnin is? It's a samurai without a master. They need a master, you see. Evie was his master now. He had two of those guys. They were his personal bodyguards. In full armour. Evie said he was going to give me some time to get my head straight. He promised great things would come. He said Emu and Bacon and Alan and Tunde had been biding their time. Plotting to do away with us. He told me I shouldn't feel bad. 'What about all the people on my estate?' I asked. He shrugged. That's it. Nothing else. All those people and all they got was a shrug. 'What about my sister?' I asked. 'There was,' he said, and I'll never forget this, 'there was a misunderstanding.' Then he quickly corrected himself, 'An unfortunate misunderstanding'.

I was locked up after that. Fed, watered, kept comfortable. Every day for a week, Evie would come to see me, with his two samurai in tow. He would ask me if I had made a decision. I'd say, I've decided to kill you. The samurai would draw their swords defensively but Evie would have them stand down. Then he'd leave and come back the next day and ask the same thing. I would reply the same way and that carried on for seven days. On the eighth day he sent Danny in on his own. No samurai. Danny was a shell of his former self. Skin and bones. Hair greasy. Unshaven. He looked ill. Worse than the last time I'd seen him. He paced about a lot, wringing his hands. Lots of hand wringing. Lots of rambling talk. Going off on complete tangents. He started talking about the Peacock Emperor in the third person. 'You're the Peacock Emperor, Danny,' I said. He just shook his head and stared at the floor with bloodshot eyes. 'I'm the Pigeon, I'm the Pigeon, I'm the Pigeon . . .' He just kept saying it over and over. He hadn't done anything to hurt anyone, but he had known about it and he hadn't done anything to stop it, and that was tearing him apart. It was twisting his mind. He had created this other version of himself and called him the Pigeon Emperor. It represented his weak, timid, gutless side. The Peacock Emperor was locked away inside him somewhere and he was scared of it. The Peacock Emperor would punish him whenever he returned. Poor Danny.

Next day, Evie came back with his samurai in tow. He told me he couldn't keep asking me the same question. He had other things to do. 'Like killing other innocent people?' I said. 'They weren't innocent,' he said. If he had done nothing at all and they had attacked first, as he knew they were planning to, then we would all be dead. I should be thanking him, he said. 'Thank you,' I said. My sarcasm was not lost on him. 'Where was his proof that they were planning a massacre of their own?' I asked. 'Foster and Ed overheard them plotting,' he said. I understood then. I knew Evie better than I knew anyone in the whole world. I knew that he could be persuaded by a silver tongue and I knew Foster had such a tongue. I never fully trusted him. He was just too clever. Too tricky. I always felt like I was missing the joke with him. That he was operating on a higher level. You know who he is? He's Iago. You know who that is? Othello. Shakespeare. Listen to me, talking about Shakespeare. La-di-da. Never read a book in my life before, not through choice anyway. There's loads of them here. I've read all sorts of things now. Lots of times, some of them. I've read Othello most of all. Didn't really understand it to begin with. But every time I read it, something else would

173

click. Some scenes I'd read over and over. Specially scenes with Iago. Othello's this general, you see. Great man, commander of armies, and Iago's supposed to be his friend but he's not. He's poison. He's a snake in human form. He's angry with Othello, you see, so he whispers in his ear: Pssst-psst-psst-psst-psst-psst. Whispering toxic nothings, making Othello see betrayal where there is none until Othello does something terrible. Something monstrous. That's Foster. Not Ed. He's not bright enough. It's Foster. He's a villain.

So Evie asked me one last time what my decision was and I said it hadn't changed. I was going to kill him first chance I got. And I'd kill Foster and Ed. 'They'll turn on you too,' I said. 'You mark my words,' I said. Evie said he was sorry but there was nothing else he could do for me. He took out the pyramid and opened up a portal there and then. He said he had convinced Foster and Ed to let me live. Exile would be my punishment. He said he had picked somewhere that meant something to the both of us. Said he had thought about it long and hard. He explained he was sending me back to the world a short time after the last of the humans had died out. There was no one else on the planet. I would be alone. He was sending me to a place he and I had been to on holiday a bunch of times in our youth. 'Good times,' he said. I had to laugh.

I went to the portal. Stopped. Looked back. 'Bye, Evie,' I said. He looked properly sad. We both knew it was the last time we'd ever see each other. I put out an arm for a hug. His samurai flinched. Half-pulled their swords. Evie waved them back but didn't respond to begin with. Obviously not sure how to play it. What's the etiquette when you're exiling a person? Then finally he comes over and we hug each other. 'I love you,' I say. I meant it. He was my best friend in the whole world. And then I killed him.

When Danny had come to see me the day before he smuggled in a cold bottle of beer for me. Sweet Danny. I drank the beer when he was gone and then I broke off the top of the bottle and I spent some hours sharpening the edge of the glass till it was like a scalpel. When Evie came in for the hug I stuck it into him, into his belly . . . twisted . . . tore. Opened his stomach up. Watched his insides come out. Those two samurai had been waiting and watching for over a week and they missed it. I stepped back. Saw the life leaving Evie as I was pulled through the portal. Five emperors became four.

I found myself here. In Corfu. No one followed. The door closed. Don't know how much time had passed since the last humans had been around. There weren't any corpses. Nothing rotting. It didn't smell. It was just like everyone had got up and left. As far as I can tell everyone had left long before the end. They all converged on the big cities, thinking that help would come there first. I walked around the island for a while. Seeing what's what. Picking a place to live. I mean, there's plenty of choice, but I came here once before with Evie. This house, I mean. Back in two thousand and something. Couple of Brits owned it. They were having a party. Me and Evie had made friends with some people who were friends with them and we found ourselves on this very terrace. The guy who owned it played the guitar, I remember. Used to be in a band years before. Bunch of his friends played too and sang. There was a barbecue and we drank wine. We all jumped in the pool, drank more wine. I remember thinking this was paradise on earth. Who could ask for more?

Obviously that was a long, long time ago. Lots of people owned it since. Lots of changes, but since I've been here I've been trying to put it back to the way I remember it from the party that night. This terrace didn't look like this when I first came back. It was all enclosed. Wasn't right. Wasn't how it had been all those years before, so I changed it back. I extended the allotment all down the hill. Plenty of food. Plenty of animals in the hills too, for when I want meat. I meant what I said earlier. I don't want to leave here. There's honestly nowhere I'd rather be. I could go after Ed and Foster and get my revenge, but I've had a long time to think and a long time for the anger to abate. I'm not ready for it to start again. Maybe, if you can, pop back now and again. Just in case I ever change my mind. If you can't, you can't. No harm, no foul.

Well, I guess that brings us up to date. Is there anything else you want to know?

Dramatis Personae (updated)

Ian 'Evie' Vincent ~~DEAD~~
'The Eagle Emperor'. Born in Hackney, east London.

Foster 'Pecker' Peck ~~UNKNOWN~~
'The Falcon Emperor'. Born in Mud Bay, South Carolina. *Star Wars* fanatic.

Ed 'Ed-Head' Cresswell ~~UNKNOWN~~
'The Magpie Emperor'. Born in Frome, Somerset. Art lover. Thief. Lives in the Palace of Versailles.

Shaun 'Dunny' Dunmore ~~EXILED~~
'The Owl Emperor'. Born in Hackney, east London. Lived in a French chateau. Now lives in a villa in Corfu.

Danny 'Larry' Lambe ~~CRAZY~~
'The Pigeon/Peacock Emperor'. Born in Fife, Scotland. Lives on a train.

Alan 'Alfonso' Lynch ~~DEAD~~
'The Seagull Emperor'. Born in Brighton, East Sussex. Loves Brighton & Hove Albion football club. Oldest of the group. Lives in a replica of the Royal Pavilion.

Tunde 'Boo' Buhari ~~DEAD~~
'The Firefinch Emperor'. Born in Port Harcourt, Nigeria. Lives in a mirrored tower.

Liam 'Emu' Rodericks ~~DEAD~~
'The Penguin Emperor'. Born in Brockley, south London. The youngest of the group. Lives in an amusement park.

Paul 'Bacon' Whittaker ~~DEAD~~
'The Swallow Emperor'. Born in Grays, Essex. Mum died when he was young. Ex-member of the Territorial Army. Lives in a replica English village.

15

Junk was silent for several long moments. There was a lot to take in.

'My sister,' he said finally.

Shaun shook his head. 'Like I said, I don't know anything about her. There were no stolen children. Not that I know of anyway.'

'What about Tolfke? You know who he is?'

'No. You mentioned him before. Name doesn't ring a bell. Who is he?'

'Just some guy. Like a fixer, you know? Wears a mask.'

'A mask?' said Shaun, his curiosity tickled.

'A red one last time I saw him, but he has others.'

'I do know him. Least I remember seeing a man in a red mask.'

'Where?' asked Junk eagerly.

'It wasn't long before things started to implode. We were all at Versailles. Ed liked to have big parties. They were fun. We would invite celebrities from the old world, use the invisible door trick, they'd never know where they were. We convinced them it was a replica of Versailles. Not the real thing. No one thought it was the real thing. That was in France. They knew they weren't in France. They just thought they were in the wilds of Sussex somewhere. No one's mobile phone worked, of course, but we just said it was a lousy signal. Anyway, at one of these bashes I got bored and wandered off. There are so many rooms in Versailles, Ed's probably still not been in all of them yet.

'I was exploring and I was at the end of a long corridor and a door opened and a man in a red mask stepped out. I saw him, he saw me. It was freaky. It wasn't a fancy-dress party or anything. He just looked like he didn't belong. I started towards him and he turned and ran. I ran after him. When I got round the next corner he was nowhere to be seen. There were a dozen doors he could have gone through so I gave up and went back downstairs.

'The oddest thing was a little later I asked Ed about it. Said I'd seen this bloke in a mask upstairs, and before Ed could say anything, Foster answered for him. Said, "Oh, that's just the phantom who haunts the halls here." He laughed. Ed and Evie laughed too. Then Foster quickly started talking about something else and the topic was ignored. So to answer your question, the man in the red mask is somewhere in Versailles and I would say Foster knows something about it, but I'd be very careful if I was you. You don't want to go there.'

'I have to go there,' said Junk. 'I left my friends there.'

'Then I'm sorry, but your friends are probably already dead.'

'What are you talking about?' asked Junk.

'Were you not listening to the story I just told you? Ed and Foster are still there.'

'How do you know? You've not seen them in how long?'

'Trust me. I know them. Know how they think. They're still there, but your friends probably aren't.'

The portal of green light opened up right there on the terrace that looked out over olive groves stretching down to the sea. Junk leaped through and vanished. The portal closed and Shaun Dunmore, Dunny, was all alone again. He whipped off his tatty shorts and naked Wednesday was able to resume.

A door opened in a hallway of Versailles and Junk stepped out. He stopped to listen but heard nothing. Silence was everywhere. He moved quickly, sticking close to the wall. The doorway closed behind him. He hurried to the bedrooms where he had left the others. The doors of each were wide open. He looked into the first room. This had been where Lasel was resting. The room was empty but he saw signs of a struggle. Bedclothes ripped from the beds and discarded. A chair on its side.

He went to the next room. It was empty too. And the next and the next. In the hallway he looked left and right. He didn't know what to do so he ran.

He reached a stairwell and looked over the top. There were no sounds of life from anywhere. Not so much as the ticking of a clock. His hands were shaking. He was scared. He wasn't sure why he believed Shaun's story, but he did. Every word.

He headed down the stairs, moving as softly as possible, taking two or three steps at a time. The treads were wide and made of white marble veined with purple. At the next floor he stopped and listened. Still nothing. He carried on down.

Each floor offered the same silent reception. When he reached the ground floor he had a choice of directions. Multiple corridors stretched away. He picked a direction at random and raced along. His eyes and ears were peeled, as aware of his surroundings as he could be.

Soon he found himself back in the ballroom where all this had started. He saw the familiar paintings in their gaudy frames and the numerous vanity paintings of Ed. He stopped to listen again. Still nothing, and he was about to leave to look elsewhere when some force, most probably instinct, drew him forward. Then he saw it. In the middle of the room was a doorway or portal. Green and shimmering. It was horizontal, lying on the floor like a rug. It hadn't been there before and somehow Junk knew it was meant for him. It filled him with dread. This had been left here to lure him somewhere, and the fact that someone – Ed, Foster, whoever – wanted to lure him somewhere meant they had probably already tipped their hand and shown their true colours. He was too late. His friends were already in danger. He stared at the doorway on the floor and searched his mind for a plan B. If plan A was doing what Foster and whoever else wanted, then plan B was something smarter, something unexpected, something . . . else. He couldn't think of anything else. He had no way of knowing where that doorway led without stepping through it, so it wasn't as if he could sneak up on them from another direction. Instinct told him time was of the essence. He had to do something and he had to do that something quickly. He shook his head. No other choice. He moved forward and stepped into the prone doorway. He fell through and was gone.

It felt as if he hadn't fallen at all. It felt as if he had just skipped off a low wall and landed on a meadow of lush grass. He was somewhere that felt faintly familiar. He was in a dense forest. All the trees had bright yellow leaves. It was like being in a giant vat of butter. Yellow as far as the eye could see. He remembered the nolic-tea vision. The yellow forest. This was it. And in the vision, this is where he found Ambeline, albeit for little more than a few seconds before she threw him off a cliff, but still. He looked around. Which way to go? He turned in a circle but everything looked identical. Leaves the colour of custard on all sides. Then suddenly a flash of red. Just like in the vision. In among the trees ahead. He only saw it for a second. He stayed still and silent and stared ahead like a hunter waiting for his quarry to reveal itself. Time passed. Seconds joined together to form a minute, then more seconds came along to make two, but before they got there Junk saw it again. Something red dancing between the trees. He started running towards it. It started running too. He would lose sight of it now and again and every second it was gone would seem like ten, but then it would reappear and Junk would keep going. He ran faster and faster until suddenly the trees ended and he stepped out into a clearing. He skittered to a stop.

Ahead were more trees, but before them was a figure dressed all in red. It was small. It had stopped running. There were only a few metres between them now.

'Ambeline?' said Junk. His voice was barely audible but the figure reacted to the name with a twitch of his or her head. It cocked an ear to listen and then slowly, ever so slowly, it started to turn to face Junk. Junk was frozen with anticipation. The figure turned all the way around and looked straight at Junk. It wasn't Ambeline. The figure was wearing a bright red featureless mask. No eyeholes or mouth. Just blank. Red and blank. It was Tolfke. Junk stepped gingerly forward as if not wanting to spook a deer or something.

'Where are my friends?' he asked. He took another step forward. Tolfke took a step back. Junk took a step forward. Tolfke took a step back. Junk held out a hand. 'I won't hurt you. Just tell me where my friends are.'

Tolfke turned on his heel and ran. Junk let out a cry of frustration and set off in pursuit. They quickly entered more trees that were even more dense than before. Tolfke ran and Junk ran after him.

The forest floor was more treacherous here, vines and fallen logs hidden under the yellow leaves. Tolfke seemed to be sure of his footing and ran with abandon. Junk tried his best to keep up, but he kept slipping and stumbling. Suddenly the ground gave way beneath him and he found himself tumbling wildly. He clawed at the ground, desperate for purchase, but the soft, mossy floor came away in his hand. The world spun around him and suddenly he was spat out at the top of a gentle slope. He somersaulted down it and lay upside down in a heap at the bottom.

A short distance ahead was Tolfke, inverted from Junk's point of view. Junk quickly became aware of more movement and focused on several other figures a short distance further on. Junk manoeuvred himself around so he was sitting up straight. He saw Pallatans first. Directly behind Tolfke were a dozen Pallatans. They were shorter, stockier and darker-skinned than Mestrowe, but no less aggressive-looking and no less scary. Next to them were ten heavily armoured warriors. They had horned helmets, full face masks designed to strike terror into their opponents, and armour covering their entire bodies. They were samurai. They each held a long, thin blade loosely in front of them or resting on their shoulder. Next to them were men wearing a lot less armour. They had armoured breastplates and domed helmets. All eyes were looking at Junk. Then all the warriors – Pallatans, samurai and Roundheads – stepped aside as if at some inaudible command, and a corridor was created. Junk saw two men. One he recognized immediately. He had seen several paintings of him earlier. He was tall, lanky, had shaggy fair hair and a lush handlebar moustache. This was Ed. The Magpie Emperor. So by a process of elimination, the shorter, bespectacled man next to him had to be Foster Peck. And beside them was their army. Part of it at least.

Something caught Junk's eye and he looked past Foster and Ed and saw Garvan, Lasel, Otravinicus and Payo–Mestrowe. Each had their wrists tied to a length of rope that stretched out before them. Each rope was tethered to a stake in the ground. Garvan and the others were leaning back over the edge of a cliff beyond and the rope was all that was stopping them falling. Soldiers clad in chain mail, wearing conical helmets with aventails (a curtain of chain mail covering their throats), hefting large axes over their shoulders, stood between Junk and his friends. They were the Varangian Guard, once an elite unit of the Byzantine army, a thousand years before Junk had been born. Byzantium had grown out of the Roman empire and the Varangians had been bodyguards to the Byzantine emperors; now they were bodyguards to Foster and Ed.

'We thought you'd never get here,' said Foster. He had lost none of his native South Carolina accent. He was the reason Otravinicus spoke the way he did. 'Where have you been? What did you do to poor little Danny?'

Junk shook his head. 'Nothing,' he said. 'He's back

on his train.' He looked at his friends, meeting the eyes of each of them in turn. They looked scared.

'You know who we are?' asked Foster. Junk nodded. 'Good. Tell us why you're here.'

'I'm looking for my sister,' said Junk. 'She'll be nine years old now. Her name's Ambeline.'

Foster and Ed looked at one another and Ed shrugged. They turned back to Junk.

'Never heard of her,' said Ed. 'Tell us why you're really here.'

'That's the truth. You took her. The Nine Emperors. One of you at least.'

Foster frowned. 'Maybe we're being too subtle here.' He gestured beyond them. Junk didn't understand what he meant and didn't move. 'Well, take a look,' said Foster.

Junk got to his feet and moved forward. The soldiers shifted in such a way that there was only one path that Junk could follow. He wasn't allowed to get too near to his friends but was directed around them to see what lay behind them, and what lay behind them was a precipitous drop into nothingness. Wherever they were right now was so high that there was a dense band of mist below them. So dense it looked like clouds.

'Now,' said Foster, 'here's how this is going to work. We're going to ask you again, and if you don't tell us what we want to know, one of your friends is going to go over the side. Trust me – it's a very long way down.'

'Please don't,' said Junk, scared now he understood the situation. 'I swear to you I am telling the truth.'

Foster shook his head. 'You're travelling with an assassin.' He turned to glare at Payo–Mestrowe.

'No,' said Junk quickly, 'I'm travelling with the man who took my sister. He was hired by him –' Junk gestured to Tolfke – 'on your orders.'

'Do you know what he's talking about, Tolfke?' asked Ed. Tolfke shrugged dismissively. Foster looked to a soldier and nodded. The soldier, maybe some sort of commander, though his battle dress was the same as the others', passed on the nod to one of his men who was standing by Payo–Mestrowe. The soldier swung his axe and cut the rope connected to Payo–Mestrowe's wrists. Payo-Mestrowe's weight took him backwards over the cliff. Lasel screamed. Garvan roared. Otravinicus looked away.

'NO!' yelled Junk. He reached out but his way was blocked by more soldiers and he could do nothing but watch as Payo–Mestrowe toppled over the cliff-edge and disappeared from view. They all heard his cry getting further away as he fell, and then suddenly his voice was silenced. It was chilling. Junk and his friends all hung their heads.

'Now then,' said Foster, 'you know we're not fooling around here, so I ask again, why are you here?'

Junk looked at Garvan, Lasel and Otravinicus for guidance. What should he say? What could he say that would appease Foster and Ed?

'I'm telling you the truth. Ask Otravinicus. You know him.' Junk looked at Dr Otravinicus, who was tied up next to Garvan. The little man was shaking with fear. His lips were moving as if he was praying, though Junk didn't know to what god. 'I come from the same time you do. Early twenty-first century.' Junk was talking rapidly now. He knew time was running out for all of them. 'The Pallatan you just killed was called Jacid Mestrowe. He was a member of the League of Sharks. Your man there, Tolfke, hired him on your behalf. He broke into my house on the night of 14 December 2010. He took my sister Ambeline and jumped off a cliff with her. I've been looking for him ever since. When I found him he told me Ambeline was still alive and that you had her. That's why we're here. That's the only reason. I don't mean you any harm. I just want to find my sister, I swear.' Junk was breathing hard when he stopped, not having taken a breath while he was saying any of that.

Foster and Ed were quiet for a few moments as they considered what Junk had said.

'He's still playing games,' said Foster. 'Cut another one loose.'

'No!' shouted Junk. 'Please, no.' He stepped forward but the soldiers blocked him again. He saw an axe slink through the air. The blade embedded in the ground and for a moment none of them could tell which rope had been cut. Then Garvan started roaring in distress as he tipped backwards, and in a split second he too was gone. Like Payo–Mestrowe before him, they heard him for a short time as he fell and then his voice was extinguished.

Junk let out a wail of distress as he stared at the

empty space where his friend had been just a moment before. He couldn't believe that Garvan was gone. He looked at Lasel. Her eyes were full of tears.

'No more,' Junk begged. 'Please.'

'Then tell us what we want to know,' said Foster. He and Ed stared at Junk, willing him to answer. Junk's mind was in turmoil. Right now he had to put Garvan's death to one side and focus on saving Lasel and Otravinicus. But how could he? It was impossible. Maybe he could save one of them but not both. Just then he heard a voice in his head. A girl's voice. It said, 'Sometimes down is better than up.' That was what the figure dressed all in red had said to him in his vision. 'Sometimes down is better than up.' An idea popped into his head. It was a really stupid idea. It had next to no chance of actually working, but right now it was all he had. The axe-wielding soldiers relaxed ever so slightly in the moments after Payo–Mestrowe had gone, and again once Garvan was gone.

'OK, we're here because . . .' began Junk, and Foster and Ed leaned forward to listen. The soldiers all instinctively did the same thing, and in that moment when their attention was split Junk twisted and started running at Lasel. Foster cried out and a soldier reacted by hefting his axe, aiming to bring it down in front of Junk and in doing so cut him off. But Junk sidestepped him and the blade of the axe sliced through the rope holding Lasel and embedded itself in the ground. Lasel started to tilt backwards. She was screaming with terror. Another soldier made a grab for Junk but he ducked beneath the

189

man's outstretched leather-gloved hand. He arrived at the edge of the cliff and reached out for Lasel but she was tipping backwards too quickly and she accelerated out of his grasp and disappeared over the side, screaming as she went. Foster and Ed looked on in disbelief as Junk didn't stop. He didn't so much as hesitate. He hurled himself over the cliff-edge after her and in the blink of an eye he was gone too. Foster and Ed ran to the edge in time to see Lasel and Junk plummeting to their deaths. They were swallowed by the clouds.

Far below, Junk held his arms out as he fell. He could see Lasel just half a metre ahead of him. The mist or clouds were all around them now and their velocity was increasing by the second. Junk reached out for Lasel. The force of the air in his face was pushing his eyes shut and they were filling with water. He could hardly see. He felt her before he could see that he had a hold of her. Junk's hand curled around the front of Lasel's shirt and he held tight, pulling her to him until he could wrap his arms around her. The clouds dispersed suddenly and Junk and Lasel found themselves plummeting towards angry, jagged rocks below. For a moment, Junk saw Payo–Mestrowe and Garvan or what remained of them smeared over the rocks. He shut his eyes. He didn't want to look. He brought his hand up to the Antricle on his wrist. A doorway opened up halfway between them and the rocks. They were sucked through the doorway and they vanished.

*

They came out in the Room of Doors through a vertical standing doorway, which caused them to decelerate sharply and they hit the black floor hard but not hard enough to break anything. Junk twisted his body so he would take the brunt of the impact. They came sliding and spinning to a stop and lay there, entwined together, breathing heavily.

'Are you OK?' said Junk.

Lasel ached all over but she was alive. She nodded.

'Come on,' said Junk, scrambling to his feet. 'We've got to save them.'

Lasel didn't understand. She watched as Junk ran to the dais, pulling the Antricle from his wrist. 'How?'

'I don't know, but nothing's definite when you can time-travel.' Junk pulled and twisted the Antricle. He wasn't even paying attention to what he was doing. It snapped back into its dodecahedron formation with ease. He set it in the indentation on top of the column and it clicked into place. 'Gatekeeper,' he called.

'Location and temporal information required,' came back the booming disembodied response.

'Where were we just now?' said Junk to Lasel.

Lasel shrugged and shook her head. 'I don't know.'

'Gatekeeper, where did we just come from?' Junk asked.

'The Martaregan Peninsula, north-west Mallia. Present day,' came the voice's response.

'Fine, I want to go back there ten minutes before I—'

The Gatekeeper didn't even allow him to finish his sentence. 'That date is forbidden.'

'What?' cried Junk. 'Why?' The Gatekeeper didn't reply. 'OK, the Martaregan Peninsula twenty minut—'

'That date is forbidden.'

Junk pulled at his hair in frustration. He looked at Lasel and shook his head in despair. Tears were running down his face. She crossed to him and put her arms round him.

'The very first time we came in here,' said Lasel, thinking back, 'you asked to go back to when Ambeline was taken and it wouldn't let you, but it would let you go earlier. I think you said the day she was born.'

Junk thought back. So much had happened since then, but Lasel's memory was spot on. 'That's right. So we could trick it.' Junk lowered his voice to a conspiratorial whisper. 'Go somewhere close by a day or two earlier, so we can travel to the peninsula in time.'

'I can hear you, you know,' said the Gatekeeper. 'Paradox protocols enforced. Travel denied.'

'What?' snapped Junk. 'What does that mean?' There was no reply. 'Answer me.' Still nothing. *'ANSWER ME!'* Junk's angry voice echoed through the cavernous room but there was no response.

16

In the direct aftermath of Junk hurling himself over the edge of the cliff after Lasel, there was a stunned silence from Foster, Ed, Otravinicus and the gathered troops. Junk's actions were most unexpected to everyone present.

'Well, that didn't quite go according to plan,' said Tolfke.

'Mr Solo, sir . . .' Otravinicus was addressing Foster whom he had first met using the pseudonym *Han Solo.* 'I can be useful to you still. Please don't kill me. I—'

'Shut up, Otravinicus!' snapped Foster. He looked at Ed. 'I don't understand. Why would someone do that?'

Ed didn't answer. He didn't know what to say.

'You know anything about his sister?' asked Ed.

Foster frowned. 'No, why?'

'You used the League of Sharks more than anyone else.'

'I don't think that's true. We all used them at one time or another. I think Evie used them most.'

Ed mumbled something, not looking convinced. He turned and walked away. Foster started to follow. One of the axe-wielding soldiers advanced on Otravinicus, spinning his axe gaily, getting ready to deploy it. Otravinicus's eyes filled with fear and he started to scream and beg for his life. The soldier held the axe up over his head, ready to bring it crashing down.

'Bring him,' called Foster, just as the soldier let the axe fall. Otravinicus screamed like an eight-year-old on a roller coaster. The axe sliced through the rope and the soldier grabbed it. He used it as a leash to pull Otravinicus away. It took the latter several moments to realize he wasn't about to die. He started giggling with relief.

Ahead he saw Foster, Ed and Tolfke stepping through a doorway of green light. The soldier led him after them. Once they were gone all the other various soldiers, samurai and Pallatans followed.

Junk woke on the floor of the Room of Doors. Lasel was curled next to him, her head nestled in the crook of his arm. He ached all over but he didn't want to move because he didn't want her to move. He could feel the gentle rise and fall of her breathing, which caused her body to move against his. He could smell her hair, which despite everything they had been through still smelled sweet. It mingled with other smells that clung to her, such as sweat, dirt and fear. Or perhaps those were coming from both of them.

Suddenly the memory of what had happened to Garvan hit him. For a few seconds there, just as he woke, he had forgotten, and the loss of the memory was delightful but it didn't last long enough. It came back quickly and violently. Its return brought pain. Real physical pain that constricted his chest. His friend was dead.

He tried to not think of it, but the act of trying not to think of something made not thinking of that particular something nearly impossible. He felt his throat drying out. He tried to concentrate on something else. He lay there, staring up at the myriad doors rising up above them. He stared into the deep, dark, all-consuming blackness at the top of the Room many levels above them. He started counting doors. Wondering what shade of green they were. They stretched up and up, looming high above him, and he wondered how high it was right at the top. As high as the cliff that he and Lasel had jumped off? And Payo and Garvan had been thrown off? Try as he might, he couldn't stop thinking about what had happened. He remembered what he had thought about just before he jumped: 'Sometimes down is better than up'. He thought back to the vision-quest dream thingy that he had experienced back in Corraway after drinking the tea that Garvan had made from nolic petals. The figure in red. Was it Tolfke? In the vision it looked like Tolfke but certainly didn't sound like Tolfke. It sounded like Ambeline. 'Sometimes down is better than up' . . . and she had said something else too. What was it now? 'Find Pirestus.' Who or what is Pirestus? Junk wondered. He had asked the others, no one knew. How could he find him, her or it? He thought about asking the Gatekeeper. Just then, a series of separate thoughts all popped into his head in quick succession. Each fleeting but triggered by the one before. Thinking about the Gatekeeper reminded him of Brother Hath, the monk who manned the big heavy door that was the entrance to the monastery perched atop the sandstone rock pillar. Brother Hath made him think about Brother Rard, who had crept aboard the *Casabia* in order to kill Otravinicus. The *Casabia* reminded him of Cascér, who in turn reminded him of diving enveloped in the commust jelly. That made him think about being under the water, which he missed. The last time he had been under water, Brother Antor was trying to attack him. He wondered what had become of Brother Antor and the other monks. The Brotherhood. The Brotherhood of the One True God, Pire. Pire. Pirestus. Could there be a connection? He needed to do something to take his mind off Garvan, and he still had to find Ambeline. That hadn't changed. He shook Lasel's shoulder gently.

'Wake up,' he said. 'I've got an idea.'

A rectangle of green light crackled into existence in an austere room and Junk and Lasel stepped through. Unadorned stone walls housed a rather basic-looking low wooden bed with a threadbare grey blanket and a pillow only a little thicker than the blanket. On the back of the door hung a black cloak and in the corner was a pile of dirty clothes. There were bowls of rotten food being strafed by a disco of bluebottles. Lasel and Junk covered their noses at the stench of decaying meat.

'Has something died in here?' asked Lasel.

'You'd think a monk would keep his room tidier,'

said Junk as he crossed to the door. He tried the handle. It was unlocked. He peered out into the corridor beyond. It was empty and silent. The last time Junk had been in this building was to steal the Antricle that was now clamped around his wrist. The time before had been to stand before Brother Antor, the leader of the order of monks for whom this monastery was home. That meeting ended badly for Junk, and Brother Antor had punished him by pushing a red-hot poker against his chest, blistering his flesh. Though the injury had healed quickly with the help of Garvan's buchelous grass remedy and the scar was faint now, Junk felt a sharp ache in his breast, a memory of the torture he had endured.

Junk and Lasel slipped out and moved swiftly and quietly, listening out for any signs of life.

'What are we looking for?' whispered Lasel.

'When I was here first –' Junk rubbed his chest unconsciously as he spoke – 'I saw a library off the main corridor, which led to the big hall where you got this.' He held up the Antricle. 'I figure if there's a reference to Pirestus, that's where we'd find it.' They came to a spiral staircase and descended.

At the bottom Junk looked out cautiously, expecting to see one of the monastery's zealous occupants, but again the corridor was empty. The only sound he could hear was that of dripping water coming from somewhere but he couldn't tell where.

'Where is everyone?' he said. Lasel was thinking the same thing: that the Brotherhood perished that day they attacked the *Casabia*. The last Junk saw of Brother Antor, he was drowning. Chances were, he was dead. Chances were, most, if not all, of the Brotherhood were dead. Did any of them come back?

Junk and Lasel turned a corner and found themselves in the main hallway of the monastery. At one end was the chapel where Junk first met Brother Antor and where Lasel later stole the Antricle. At the other end was the massive front door that had been manned by Brother Hath. Now it stood wide open and a cold wind blew in.

'I think the place is deserted,' said Junk, not bothering to whisper any more.

'Where was the library?' asked Lasel.

'One of these doors,' said Junk, gesturing to three tall, broad wooden doors running along the left wall. They tried the first. It was a storeroom. Some cleaning products, brooms, mops, that sort of thing. The second door opened into a long narrow corridor that led away from them. So the third door had to be the library. The door opened and they saw a high bookcase stretching out in front of them. Success. They hurried incautiously into the room and stuttered to a stop. A small fireplace at the end of the room was ablaze and lying prostrate on a couch in front of it was a sleeping monk. Junk didn't remember seeing this man before. He was bigger even than Brother Antor but his girth was not as solid. He lay on his back with his mouth wide open and his huge gelatinous belly juddered in time with his snoring. There were bits of food lodged in his hedge-like beard. As Junk edged closer he accidently kicked a bottle with his toe. It rolled forward, colliding with more bottles, and made for a clamorous alarm. Junk and Lasel froze on the spot, holding their breath, expecting the sleeping monk to leap up and start shouting. He didn't do that. He let out a little squeaky trumpet of a fart and carried on snoring.

Junk saw the floor in front of the couch was littered with bottles and all were empty. The monk was drunk. He gestured to Lasel to check out the books.

The shelves ran the length of the room and stood six rows high. They could easily have displayed a thousand books. As it was there weren't even a hundred so the shelves looked feeble and bare.

Keeping an eye and an ear on the sleeping monk, they started to flick through one book after another. The books were old and heavy. Their pages were thick and the typeface small and monotonous. Junk had expected weighty tomes filled with elaborate calligraphy and sumptuous illuminations, but it was just pages and pages of text. Plain and uninspiring.

'Can you read any of it?' asked Junk quietly. Lasel shook her head. They tried a few more books, hoping for illustrations, but no luck. 'I don't even know how to spell Pirestus in their language, do you?' Again Lasel shook her head. 'We maybe should have thought this through a little more.'

'Punté-intaré-unstass . . .' Junk and Lasel spun around to find Brother Antor standing in the doorway. '. . . enstash-sussa-tal-ust-sussa . . . is how you spell Pirestus in my

199

language.' Brother Antor looked different from the last time Junk had seen him. He had let his hair grow, so what had been criss-crossed strips was now starting to become a little unruly and was in desperate need of a wash. He was unshaven but did not yet sport a beard.

Just then the inebriated monk on the couch snored louder than ever. 'Biroc,' Brother Antor called to him, but he didn't respond so Antor picked up a book and flung it across the room. His aim was keen and he hit Biroc on the side of the head. The corpulent monk roared angrily, suddenly awake, and leaped to his feet barking what were clearly obscenities in Uuklynian (the language of the monks) until he looked up and saw Junk, Lasel and Brother Antor. He stayed his tongue and rubbed his head.

'So the desecrators have returned,' said Brother Antor, turning his attention back to Junk and Lasel. 'How did you get in this time?' He leaned back and looked along the corridor to the open front door. 'Oh, we left the door open. Oh, well.' He shrugged. 'Take what you want. It doesn't matter any more.' And with that, he turned and walked away. Junk and Lasel frowned at one another. That was unexpected. Junk hurried out into the corridor in pursuit of Brother Antor. Lasel followed.

'Wait,' called Junk, but Brother Antor didn't wait. He carried on to the chapel. The fire that had once been a hidden security feature designed to protect the Antricle was now alight and used to heat the large room. There was a massive table running the length of one wall and it was laden with food. Roasted meats, a dozen varieties of vegetables, the same of fruit, bread, potatoes or something that looked very much like potatoes and scores of other things that Junk had never seen before. There were also lots of bottles of wine and other types of alcohol. It was a sumptuous banquet that wouldn't have looked out of place if Henry VIII popped in for a quick side of mutton. However, there was something missing and Junk realized quickly what it was: joy.

Far from all being dead, the monks, about forty of them, slouched in broad, cushioned chairs, eating and drinking. Like Antor, all that could had grown their hair. Not one of them had kept the Mohican strips. They ate, they drank, they drank some more, they talked, they shouted, they argued, but they didn't laugh or sing or do anything that suggested they were enjoying any of this.

Brother Antor took his place at the head of the table, ripping a leg from a roast bird and snatching up a new bottle of wine. As he sat he said something to the other monks that Junk and Lasel didn't understand, but evidently it was about them because almost all of them turned to look at the 'desecrators'. However, no one seemed angry or happy or sad or anything else. They just regarded them with mild disinterest before turning back to what they had been doing.

'Brother Antor,' Junk said as he moved closer to the head of the table.

'Not Brother any more,' said Antor. 'After we failed in our duty to protect the key –' that's what the monks called the Antricle – 'we were no longer fit to call ourselves

Brother. Now just Antor.' He started to point to the people around the table and name them. 'Now just Veb. Tuca. Lask. Rard. Oh! You know Rard.' They looked to where Antor was pointing and Junk saw the former Brother Rard. He was leaning forward, his head resting on the table. He was asleep, snoring softly in contrast to Biroc back in the library. A steady trickle of spittle was running out of the corner of his mouth and puddling on the table beneath him. He looked utterly pathetic. Junk remembered the proud and vital young monk who had snuck aboard the *Casabia* to kill the heretic Otravinicus. A mixture of guilt and pity filled Junk then as he looked at the Brotherhood. They were men without purpose and he was the one who had taken that purpose away when he stole the Antricle.

'What can you tell us about Pirestus?' Junk asked Antor. Antor filled his glass and drank. Blood-red wine snaked through the stubble on his chin. He dragged his sleeve over his mouth and laughed. It was a dry, empty laugh.

'Pirestus is the kingdom of the one true god, home to Pire.'

'So it's . . . heaven, you mean?' said Junk. He said the word in English. Antor looked blank. It meant nothing to him. Junk looked to Lasel with a frown. Lasel shrugged back. She didn't know what heaven was either. Junk searched his memory for the translation in Jansian. He had heard Garvan say it once: 'Tarramaruum' in Cantibean. In Jansian . . . 'Kaneno,' he said. Lasel understood. So did Antor.

'Yes, Pirestus is kaneno.' He glanced at the metal goblet in his hand and Junk saw that his once golden eyes were as dull as tarnished brass. There was an engraving on the goblet. It depicted a tree, something like a mighty oak, the top of which turned into a fiery sun with jagged flames shooting out of it. 'A place we will now never see.'

Junk gasped. He had seen this image before. 'That represents Pirestus?' he said to Antor, who nodded. Junk looked at Lasel and let his eyes sparkle. She understood that he recognized it. It was time to leave. They stepped back from the table and edged towards the door. No one tried to stop them. No one even seemed to notice or care. Junk stopped and looked back. It felt wrong to leave like this. This was his doing. Not vindictively, but he had done this to the men around the table. He had taken the meaning out of their existence. He felt responsible. He put a hand on Lasel's arm to stop her and headed back towards the table.

'Antor,' said Junk, 'you didn't fail. You were tested and you passed.' With that Junk subtly touched the Antricle on his wrist and a doorway blazed into life behind him and Lasel. The monks reacted immediately. All shot to their feet, mouths open, eyes wide with astonishment. Junk held out his arm and the Antricle band moved from his wrist, spiralling around his hand, enclosing it like a glove once more before growing up out of his palm and mimicking their tree becoming the sun, the symbol for Pirestus. Junk's connection to the Antricle was becoming stronger all the time and he could make it assume any form he pictured in his mind's eye. For a moment the monks stared in disbelief, and then one by one they dropped to their knees with their heads bowed. Brother Antor was the last man standing. He stepped out from the table and walked towards Junk. He had a stern, angry look, his thin lips a black slash in his weathered face, and Junk was starting to think that maybe he had made a mistake. Nonetheless he stood his ground. Antor reached him and stared at the Antricle sun-tree in his hand before he too fell to his knees. He bowed his head.

'You are an emissary. You are a walker. Forgive me!' he sobbed. 'I was blind. Blinded by my own arrogance. I will repent. I will cut out my eyes as penance.' He reached up to the table and snatched up a knife.

'Whoa!' shouted Junk. 'Stop!' Brother Antor stayed his hand. Junk took the knife from his grip and tossed it back on to the table with a clatter. 'Don't beat yourself up about it and definitely don't go blinding yourself. What sort of craziness is that? What sort of god would want anyone to blind themselves?'

'But in the Book of Brask, Pire told Rundin to pluck out his eyes and the eyes of his children.'

'What?' Junk sounded horrified. He didn't know what the Book of Brask was but he figured it was the Brotherhood's version of the Bible. 'Why would he do that?'

Brother Antor frowned, assuming Junk, a walker, an angel, would know the Book of Brask inside out. Brother Antor wondered if this was another test so he answered, 'Because he had eaten fish on a holy day.'

'Are you kidding? Ah, don't believe everything you read. Pire's not like that. He's a pretty cool guy. He's more into love than war. Happy rather than angry. That sort of thing.'

Junk was running out of things to say now, so he looked at Lasel and gestured with his eyes for her to leave. Junk turned back to Brother Antor. 'You must hold on to your faith, Brother.' Antor looked up at Junk. His eyes blazed golden once more and tears were flowing freely down his cheeks.

'What do we do now?' asked Brother Antor. 'We are protectors but we have nothing to protect.'

'Don't get so caught up with material things. The whole planet's the work of Pire, right? Go protect that. Look after some rabbits or something. Make a difference.' Junk realized he was just riffing now and in danger of saying something stupid, or more stupid at least. It was time to go but he felt like he needed a parting gesture, so he reached out and patted Brother Antor on the head. Then he stepped back through the doorway and it closed after him.

The monks stayed where they were, all feeling as if they were in a state of grace. Just then Brother Rard, who was still slumped at the table, awoke. He sat up, wiping the drool off his chin and rubbing his eyes. He looked around him and was understandably surprised to find his brethren kneeling in worship to nothing he could see.

'Did I miss something?'

*

Junk and Lasel were back in the Room of Doors and Junk was excited. The Antricle transformed in his hand and became a sphere.

'I've seen that symbol before,' he said to Lasel, 'in my vision. On a button. In here.' He held up the Antricle. They both looked at it and the Antricle started to disrobe, layer after layer peeled back like a flower blooming. Junk had pictured this happening in his mind and so the Antricle was obliging him. Leaves drew back from the centre and folded under themselves. This carried on for longer than seemed possible without reaching the centre, but eventually the heart of the device started to appear. The layers became increasingly thin until something faintly green could be seen rising to the surface. And then the final leaf curled away, revealing a small emerald-green button that bore the symbol of the sun-tree. It was just as it had been in Junk's nolic-tea-induced dream.

'Shall we go and see what heaven's like?' he said, and he stabbed his finger down on the emerald button.

Nothing happened.

They waited and still nothing happened. Junk felt deflated. That had been decidedly anticlimactic. He pressed the button a few more times. Nothing continued to happen.

'Oh,' he said to Lasel, a little embarrassed now. He had probably made too big a deal of it, with all that brash talk of going to see what heaven's like, but he had been sure it was going to do something spectacular. Only then did he notice Lasel wasn't looking at him. She was staring past him into the distance. 'What's wrong?' he said.

'The lights are going out,' said Lasel. Junk turned to look at what she was looking at and after staring into the distance for only a few seconds he noticed what she meant. The hundreds of thousands of doorways that stretched out around them as far as the eye could see were vanishing. In quick succession they were all going black. Junk turned the other way, looking past Lasel, and the same thing was happening.

'Maybe I shouldn't have pressed that button. Gatekeeper, what's happening?' There was no response. 'Gatekeeper?' Still nothing.

'I think we should get out of here,' said Lasel.

'I think you might be right,' said Junk, 'but without the Gatekeeper there's no way to know where we're going.'

'Let's worry about that when we're out.' The prevailing blackness had consumed more than half of the Room now and it showed no signs of abating. More and more lights were going out every second. Junk took Lasel's hand and they ran to the nearest doorway. Without hesitation they leaped through.

And went absolutely nowhere. They were still in the Room of Doors. The speed that the outer darkness was approaching at continued to increase.

'What do we do?' said Junk.

Lasel led Junk to another portal and they tried again. The same thing happened and they just passed through, remaining in the rapidly extinguishing Room of Doors.

Now the portals were just impotent rectangles of green light that didn't lead anywhere.

'Wait,' said Junk, squinting at the doorways, the furthest of which was now only a hundred metres away and closing rapidly. 'They're not going out, they're merging.' Lasel strained to focus and she saw what Junk had seen already. From a distance it had looked as if the doors were closing, their lights extinguishing, but now they saw that the doors were in fact joining together with their neighbours and then they would join with their neighbours, doubling in size each time. Thirty-two giant-sized doorways merged to make sixteen. Those sixteen merged to make eight. Then eight became four. Four towering doors surrounding Lasel and Junk. Still approaching at speed. Then the four became two even larger and those two finally became one gargantuan single portal. It stood before them like a vast monolith of light.

'Now what?' asked Lasel. No sooner had the words left her lips than the last doorway started coming rapidly towards them. It gained speed. Lasel and Junk were scared and instinctively tried to outrun it, but it was impossible. Whichever direction they ran, the doorway was hot on their trail and closing the gap by the second.

Then finally they ran out of time and the doorway washed over them. They blinked out of existence and a moment later the doorway was gone too. The Room of Doors was empty.

17

The journey took no time at all. Less time than it took to blink or breathe or even to think about blinking or breathing. One moment Junk and Lasel were in the Room of (one big) Door and a nanosecond later they were somewhere else entirely. Their new location was easily as vast as the place they had just left, but there the similarities ended. Towering dirty metal walls streaked with grease and faded signage in an alphabet that neither Junk nor Lasel recognized surrounded them. It was bright (too bright, blindingly so), mechanized, with lots of machinery as big as houses. There was much noise and activity. It was like a bustling factory floor when everything had long been automated. Junk wasn't entirely sure why, but he had the impression this was some sort of sorting room. Robotic arms swivelled repetitively on platforms, picked up gigantic containers and moved them to conveyor belts that would take them away in various directions where they would then be picked up by magnetic clamps and moved on elsewhere. The conveyor belts rose this way and that but all ended in high-up openings that the containers would pass through, vanishing from view. Steam belched out of vents the size of buses. Everything here was on a gargantuan scale. A light started flashing over their heads. It was orange and pulsed hypnotically. Incomprehensible sounds were played at deafening volume over some kind of tannoy system. It sounded like words, a language, but spoken at triple speed and by a machine pretending to be a person or maybe a person pretending to be a machine.

'Ankhoonkperuperterlucunderhunderrundertun-pungpung,' said the announcement. Or that's what it sounded like to Junk and Lasel.

'What happened?' asked Lasel. 'Where did the Room of Doors go?'

'I don't think it went anywhere,' said Junk. 'I think we did.'

'But where? Where are we?' They looked down and saw they were standing on a platform of scuffed metal covered in raised markings in more of the unfamiliar letters. They couldn't read these ones either of course, but right in the middle of the platform they saw the now familiar sun-tree symbol.

'Pirestus,' said Junk. Was this it? Was this heaven? He hadn't expected it to look so . . . industrial. They heard something approaching. Something mechanical. Metal on metal. Iron footsteps. Lasel grabbed Junk by the hand and pulled him out of sight, behind some metal crates, each as big as a garden shed.

'Why are we hiding?' asked Junk.

'I'm not sure this is heaven, and if it is I'm not sure

we should enter without being invited . . . or dead.' It was a fair point. They hid in the shadows and watched as the iron footsteps grew louder and closer, shaking the ground. Then a huge figure came into view. Junk and Lasel looked at one another open-mouthed. Both were finding it hard to accept what it was they were seeing. In front of them was a man thirty metres tall. Not a man. Part man, part machine. A cyborg. He was humanoid in shape but his legs were robustly mechanical. Robot's legs. They were broader at the base than the waist, jointed at the ankles and knees. Pistons on his thighs and heels pumped as he marched into view. A series of semi-opaque tubes enveloped both calves like fat varicose veins. A viscous milky substance could be seen sputtering through them in staccato bursts. Coughs of steam were exhaled from small slatted vents dotted down the length of his out-seam. His paintwork had once been teal in colour but was badly scratched and faded now. At his waist was a metallic cummerbund. It was black and made from a material that looked similar to the floor in the Room of Doors. In sharp contrast to the metal of the cyborg's legs it was pristine. It glistened.

Above that his torso appeared to be mostly organic. He was wearing a grubby, sweat-stained, close-fitting tunic that covered his chest and arms. All three of them. He had two muscular flesh-and-blood arms, ribbed with bulbous blue veins, that ended in a pair of oversized hands, disproportionate to his already vast frame. Each hand had six digits, a fat thumb and five rough calloused

211

fingers. Then there was a third mechanical arm that grew out from his lower back, evidently supported by the cummerbund. This third arm was made from the same flawless black material but it was formed of numerous components that slid, twisted and moved with silent precision. This mechanical hand was sleek in comparison to his other two. The thumb and five fingers were long and thin.

Strangely though, neither his metal legs, nor his three arms nor his immense size were the most astonishing aspect of him. That would be his face. Or rather, faces. His head was completely bald, his skin devoid of any pigment, which gave him a translucent glow, and each plane, four in total, was a discrete face. Four sides, four chins, four noses, four mouths. However, he had no ears at all and only one pair of eyes, that flitted from front to back and left to right depending on where he wanted to look. When the eyes were absent from a face, there was only the merest suggestion of eye sockets, but when the eyes appeared the skin that had looked smooth and complete a moment earlier split apart into eyelids and revealed two orange-rimmed eyeballs. He was looking forward one second and then his eyeballs darted with lightning speed first to his left, then his right and then back to the front. It was the same movement anyone would make when crossing the road, say. The only difference being that the cyborg didn't have to turn his head to achieve it.

Junk and Lasel looked at one another, as if to say,

'Are we really seeing this?' The cyborg reached the platform and his eyes flitted from one side of his face to the other and back again. Then one of his big flesh hands came up and scratched one of his chins as if he was considering what to do next. His eyes moved to the back face as the black robot arm reached out and pressed a greasy red button on the wall behind him next to a screen.

The screen hiccuped to life and another four-faced being appeared. This one was fatter and sported a small turd of hair on top of his head. His eyes popped open as he looked up from the desk he was sitting at. The two cyborgs spoke to one another rapidly. The cadence of their language was strangely melodic and not unpleasant, but Junk and Lasel didn't understand a word of it. If they had to guess, they would say that the cyborg standing in front of them was telling his colleague on the screen that something that he expected to be here was not and his colleague was insisting it had to be. This they gleaned mostly from body language. The cyborg in front of them liked to gesticulate wildly with all three of his arms, stabbing them in the direction of the empty platform. Their conversation only lasted for fifteen or twenty seconds and then the screen went black and the cyborg let his eyes move from one of his faces to the next. They stayed on each face for a few moments, scanning the area within their field of vision.

The cyborg started to mutter to himself. There was an irritated tone to his voice. His muttering started at one mouth and was joined by another, working its way around until all four mouths were grumbling together but all saying something different.

He started searching the area for something, looking behind every crate and stack. He was coming closer to where Junk and Lasel were hiding and there was nowhere else for them to go. They were backed into a corner. It was only a matter of time before he found them.

'We're going to have to make a run for it,' whispered Junk. As Junk spoke, the cyborg stopped and leaned his four-faced head to the side as if he was listening. Though seeing as he had no ears it wasn't clear just how he could do this.

Lasel nodded to Junk to show she understood. Then Junk counted on his fingers: one . . . two . . . three! Lasel was faster out of the blocks. She grabbed Junk by the hand and set off, pulling him after her. The cyborg was looking to the left when they sprang up but before they had taken a full step his eyes flicked to his front face and he was looking directly at them. Those eyes grew wide with astonishment as if these little people were the last thing he had expected to see. He tried to grab them, but they ducked out of reach of his clamshell hands. He said something in his impenetrable rapid language, but of course neither understood. They just kept running. Then the cyborg started after them, calling out in a variety of languages. Junk and Lasel weren't listening however. All their focus was on running.

A colossal door, a hundred and twenty metres high, was standing open in front of them, but as they neared it something must have happened, maybe the giant cyborg activated it remotely, because it started to close. Junk and Lasel accelerated as hydraulics hissed and the two sides started to slide together. They turned to see the cyborg coming towards them, covering the ground between them in just a few long, reaching strides. As they reached the doors there was just enough room for the pair of them to squeeze through but not enough for the cyborg to follow.

They were on the other side and thinking they were free when the cyborg's mechanized hand darted through the narrowing gap and clamped around Lasel. She screamed as she was snatched back through the doors.

Junk turned immediately and jumped towards her, stretching out his hand.

'Lasel!'

She reached for him and their fingertips kissed just as the massive hand retracted and the door crunched shut. Junk hit the vast metal barrier. He hammered his fists against it, but it was so big and so dense that it was as useless as hammering against a mountain.

The Antricle on Junk's wrist caught the light and he realized he had a way through. Just as he had done in the forest outside the mirrored tower, Junk touched his left palm to the door and placed the fingers of his right hand purposefully on the Antricle. Nothing happened. No opening magically appeared. Junk tried again and nothing continued to happen. He stepped back and placed his fingers in a different configuration. One he knew well.

The way to open the Room of Doors. But again there was no response.

Junk turned in a circle, pulling at his hair, groaning with frustration. What was he going to do? How would he get to Lasel?

He glanced around at his surroundings. He was in a corridor as wide as a football pitch and as high as a cathedral. Everything in this place was on an incomprehensibly massive scale. Built to accommodate people the size of the four-faced cyborg who had Lasel. They were in a land of giants. Junk was expecting to hear some sort of alarm but there was nothing. Announcements were being constantly broadcast over the tannoy system high above him in the same rapid, indecipherable language they had heard the cyborgs speaking earlier. Junk still didn't understand a word of it. However, the tone of the broadcasts didn't sound urgent. Didn't sound like a call to arms or an alert that there were intruders in the halls of heaven or wherever this was.

Then Junk's gaze settled on what appeared to be an activation panel alongside the door, but it was fifty metres above the ground. Forty-eight metres too high for him to reach. He wasn't going to be opening it any time soon.

'Come on,' he growled to himself, 'think! Think, think, think!' But he couldn't think. He could feel the panic within him starting to take over. The adrenalin was bubbling up. White noise in his ears. His vision flickering. Concentration wasn't happening. 'OPEN THE BLOODY DOOR!' Junk attacked the door frenziedly, kicking, pounding, punching. It was all pointless. He stopped. He was panting from the exertion and it was a few moments before he became aware of a new sound coming from behind. He turned to see a vehicle trundling towards him. Its fat tyres were as high as a double-decker bus, but the floor of the chassis lay low to the ground. It was some sort of transporter like a forklift truck. There was a platform at the front and the cab was behind. It was almost as wide as the corridor and Junk had nowhere to go. The driver was another quad-faced cyborg. This one had four arms, of which only one was organic. The other three were mechanical. Two grew from his back and came around his body like a pair of wings. They seemed old and clunky in comparison to the other arm, which was sleek and red. It was the red arm that reached out to press a button and Junk heard the colossal door behind him start to open. A surge of excitement rang through him. Luck was on his side.

The moment the gap in the door was wide enough, he squeezed through. He turned, looking for Lasel and her cyborg abductor, only to find himself staring at a foot the size of a small car. He looked up and saw the first cyborg towering over him. The cyborg reached down and grabbed hold of Junk. Junk started to roar and squirm, desperate to get free. The cyborg raised him up so he was right in front of his face.

'Please be silent,' said the cyborg in English. Junk was stunned to hear this man-machine speaking his own language.

'You speak English? Lasel? Where's my friend? What have you done with her?'

The cyborg's eyes vanished from the face looking at Junk, moved to the side to look at the opening door and then back to Junk. 'I'm sorry,' he said, and suddenly a crackle of electricity enveloped his black mechanical hand and Junk. Briefly Junk cried out but fell silent as he lapsed into unconsciousness.

18

Junk woke slowly. It took him several moments to get his bearings. His first thought was that he was in a coffin. He was dead. Then his rational mind kicked in and realized he clearly wasn't dead because dead people don't lie around thinking they're dead. At least he didn't think they did.

Plus he wasn't in a coffin. He was wrapped in some sort of cocoon that enveloped his head and, as far as he could tell, his body completely. Light seeped in from outside, but he couldn't see anything, not even vague shapes. He tried moving his hand, and whatever the cocoon was made from stretched with him. He strained harder and the cocoon started to tear. A little more and his hand was free. He stretched out his fingers, digging his nails into the rubbery material, and started ripping. Bit by bit it came away, until more and more of him was uncovered. Eventually both hands were free and he was able to pull the membrane from his face. Strands of whatever it was clung to his otherwise naked body. He sat up and took a moment to get his bearings.

He was in a relatively small room, compared to the other room and corridors he had seen, but it had a ridiculously high ceiling so he knew he was still in Pirestus. He guessed it was someone's living quarters. He was on an expansive cot-bed that had slid out of the wall. It was like being on the wing of a 747. There was a table but no chair. One wall was a screen full of indecipherable scrolling text. On the adjacent wall was an indentation in the shape of a huge arm.

There was movement next to him and he turned to see another cocoon. The movement was coming from within. The fabric of the cocoon tore and a hand emerged. Lasel's hand. Junk moved to help her. As she ripped from the inside, he tore from the outside. In a few moments her face was free and she gulped down as much air as she could consume, coughing violently.

'Where are we?' she asked after a moment.

'I'm not sure,' said Junk. He moved to look over the edge of the bed. It would be low for the lofty occupants of this place, but it was still dizzyingly high for Junk and Lasel. Junk turned back and found Lasel pulling off bits of the cocoon that were stuck to her skin. Junk caught himself staring at her naked body. He knew he should look away, but it was a struggle. Then he realized that he was naked too and he became embarrassed.

'What's wrong?' asked Lasel. Clearly she had little concern about their state of undress. Junk wished he could be as cool about it, but he was a kid from Ireland. Nudity didn't come comfortably. He covered himself up but tried not to look like he was covering himself up.

Just then a door on the far side of the room slid aside and the cyborg that had captured them earlier entered. His eyes were on his left face, so even though he was walking straight ahead he was looking to the side. He smiled.

'Ah, you're awake,' he said in English. His eyes vanished and reappeared on the back face as he closed and locked his door. His eyes moved with him as he turned and approached the cot-bed, carrying a grey bag. He stood looking down on Junk and Lasel, who edged closer to one another, frightened that this giant might crush their bones to make his bread.

The cyborg reached into the bag and retrieved their clothes. He laid them on the bed in front of them.

'I took the liberty of having your clothes cleaned while you recovered.' He spoke quickly and retained the same undulating, musical cadence as when he had spoken his own language earlier. Junk reached out cautiously, grabbed the clothes and yanked them towards them. He and Lasel started to dress speedily. Junk noticed then that the Antricle was no longer on his wrist. He searched among the clothing but it wasn't there either. He caught Lasel's eye and drew her attention subtly to his bare arm.

The cyborg pulled at a series of clasps holding the black cummerbund in place around his waist. The cummerbund whirred and hissed as it powered down. He removed it and the attached sleek black appendage and slotted the whole contraption into the arm-shaped indentation on the wall. It clicked into place perfectly. Then he put his hands on a pair of dials, one on each thigh, and turned. His mechanical legs moved from a standing to a sitting position in a few seconds, accompanied by the industrial sound of heavy metal rubbing against more heavy metal. The cyborg sat in front of Junk and Lasel.

'My name is Espa Hara-kayan and I am very excited to meet you. Very excited indeed.' The cyborg smiled a little lopsidedly. He seemed to realize then that his smile wasn't the best and so turned his whole body at the waist so a different face was pointing at them. His eyes followed and he smiled again. This smile was better.

Junk and Lasel looked at one another, both saying wordlessly, What do we do? Junk turned to Espa.

'How come you speak English? And where are we? And how did we get here?'

'They are separate questions, yes?' said Espa, not waiting for an answer. 'Which to answer first? In order, I suppose. I speak English because I was part of the linguistic development team. Where are we? Pirestus Octonary. Crew deck. How did you get here? I brought you here. I had to administer a mild electric shock in order to keep you quiet. You're not supposed to be here. It would have been problematic had anyone else seen you. I hope I didn't hurt you. I put you in the reju-sacs –' he nodded at the remains of the cocoons littering the bed – 'to hasten your recovery. Are you recovered?' Lasel and Junk both nodded.

'You're very big,' said Lasel.

Even though she spoke in English, Espa replied in Jansian. From then on he would address Lasel in Jansian and Junk in English, switching effortlessly. 'No, you're very small,' he said. 'We're getting better. You're getting bigger but life is a complicated being.' He paused then and looked a little melancholy. 'Not my department any more.' He sank into his own thoughts for a few moments and Junk and Lasel shared another questioning look. 'This is a first,' said Espa. 'No one from the anomaly has ever come to Pirestus before. How did you get here?'

Junk and Lasel furrowed their brows in thought as they replayed Espa's words back in their minds.

'I don't understand,' said Junk. 'What's the anomaly?'

'The third planet. Where you came from?'

'Earth?' said Junk.

'Jorda?' said Lasel at the same time.

'It has many names,' said Espa.

'Why's it an anomaly?' asked Junk, sounding a little put out.

'Because of you,' said Espa. 'Life grew when it wasn't supposed to. It took Pirestus Prime into a whole new direction.'

Talking to Espa was not easy. Everything he said caused dozens of new questions to form in Junk and Lasel's heads.

'Listen, forgive me but I'm lost. I really don't know what you're talking about. What's Pirestus Prime? What's Pirestus Octonary? Who are you?' Junk had reached the conclusion that this place wasn't heaven, but that didn't mean he knew what it was.

Espa took a moment to consider Junk's questions and he nodded. He understood why he would ask them. 'Pirestus Prime is our parent company. They own all the outlying creation rigs. This is one of them – Pirestus Octonary. The eighth platform. We are universe-builders.'

'Y-you build universes?' said Lasel, struggling to make sense of what Espa was saying, certain that he couldn't mean it literally.

'Yes, that's right,' he said. Apparently he did mean it literally.

'And you built ours?'

'We did. For the Daga Mining Corporation, but unfortunately they went out of business before completion. The whole thing was going to be scrapped. Then next thing we know, life starts to flourish on the third planet when it wasn't supposed to. It wasn't in the plans. Ordinance says we can't do anything about that. We're stuck with you. Me, I'm thrilled. I transferred to development as soon as the news broke. It's what I always dreamed of doing, but I don't live in the centre. I'm all the way out here in the outlands. There's not supposed to be any life out here. You're not supposed to exist. This is strictly mining country, or at least will be when it's mature, but then you happen. It's unprecedented. The anomaly. Best day of my life.'

Junk was struggling to understand what they were talking about. 'So you . . .' he started to say but stopped.

'The . . . Are you saying . . . When you say universe-builders . . . what do you mean exactly?'

'We create planets and stars. Solar systems. Galaxies. Multiple galaxies make universes and we do all the bits in between.'

'But that's impossible,' said Lasel.

'No,' said Espa, 'not at all. It just takes time.'

'Like billions of years,' said Junk.

'Oh yes,' said Espa in agreement. 'Yours, I believe, is somewhere around fifteen billion by your quantification.'

'And you said before, it's not mature yet,' said Junk.

'That's right. Another five or ten billion years should do it.'

'And do you live for that long?'

'No, of course not. That would be a very long time.'

'And what happens when it's mature?'

'Then we hand it over to whoever paid for it in the first place, but as I said before, I'm not sure what will happen with yours. Well, we'll find out soon enough.'

'In five or ten billion years!'

'That's right,' agreed Espa.

'Are you gods?' asked Lasel.

'No,' said Espa, 'just an engineer from D'Krin.'

'What's that?' asked Junk.

'My home.'

'Another planet?'

'Of course.'

'There are other planets with life on them?' asked Junk.

'In your universe or all of the universes?'

'There's more than one universe?'

'There are thirty-seven universes, with applications pending for nine more. Last time I checked anyway, but that was a while ago.'

'How come you're part machine?' Junk sounded a little wary asking the question. He wasn't sure if Espa would take offence.

'Part fashion, part tradition. It's what we do. It's what we've always done on D'Krin. Usually something a bit more stylish that these old gumbertuns.' He chuckled, tapping his metal legs. Junk and Lasel looked at one another, wondering if the other knew what a gumbertun was. Neither did. 'But they're practical for this sort of work.'

'I thought you said you worked on language.'

'I used to. There were cutbacks. Half the department got sent home. I really wanted to stay, and fortunately I used to work haulage on the moons of Triagnon so I had valuable experience. They reassigned me.'

'Why did you want to stay so much?' asked Lasel.

'Because of you,' said Espa, excitement twinkling in his eyes. 'Planets are bred to support life all the time. It's what we do. Nothing special. But you weren't. The third planet was supposed to be barren. You were designed to be a water planet. No life. Just water. There are a trillion of those across the universes that have been grown in exactly the same way as you, but for some reason life snuck in. There are so many precautions, safeguards that mean that can't happen, but it did and just look at you.

Two of you from the anomaly, in *my* quarters.' He looked giddy with delight.

'Where are we?' asked Lasel. 'I mean right now, where in the universe are we?'

'I told you already, you're on the crew deck of Pirestus Octonary.'

'And where is that?'

Espa leaned back and grabbed a small (to him anyway) puck-shaped box. It was black with no markings. He pointed it like a remote control at the screen on the far wall and the scrolling text vanished as the screen concertinaed upwards like a blind, revealing a panoramic window. They were on some sort of space station. From their position they could see some of the vessel's pale grey outer walls stretching away from them. They looked out into the blackness of space. A hazy pink, green and blue mist of gas and dust danced not far away. Beyond and above that was a great ball of spitting fire. They were looking up at the sun. Their sun. Espa manipulated the puck in his hand and the resolution of what they were seeing magnified. The sun came closer. They could see some of the planets beyond. Mercury looked close enough to touch. There was Venus and, much further away, Earth. Lasel and Junk walked to the edge of the cot-bed. They stared in awe at the view that greeted them. The panoramic window was not much bigger than the display screen for Espa, but for Junk and Lasel who were one-fifteenth his size it filled their entire vision.

'This is a magnified view, of course,' said Espa.

'We're not really that close to any of it. We're about the same distance away from the sun as the sun is from the anomaly. It all pretty much takes care of itself now. We just maintain. Make sure moons keep to their orbit, that sort of thing.'

Lasel reached down and took hold of Junk's hand. They both needed to touch the other to know this was real. They were actually seeing this. They looked at one another and smiled before turning back to the window.

'It's so beautiful,' said Lasel.

'Yes, it is, isn't it?' said Espa. 'I never tire of looking out there.'

19

Espa looked so happy at that moment and seemed unlikely to want to eat Junk and Lasel, so Junk decided he would ask about the Antricle. 'I was wearing something on my wrist.'

'Yes, an Antricle,' said Espa. 'However did you come across one of those?'

'It's a long story. Do you have it?'

'Yes, I do.'

'Can I have it back, please?'

'No. I'm sorry. I know it's pretty, but it's not just a trinket.'

'I know,' said Junk, sounding a little insulted. 'I know what it does.'

'I don't think so.'

'We've been in the Room of Doors.'

Espa frowned. 'The Room of Doors?' He considered those words for a few moments and then nodded. 'Is that what you call it?'

'What do you call it?'

'The Rammaniac, but actually Room of Doors is a

better description.' He considered the phrase. 'Hhmm, Room of Doors. It is that.' A new thought occurred to him. 'So you've been in there, have you?'

'Quite a few times. We're on first name terms with the Gatekeeper and everything,' said Junk.

Espa looked shocked. 'The Gatekeeper has spoken to you? That's not supposed to happen.'

'What *is* the Room of Doors?' asked Lasel. 'Why does it exist?'

'It is . . . how to define it? . . . backstage. You know what this means?' Lasel and Junk nodded. 'In order to maintain your world we sometimes need to adjust things. Alter moments in time. Fix flaws in the construction. We didn't know anyone from the anomaly had found their way inside.'

'How come?' asked Junk. 'How do you not know?'

'Well, the Rammaniac is not used so much any more. It's a . . . creepy basement that is rarely visited. It was never unoccupied for the first few billion years of your planet's construction, but then there's a point in any planet's maturation where we take a back seat.' Espa changed the subject slightly. 'And you've travelled the pathways? Tell me – what does it look like when you're in there?'

'Black. Lots of doors. Like billions of them, all made from green light,' said Junk.

'How big?' asked Espa.

'Door-sized,' replied Junk with a shrug.

'*Your* door size?'

'Yeah.'

'How interesting,' said Espa. 'I've been in there myself, and the doors, and there are a lot of them as you say, are the right size for me. It seems the Rammaniac is intuitive.'

'You didn't build it then?' asked Lasel.

'No, it's a standard installation. All planets have them.'

'Last time we were in there,' said Junk, 'all the doors came together and made one really massive door that brought us here.'

'Fascinating,' said Espa.

'Is that supposed to happen?'

'Yes,' said Espa. 'In order to open the door to Pirestus Octonary it is necessary to close the rest. When you return, the door here will close and the others will re-open.'

'It wouldn't work once we got here,' said Junk. 'The Antricle, I mean.'

'No, it doesn't. The only way to embark or disembark is via the platform in the room where I first saw you.'

Espa pressed another dial on his legs and the motors powering his lower half started up again and he transformed out of his seated position. He crossed to a cupboard and the front slid aside at his approach. He retrieved Junk's Antricle from within and returned to sit again. The Antricle looked minute in his oversized hands.

'What else can you do with it?' asked Espa.

'I can make it change shape,' said Junk.

'How?'

'By thinking about it. We're kind of in tune with one another.'

Espa looked from the Antricle to Junk and back again a few times.

'There were hundreds of these once. Most have been recalled, now that there aren't that many left who need them. A few got lost over the years. Clearly you found one of them. There'll be others. One or two maybe. The thing is, it's not really supposed to talk back to you, but it has been heard of in the past. There are stories of some D'Krinians who could interact with an Antricle, but never an anomaly dweller.'

'What sort of stories?' asked Junk.

'Certain individuals who would allow the Antricle into their minds. They would bond. They would become one. The Antricle would show them how to work the Ramm— the Room of Doors. It is capable of so much more than most D'Krinians realize.'

Finally he reached out, holding the Antricle between huge thumb and vast forefinger and deposited it precisely and gently on Junk's outstretched palm. Junk slipped the Antricle back on to his wrist, sliding it over his hand. It didn't open and close as he wanted it to now. Espa went on.

'There's little that you can't make the Antricle do for you once it's accepted you. I think you've just got to ask it nicely. However, a word of warning. Be cautious. You must avoid paradoxes at all cost. These will be noticed up here. There's a whole department dedicated to making sure paradoxes don't occur, and they're a humourless bunch. The Paradox Police, we call them.'

'What does "paradox" mean?' asked Lasel.

'You have to be careful what you change. If changing one thing has a knock-on effect, it can quickly spiral out of control. I remember paradoxes that nearly caused whole solar systems to implode.'

Junk thought about that. He thought he understood something now that he hadn't before.

'That's why some dates are forbidden. That's why it wouldn't let us go back and save Garvan or my sister.' He verbalized his thoughts as they came to him. 'If I had gone back to the night Mestrowe took Ambeline and stopped him somehow, then I'd never have left, never have found the Room of Doors and never then been able to go back to stop him to begin with.'

'Precisely,' said Espa. 'Paradox. Most work themselves out and aren't dangerous, but there's no way of telling until it might be too late and all thirty-seven universes are being sucked into a black hole. That would be bad.'

'Is there any way of getting around that? Any way to negotiate with the Gatekeeper?'

Espa shrugged. 'Of course. The Gatekeeper stopped you for your own good. Making such a journey would have brought you to the attention of the Paradox Police and they are, as I mentioned, an unforgiving lot.'

'So the Gatekeeper was helping us even then,' said Lasel.

'If,' said Junk, the thought forming as he spoke, as the words came tumbling out, 'there was a scenario where you could change something more recent,' he was thinking

233

now about Garvan and Payo–Mestrowe, 'that hasn't had time to impact on other subsequent events, then—'

Before he could complete the sentence an address blared over the tannoy system. The intrusive voice spoke in Espa's rapid-fire language, sounding more urgent this time. Espa listened carefully to the announcement, the brow on all four faces furrowing as he did so. When it finished he looked troubled.

'What did it say?' asked Lasel.

'The transport driver has reported seeing you. The station's on high alert and Security's looking for you.'

Junk and Lasel looked scared. 'What do we do?' asked Junk.

'It won't take them long to find you. Our only option is to try and make it back to the platform room. The place you arrived at. The transport will be disabled because of the alert but the Antricle will work again on the platform. Only place on the station it isn't blocked.'

Espa marched along the wide corridors. His metal legs stamped rapidly, uniformly, always rising to the exact same height, every stride always exactly the same as the one before and the one yet to come, the pistons and gears inhaling and exhaling as he went. There was much activity around him now. More of the station's personnel were whizzing to and fro, all on the look out for the intruders. Pirestus Octonary's Security were recognizable by their sleek metal limbs made from the same substance as Espa's third arm, but dark blue rather than black like his. The guards were all at least seventy-five-per-cent machine. All had mechanical arms and legs. They wore mirrored visors that circled the eye sockets of all four of their colourless faces.

Espa carried what looked like a canvas work bag with him. In the bag, Junk and Lasel were being tossed about as if they were on the world's worst fairground ride. They held on to one another and it eased the roughness of the ride.

'Can't say I ever expected to be doing this in my lifetime,' said Junk.

'Doing what?' said Lasel. 'Riding in the bag of a giant alien cyborg who built the universe? Really? I always knew it was bound to happen one day.' They shared a smile.

The bag opened above their heads and one of Espa's faces peered inside.

'You still OK in there?' he asked in a whisper.

'Peachy,' said Junk.

'We're coming up to the platform room now.' Junk gave him a thumbs-up. 'What does that mean? Have you hurt your thumb?'

'No, it means OK,' said Junk.

Espa thought about this and nodded. 'OK,' he said, and closed the bag.

The door to the platform room opened and Espa walked inside. Two serious-looking security guards were standing in front of the platform. They didn't move their heads and their eyes were hidden behind their mirrored visors so it was hard to tell where they were looking. They barked at Espa in a fast, aggressive tone. Espa answered calmly, but his cadence was no less speedy and direct. The guards clearly accepted whatever it was he had said to them and stepped aside to allow him on to the platform.

He crossed to a control panel on the far side and laid the canvas bag down carefully. He studied the panel briefly, letting his eyes flit to his back face so he could take a quick peek at the guards. They had their backs to him but that didn't mean they weren't looking his way. Espa crouched down and opened the bag. Junk and Lasel looked up from within.

'You'll have to activate it from in there,' he said as quietly as he could. 'Safe journey and I hope we'll meet again.'

One of the guards spoke and Espa's eyes moved to look at him. They spoke about the bag. The guard pointed to it. He stepped up on to the platform and strode towards Espa, who started to get up but the guard's mechanical right arm extended suddenly and his large metal hand clamped on to Espa's shoulder, keeping him pinned to the ground. The guard used his mechanical left foot to kick open the bag and peer inside. It was empty. Junk and Lasel were gone.

'Do you think he'll be OK?' asked Lasel as they stepped through the one massive portal into the Room of Doors. Almost immediately the big door started to separate and multiply. Junk and Lasel watched as the dabs of green peppered outwards and upwards like a contagion.

'I'm sure he'll be fine,' said Junk.

'What do we do now?' said Lasel.

'We get our friends back.'

'What? How?' said Lasel. 'You heard Espa – the Gatekeeper won't allow it in case it causes a paradox.'

'I think I understand this now,' said Junk. He looked at the Antricle on his wrist. 'Like Espa said, it's how you ask that's important.'

Junk held out his hand in front of him. The Antricle started to grow. It spread out, covering Junk's hand, and then began to move up his arm and across his torso, encasing his body.

'Are you doing that?' asked Lasel.

'Yep.' Junk winked at her. 'Back in a mo,' he said, as the Antricle covered his chin and then wrapped itself around his face. He closed his eyes as the Antricle skin enveloped him completely. He stood in front of Lasel, looking like a knight encased in copper-coloured armour.

Inside the Antricle suit, Junk opened his eyes. He could see out, could see Lasel staring at him. His view was tinted. Everything was a little yellow. His breathing made it sound like he was in a spacesuit.

'Can you hear me?' His voice sounded muffled to him.

'I can hear you fine,' said Lasel.

'Can you see me?'

'All I can see is the Antricle. You're completely covered. Can you see me?'

'Yep. This is what the Antricle is. It's not a cube or a dodecahedron or a bracelet. It's a full bodysuit.'

'How do you know?' asked Lasel. She circled him, examining him from all angles.

'It told me. It tells me a lot of things. I just need to learn to listen better.'

Lasel stood in front of him and nodded. 'Now what?'

'You should probably stand back a little.' Lasel stepped back a couple of paces and Junk looked around at the myriad of portals stretching out in front of him. He waved his hand in a wide arc in front of his face and suddenly his view of the room changed as if he was now looking through a red filter. The number of doorways he could see tripled. He turned in a slow circle, looking all around.

'What? What do you see?' asked Lasel.

'There's a lot more to the Rammaniac than we usually see,' said Junk. He continued turning until he came back around to Lasel and as he did so he jumped, startled. There was a tall, slender jet-black figure standing behind her.

'What's wrong?' asked Lasel. She looked behind her but saw nothing.

The figure was like a person made of shadow. Junk couldn't be sure if he was in three dimensions. Possibly not.

'Gatekeeper?' said Junk.

'That's right,' said the shadow man.

Lasel reacted to the sound of the disembodied voice. It sounded as if he was right behind her, which he was.

'The Gatekeeper's real?' Goose pimples skittered up her arms.

'You've found your way,' said the Gatekeeper to Junk. 'You're the first in a very long time. Are you ready to embrace everything I can offer?'

'Yes,' said Junk without hesitation. Though the Gatekeeper had no features, it was clear from the way he tilted his head that he was surprised by Junk's answer.

'You don't know what it entails,' he said.

Junk shrugged. 'Not exactly, no, but I'll find out, won't I?'

'And you're not scared?'

'A little, maybe,' said Junk, 'but the time to turn back has long gone.'

The Gatekeeper nodded in agreement. 'Forward it is then,' he said. 'Let's see what you're capable of. Let's see how you wield the power I offer. Where to first?'

'The Martaregan Peninsula.'

'To save your friends. You tried to do that before.'

'Yes, but now I know what I'm doing and I know what I'm not doing,' said Junk. 'And I assume you'll stop me if I try to do something dumb.'

'Maybe, maybe not,' said the Gatekeeper. 'It depends on how dumb.' Junk wondered if the Gatekeeper was joking. 'Well then,' said the Gatekeeper, 'it's all yours.' He waved a hand towards the doorways as if he was a performer giving Junk the stage.

Junk took a moment to gather his thoughts and then he lifted his head. A pinprick of light appeared in front

239

of him and immediately started to grow into a round doorway. Unlike all the others, this one had a blue tinge to it rather than green. It hovered in the air, vertically, just above the floor.

On top of the Martaregan Peninsula at an earlier point in time a soldier swung his axe and cut a rope connected to Payo–Mestrowe's wrists. Payo–Mestrowe's weight took him backwards over the cliff. Lasel screamed. Garvan roared. Otravinicus looked away.

'NO!' yelled Junk. He reached out, but his way was blocked by more soldiers and he could do nothing but watch as Payo–Mestrowe toppled over the cliff-edge and disappeared from view. They all heard his cry getting further away as he fell, and then suddenly his voice was silenced. It was chilling. Junk and his friends all hung their heads.

'Now then,' said Foster, 'you know we're not fooling around here, so I ask again, why are you here?'

Junk looked at Garvan, Lasel and Otravinicus for guidance. What should he say? What could he say that would appease Foster and Ed?

'I'm telling you the truth. Ask Otravinicus. You know him.' Junk looked at Dr Otravinicus, who was tied up next to Garvan. The little man was shaking with fear. His lips were moving as if he was praying, though Junk didn't know to what god. 'I come from the same time you do. Early twenty-first century.' Junk was talking rapidly now. He knew time was running out for all of them. 'The

Pallatan you just killed was called Jacid Mestrowe. He was a member of the League of Sharks. Your man there, Tolfke, hired him on your behalf. He broke into my house on the night of 14 December 2010. He took my sister Ambeline and jumped off a cliff with her. I've been looking for him ever since. When I found him he told me Ambeline was still alive and that you had her. That's why we're here. That's the only reason. I don't mean you any harm. I just want to find my sister, I swear.' Junk was breathing hard when he stopped, not having taken a breath while he was saying any of that.

Foster and Ed were quiet for a few moments as they considered what Junk had said.

'He's still playing games,' said Foster. 'Cut another one loose.'

'No!' shouted Junk. 'Please, no.' He stepped forward but the soldiers blocked him again. He saw an axe slink through the air. The blade embedded in the ground and for a moment none of them could tell which rope had been cut. Then Garvan started roaring in distress as he tipped backwards, and in a split second he too was gone.

Garvan felt his stomach pitch as he fell through the air. He bellowed as he dropped. His hands snatched at nothing as he was swallowed up by the thick mist. He felt his speed increasing. The force of the air was driving into his throat, contorting his face, forcing his eyes closed. Garvan managed to half open one eye and for a split second saw a large circular blue portal of light below him. It drew him in.

In the Room of Doors a second later Garvan came flying out of the blue doorway.

'AAARRRRGGGGGHHHHHHhhh-h-h-h-hhhh.' His scream died away as he skidded along the polished green-black floor. Lasel, who had been helping Payo–Mestrowe, ran to Garvan. She threw her arms around his big neck. She was crying with joy. Garvan was frowning. He looked at Junk clad in his Antricle armour.

'Junk?' said Garvan. The armour receded, exposing Junk's head and face. Garvan frowned. 'You two were up there just now.'

'We still are,' said Junk. He held out his hand to the blue door and it vanished. 'We're about to do the same thing you've just done, but a few hours earlier.' He looked to Lasel. 'No paradox.'

Garvan looked at Payo–Mestrowe. 'I have a feeling we've missed something,' he said.

'We'll explain as we go,' said Junk. He picked another doorway and held out his hand to it. It turned blue.

'Where are we going?' asked Garvan.

'We're going to pick a fight and we're going to raise an army,' replied Junk.

'Where do we get an army from?'

'Cantibea.'

Garvan frowned and shook his head. 'I can't,' he said.

'But you can,' said Junk, adding, 'The king can do anything.'

20

Foster Peck slept fitfully that night. He was plagued by disturbing dreams. In one he saw Rusty, the dog he had had as a boy back in Mud Bay. Rusty was lying on the highway, cut in two by a truck. He was dying. Foster was next to him, crying, listening as Rusty's breathing slowed and slowed some more. Foster looked into his dog's eyes as the light of life started to fade. Then on the tip of his last rasping breath, the dog spoke:

'I . . .' and the word stretched out, lasting for a dozen seconds. Then there was a pause. '. . . saw!' Foster frowned and the dog closed its eyes for the last time.

Foster woke sharply, pulling in a bubble of air. He sat up in bed, holding his chest, which ached. The room was pitch black. In reality, Rusty hadn't died like that. In real life, he'd gone to live with Foster's dad when his parents split up. His dad got Rusty and Foster's sister, Brady. His mother got Foster and got angry. Rusty lived to a ripe old age and died peacefully in his sleep. When they were a family, the dog had been his dog. Afterwards, when Foster would go and visit, Rusty would growl at him and keep his distance, as if holding a grudge, blaming Foster for leaving him.

Foster's eyesight was acclimatizing to the lack of light. He started to make out shapes around the bed. It took him a moment to realize there shouldn't be anything there. He reached to turn on a lamp, but a cold, clammy hand clamped on to his wrist.

'Who's there?' he called.

'Tomorrow morning,' said a voice from the darkness. An Irish voice. 'At first light. I'm coming back for my sister.'

Foster's sight improved further and he could see Junk and Payo–Mestrowe standing over him.

'I-I told you,' said Foster, faking the confidence in his voice, 'I don't know anything about your sister.'

'Well, you better find out,' said Junk. 'By first light.' Foster didn't feel Payo–Mestrowe's hand leaving his wrist. It took him a few moments to realize the intruders had gone. He reached out and turned on the lamp. He was alone.

Cantibea was an island nation situated in the middle of the Sitan provinces. It was considered part of the Greater Sitan Confederacy but at the same time it liked to retain a little distance and its own identity. What had been continental Africa in Junk's day had broken up into four smaller continents over time. To the north was the Agip Sea and Glarn Sita; to the east were the Barden Straits and Unta Sita; to the south lay the Sitan Channel and Cul Sita;

and to the west could be found Tulon Bight and Daté Sita. Each land mass was a collection of countries. Cantibea was physically tiny compared to its neighbours, only about a thousand kilometres from north to south and a little less from east to west, but because of its position, history and wealth it wielded more power than its size would suggest.

Junk, Garvan, Lasel and Payo–Mestrowe stepped through a doorway at the bottom of a hill. There was a road that snaked up the hillside to a walled city. This was Edrin, the capital of Cantibea and Garvan's childhood home. The city was built up in layers and at the very top was a citadel. The royal palace. It looked down on the bustling city, a watchful sentry.

'I could have opened a door up there,' said Junk.

'I used to walk this road every day as a boy. I want to do it again, just one more time,' said Garvan.

'You can walk it as often as you want after today,' said Junk.

Garvan didn't look convinced. 'Fine,' he said coolly. 'Tell me what I have to do.'

As Garvan and the others entered the city through a pair of huge doors more than a metre thick and twenty-five metres high, that were always left wide open, they found themselves in a vibrant and bustling metropolis. A sprawling marketplace was the first sight that greeted them. It was a dizzying collection of noises, smells and colours.

The people of Edrin were all shapes and sizes. Many were as big as Garvan, many others were no taller than half a metre and many were in between.

'Do you think you'll be recognized?' asked Lasel.

Garvan shrugged. 'I doubt it. It's been a while since I was here last.'

Just then a huge woman who was as wide as she was tall, and she was very tall indeed, walked around the corner, straight into their path. She glanced once at Garvan and instantly her eyes lit up. She did a double take and her meaty hand came up to her broad mouth. Her dark skin turned the same shade of deep red as her voluminous muumuu and she jittered on her tiptoes for a moment before collapsing to the ground in an inelegant curtsy.

'Gomba Needy!' she said.

'What's she saying?' asked Junk.

Garvan looked embarrassed. 'Your Highness,' he said quietly, and bent to talk to the woman, trying to persuade her to get up, but she was having none of it. She kept saying 'Gomba Needy' over and over, and every time it seemed that she was about to get up, she sank back to the ground, reaching for Garvan's feet, which he kept having to move out of her grasp.

Naturally such a display drew attention and more and more people turned to look. An excited murmur of recognition spread. Clearly Garvan wasn't as forgotten about as he had thought. More and more Edrinites crowded around him, pulling at him, wanting to touch

246

him or falling to the ground in front of him. They were all talking to him at once and Garvan looked overwhelmed.

'I'm not sure walking was the best idea,' said Junk to Lasel. Lasel looked to Payo–Mestrowe and gave him a nod. He understood and waded into the crowd.

Payo and Mestrowe worked together to extricate Garvan. 'Excuse me,' Payo called politely, as Mestrowe shoved people out of the way. 'Coming through,' Payo warned, as Mestrowe grabbed collars and pushed them aside. As soon as they had cleared a path to Garvan, Junk created a doorway in the ground. They all jumped through. It closed immediately and the townsfolk were left scratching their heads as to what had happened to the crown prince.

The doorway took them directly into the royal residence overlooking the city. They stepped out on to a quiet terrace at the side of the palace itself. From here they could look down on Edrin. They could see the puzzled townsfolk they had just left. They could see them searching for Garvan, trying to figure out what had become of him.

'Where now?' asked Junk. Just then a clock in the town square far below chimed.

'Four bells,' said Garvan. 'Come on, this way.'

Junk, Lasel and Payo–Mestrowe followed Garvan to a broad spiral staircase. The palace had been built for Garvan and his family, so nothing was tight or constricted. Corridors were broad, rooms were expansive and doorways wide and high.

At the top of the spiral staircase was a long corridor that led to a pair of double doors. There were two uniformed guards outside and they were tensed for trouble the moment they saw Garvan and the others. It wasn't until Garvan drew closer that the guards started to frown. They recognized him, but he was the last person they had expected to see. Both men bowed.

'Gomba Needy, jing jaroom?' said one of the two.

'Darra ooma,' replied Garvan. 'Hes te nud barracoombe.'

'Tens, Gomba Needy. Stuum varracoombe.'

Garvan looked at Junk and the others and translated. 'He asked if it was me, I said it was and asked if my father was inside, he said he is and my mother is too.'

'Then let's go,' said Junk.

'Are you absolutely sure about this?' asked Garvan.

'Trust me,' said Junk.

Garvan nodded. 'I do already.'

He turned back to the guard. 'Eirum daaroomay taruumpt ahmey,' he said. He translated again. 'I said he had better announce me. Might as well get this over and done with.' He was finding it difficult to hide the reluctance in his voice. His mouth was dry and tasted medicinal for no reason he knew. Right now he was putting a lot of faith in Junk. He didn't really know if this was going to work, but he figured the time had probably passed to turn back.

The guards opened the double doors and stepped inside. One cleared his throat and announced loudly and clearly that Crown Prince Garvan had returned. Everyone in the room stopped what they were doing instantly and looked up, frowning. Had they heard correctly? Surely not.

It was a massive room that was half covered and half exposed. The open side looked out over Cantibea's breathtaking landscape. It was richly vegetated. Snow-capped mountains to the west. A series of waterfalls to the north. Flocks of brightly coloured birds soared majestically across the expansive sky.

There were various aides and assistants in the room but anyone could see straight away that the focus of their attention was directed at two people: the king and queen. Garvan's parents.

King Cadrew was an older, heavier version of Garvan. He wore a perfectly tailored blue suit and his hair was cut short, an almost military-looking style. To Junk he was what a king should look like: magisterial.

Queen Adilla was small in comparison to the king and her sons. She looked younger than the king and had a lot of very lustrous blonde hair that hung to below her waist. She stared at Garvan, blinking and open-mouthed, looking thoroughly shocked like pretty much everyone else in the room. Then she jumped up from her desk and ran across to him, throwing her arms around her son.

'Nearnud,' she said, hugging him.

'Varracoombe,' said Garvan, closing his eyes and savouring the embrace. Garvan's cold and severe-looking father marched over to him and Junk was surprised to see he was crying. He too threw his arms around Garvan. Turned out he wasn't as cold and severe as he looked. Junk watched this heart-warming family reunion with mixed feelings. He was happy for his friend but how he longed for a similar reunion with his family. The king said something in Garvan's ear that immediately drained the joy out of him. He looked to Junk.

'My father wants to know if I'm here to kill him,' he said miserably.

'Tell him you most certainly are,' said Junk cheerily.

'Tens,' said Garvan to his father.

'Vavuvavuva,' said the king with a broad smile.

It seemed that there would be no hanging about. Junk got the impression that the king was eager to get this over and done with before Garvan changed his mind. Garvan and his father walked in the royal gardens and the king passed on a few words of wisdom to his son to make his time as monarch easier.

'When I'm king,' said Garvan, 'I'm going to make some changes.'

'But of course you will,' said his father. 'That is your prerogative. You will be king.' He paused. 'Hopefully.'

'What does that mean?'

'Well, it means I'm not just going to offer you my head. You have to take it or I'll take yours.' He said it in

250

a very matter-of-fact sort of way, as if they were talking about cheese or something.

In less than an hour from the time they had arrived, Garvan and his father were standing in the great hall, both wearing the royal armour. The streets of Edrin were deserted. All of the residents had gathered to watch a moment of history.

Garvan's brothers and sisters were present and Junk recognized Jadris and Kyril. They waved at him and Lasel in a friendly manner. Everyone was treating what was about to happen as a happy event. Everyone but Garvan. He looked deeply troubled. Junk crossed to speak to him.

Garvan was being strapped into the last pieces of his armour by his adjutant, a jolly but wizened old man called Mingo. He whistled a happy tune as he went about his duties and broke off from time to time to reminisce about moments from Garvan's childhood. Mingo, it seemed, had been around for a very long time indeed.

'Are you OK?' asked Junk of Garvan.

Garvan nodded. 'I'm fine. I'm just not relishing what I'm about to do. He's my father.'

'I understand,' said Junk. 'But you know it will be fine. It'll all be over soon. Remember, this is what your destiny dictated. The nolic tea told you I would bring you back to your throne.'

Garvan nodded. 'I know,' he said.

Just then a horn sounded and the excitable chatter filling the room vanished and all eyes turned to an official who had stepped into the middle of the arena. He addressed the gathering. Junk of course didn't understand, so Garvan whispered a simultaneous translation in his ear.

'Blah blah blah, official this, official that. When I'm king I'm going to limit the length of proclamations. Now he's setting out the rules. It's a fight to the death, only one victor, no mercy to be shown. No outside help from the crowd. That's it. Now we fight.'

Garvan gave Junk one last look and took his place in the middle of the room facing his father. The king stood there clutching a massive four-bladed broadsword, just like the one Jadris had used to try and behead Garvan back in Ollamah. Mingo shuffled out, hefting Garvan's similar sword, struggling under the weight of it. Garvan moved to help him but the old man refused. This was his duty and he was going to see it through to the end. Everyone waited until the old man reached the centre of the arena and finally presented Garvan with his weapon. Garvan smiled at him and watched him shuffle back again. He turned to his father.

'I'm proud of you, son,' said the king. 'For coming back. For doing your duty. You'll make a fine king, Garvan.'

'Thank you, Father,' said Garvan.

The king turned to the onlookers and made a short speech that Junk, Lasel and Payo–Mestrowe didn't understand, but it generated enthusiastic applause from the crowd and tears from his family. Then the king and

252

his son faced one another. The king raised his sword. Garvan raised his and the duel began.

It was far more ferocious that Junk had anticipated and he couldn't be sure that the king wasn't going to win. He hacked and slashed at Garvan with his broadsword and Garvan had to rely on defensive manoeuvres for the first few seconds of the battle. But soon the king started to tire. He was a powerful and vital-looking man, but not as young as he once was. He swung the broadsword, Garvan blocked it, spun on his heel and moved in for the kill. He brought his sword down repeatedly, forcing his father to take a defensive stance, giving him no opportunity to fight back. Then Garvan saw his chance, kicked the king's legs out from under him and whipped his broadsword swiftly from right to left, thus separating his father's head from his body.

There was a hush in the hall. Garvan froze on the spot and watched as the king's suddenly lifeless body fell first to its knees and then keeled over. His father's head took half a second longer to hit the ground. The fight was over.

In total, it had lasted for just a handful of seconds. The official who had announced the rules earlier appeared again and made an announcement. Even though Junk didn't speak the language, he knew what the man was saying:

'The king is dead, long live the king.'

A great cheer went up around the hall. A pair of servants approached the dead king. Garvan jumped at them and barred their progress. He looked to the long-winded official and asked him if he had fulfilled his duty to the satisfaction of the royal charter. The official looked at the old king's decapitated corpse and agreed he was very dead. Garvan turned to Junk.

'Over to you, Junk,' he said. Junk stood up and all eyes turned to him. Questioning whispers spread around the gathered Edrinites: *Who's he? What's he doing?* Ignoring everything else, Junk focused on the job at hand and a large blue doorway appeared next to the old king's corpse. It started to pulse and then expand, growing fatter. As it progressed over and beyond the king, time started to reverse itself but only within the confines of the coruscating doorway. The king's head shot up into the air. The crowd gasped. The head arced across the arena floor until it found the old king's neck and reattached itself. The rivulets of blood that had flowed out coursed back into the veins whence they had come. The skin around his throat healed itself and the old king let out a cry of surprise. He was alive when he was quite certain he had been about to die.

Garvan turned to the official and asked if there was anything in the royal charter that said the old king had to remain dead. The official stared open-mouthed. He didn't know what to say. A debate started and the old king waded in with his thoughts but Garvan shouted them all down. He pointed out that he had fulfilled his duty. What he did after that was up to him. After all, he was king now. No one could argue with that. His mother was very pleased. She didn't want to be a widow just yet. His father would come around eventually.

Garvan felt much better now all that horrible business of having to lop his father's head off was over and done with. He turned to Junk.

'I owe you so much,' he said.

'That's what friends are for, Your Majesty.'

Garvan smiled. 'Right then,' he said. 'Let's go and get your sister, shall we?'

21

The Palace of Versailles stood swathed in the icy mist of first light. The landscaped gardens encircled it for an acre in every direction. Beyond that the plains of Cul Mallia (once upon a time South America, Argentina to be precise) stretched out to the horizons. Flat, featureless grasslands.

A Roman cohort, numbering just under five hundred soldiers, stood in full battle dress, shields held in one hand, spears in the other. Their most senior officer, Gaius Arrias, the pilus prior, a stocky man with silver hair, glanced around him. He looked at the dewy grass beneath his feet and the clear sky above. He was quite certain that this was Elysium, that he and his men were dead already. They had been chosen by the gods, honoured for their bravery. In Elysium, it is said, a person spends eternity doing whatever it was he loved doing in life, and Arrias loved battle, so here he was preparing to fight once more.

Only two things concerned him. One, he had no memory of dying. One minute he and men had been camped in a field in Gaul, and the next they were here. He assumed he must have died a valiant death in order to be admitted to Elysium, but it bothered him that he couldn't remember it. Or even the battle.

The other concern was everyone else. It appeared that the gods would let just about anyone into Elysium. To the right of Arrias's cohort were Tayanan Pallatans. He had never seen their like. Long knives, like machetes, were their weapon of choice. No armour, just ragged clothes. On the left of the Romans were the Varangian Guard of Constantinople, with their domed helmets and chain-mail aventails. They brandished battleaxes and morning stars. Next to them, samurai eager to redeem themselves and prove their worth to their new daimyo. On the other side of the Pallatans were the Roundheads. Kept away from the Cavaliers, who stood beyond the samurai. In front of, behind and above all of them were the twenty-third-century super-soldiers, wearing full battle-dress exoskeletons, designed to protect and enhance their speed and agility. They hefted boxy machine guns that could fire a thousand rounds a minute and hummed with quiet intensity.

Gaius Arrias had never come across any of these warriors during his lifetime, but he tried not to question it. They had been brought here by the gods just like he had, and who was he to question the gods?

Back in the palace on an upper terrace, far away from the battleground to be, Foster, Ed, Tolfke and Otravinicus stood and watched.

'Maybe they're not coming,' said Otravinicus.

'Of course they're coming,' said Foster. Otravinicus was annoying him. He had annoyed him when they were travelling together and that irritation had quickly resurfaced. Otravinicus was weak, cowardly, conniving and self-serving. He represented everything Foster hated in other people. Mostly because they were character traits he thought he might possess himself, though he made sure never to reflect too deeply on the subject. He never wanted to know for sure if it was true.

'Are you sure it wasn't a dream?' said Ed, and it took all of Foster's self-control not to throw him off the balcony.

'Might I suggest that you just give him what he wants?' said Otravinicus.

'We can't do that,' said Foster.

'But why?' asked Otravinicus.

But before Foster could answer, Ed stood a little straighter and said: 'Something's happening.' They all looked out to the grassland beyond their troops.

A single doorway of blue light appeared for a moment and then vanished, leaving a lone figure. It was Junk, wearing the copper-coloured Antricle armour. It covered his body and head, but left his face exposed. He walked casually and calmly towards the frontline of the emperors' imposing army. Fifteen hundred assorted warriors on one side versus Junk on the other.

*

258

Up on the terrace, Foster and the others looked down on the battlefield. Foster smiled and looked at Ed. Ed smiled back, but both smiles were uneasy.

'This should be quick,' said Ed.

'I thought . . .' said Foster, 'he'd have an army with him.'

'He has an army with him,' said a female voice from behind them. They all whisked around to see Lasel, Payo–Mestrowe and Garvan. Another blue door stood glittering behind them. Tolfke drew a sword and sprang forward to attack. Payo–Mestrowe moved quickly, dodging his thrust and releasing a mighty backhand that lifted Tolfke off his feet and sent him spinning over the edge of the terrace. He fell screaming to the ground below. Otravinicus darted to the balustrade to look over and saw Tolfke lying upside down in a bush, groaning and dazed. His mask had been pulled away to reveal a horribly disfigured face. Otravinicus turned away with a look of revulsion.

'Aren't you supposed to be dead?' said Ed.

'Funny thing happened on the way to the ground,' said Garvan.

'We're here to give you a chance,' said Lasel. 'All we want is Ambeline.'

Foster and Ed shared a look. Silently considering how to handle this.

'Is it just the four of you?' asked Foster. He smirked. 'Against two thousand.' He nodded his head towards his troops.

'More like fifteen hundred,' said Garvan.

'Odds are still in our favour,' said Foster, and with that he pulled a small black box out of his pocket and pressed its lone red button. Somewhere in the grounds a siren blared. It was the signal for the battle to begin. The Roman legionnaires, the Varangian Guard, the Cavaliers, Roundheads, samurai, Pallatans and super-soldiers all started to run towards Junk, all screaming their various battle cries at the top of their lungs. There was a distance of five hundred metres between them. Junk watched impassively as they advanced.

The genetically reprogrammed super-soldiers, the former 82nd Infantry Company, were the quickest by far, aided by their full-body exoskeletons, mechanical rigs made from falakite, the same indestructible synthetic metal that had been used to rebuild the Eiffel Tower in Arrapia/Paris. The rigs were solar-powered, made up of broad strips of falakite that swathed the soldiers' limbs and torsos. Their faces were protected by blast shields that could stop a hundred bullets fired at close range. In twelve tours of duty in the Third Korean War of 2256 the 82nds had suffered zero casualties.

They surged ahead of the others and were bearing down on Junk. Not one of them questioned their orders. Independent thought had been bred out of them on a genetic level. They had a job to do: annihilate the enemy. Didn't matter it was just one kid. They raised their boxy machine guns, which started to power up, emitting a whirring turbine hum, ready to unleash total and utter destruction. So focused were all the soldiers on their target that not one of them noticed the wide blue portal that materialized to their right until it was too late. The portal was larger than normal, about the size of the doors of an aircraft hangar. The soldiers did not become aware of its presence until a twentieth-century Alaskan high-speed goods train rocketed out, scattering snow like dandruff, as it ploughed through them, bellowing like a rabid bull as it went. The ground quaked seismically. Tracks materialized in front of the train as it roared across the plain, obliterating the super-soldiers in its path.

The engineer and conductor in the cramped cabin of the train wailed with fear, confusion and panic as they heard the liquid *crunch-splat-crunch* of the soldiers as they bounced off the iron beast or were sucked underneath. A moment before it had been 1981 and the engineer and conductor had been two hours outside of Juneau, listening to the J. Giles Band singing about a centrefold and thinking about having a cup of coffee. The engineer grabbed the brake handle.

Another large blue doorway opened ahead of the train and it was swallowed up. Seconds later it was back in Alaska, screaming to a stop. The engineer and conductor looked at one another, both wondering if that had really happened. They decided to have whiskey instead of coffee.

Back on the battlefield, what remained of the super-soldiers were freaking out and running in screaming circles, total panic having taken over. Had they seen a train? And if they had, where had it come from? Where did it go? Would it be back? Their commanding officer was the only one to keep her head. She barked orders into a microphone embedded in her helmet and managed to coax the dregs of her company into a defensive huddle. There were just eighteen of them left and they came together in a tight square, backs together, weapons aiming out. Nothing was going to creep up on them.

Another blue doorway popped open a short distance above them and a stampeding herd of snorting, braying brachiosauruses from the Jurassic era thundered out, as startled as the Alaskan train drivers had been that they were no longer where they had been a split second before. The dinosaurs were wide-eyed with terror and their cries started in their bellies, echoing up their jib-like throats before bursting out in a shrill howl of distress. Their mottled orange-brown skin exuded a mustard-green discharge, a panic sweat, and the entire herd, all fourteen of them, seemed to evacuate their bowels simultaneously. Several tonnes of foul-smelling, molten herbivore faeces cascaded down on the huddled super-soldiers, who managed to get off a few shots, which did little but annoy the dinosaurs, who trampled them into the ground. The soldiers' reinforced exoskeletons were crushed as if they were made of dry leaves. Another door appeared to take the startled creatures back to where they belonged.

The rest of Foster and Ed's army stopped in their

tracks. Collectively they had been on a thousand battlefields, but that had been something none of them had seen before.

On the terrace, Foster, Ed and Otravinicus were looking on in disbelief.

'Last chance,' said Lasel. In response, Foster stubbornly pressed the button on his little black box and sounded the horn again. Lasel, Garvan and Payo–Mestrowe stepped back into the portal and vanished. Otravinicus thought about going with them, thinking maybe he had picked the wrong side, but it was too late. The doorway closed. He glanced over the balustrade to where Tolfke had fallen, but now there was no sign of the man in red.

'You have an escape plan, right?' said Otravinicus, turning back to the others. They ignored him. Foster pushed past Ed and went inside. He came back a moment later with a long-barrelled gun. It looked like something the twenty-third-century super-soldiers would have in their arsenal.

'There you go,' said Foster. 'If it looks like we're going to lose, I'll shoot him myself.' He put the rifle to one side and looked back to the field of battle.

Ed edged back towards the palace unnoticed and slipped inside. He crossed to a large safe with nine combination dials on the solid-looking front door but he ignored them, pressed a concealed button and the back panel opened up. Inside was their Antricle in its pyramid formation. He took it out and placed it on a table so that it was close to hand should they need to escape.

Down in the field, the samurai bridled their fear, not of death but of the insanity they had just witnessed, and charged at Junk. They assumed the boy was some sort of warlock. These were just tricks. He was playing with their minds. Let him taste their Japanese steel and see how he played with their minds then.

When the samurai charged, the others did too. The Varangian Guard hated to be left out of a fight. As did the Pallatans. The Romans and the Cavaliers and Roundheads were less eager, but they were jobbing soldiers and this was easily the cushiest gig ever. Plus it was only one boy and some witchcraft. How hard could it be?

The collected soldiers trampled over the remains of the twenty-third-century super-soldiers, most of whom had already been driven into the ground by the weight of the dinosaurs. They converged on Junk, wary of surprises that might jump out on any side of them.

Junk looked at the rampaging hordes impassively. He waited until they were almost on top of him and then he stepped back through an invisible doorway and vanished. The soldiers clattered to a halt and turned around in circles, wondering where the boy had gone.

Junk reappeared almost immediately behind the soldiers. They had effectively swapped positions. He was where they had started and they were where he had started. One of the Roundheads was the first to spot him.

'There he is,' he shouted in a reedy voice and gradually the news spread through the rest and they all turned and started running back the way they had come, roaring in anger now. It would have been almost amusing to any impartial observers but there were none. The only onlookers were Foster, Ed and Otravinicus, and they didn't find it funny at all.

Junk held his hands up and a blue doorway twenty-five metres square appeared high in the sky above his head. Out of it came three Supermarine Spitfires, flying in formation, their wing-mounted Browning machine guns firing already. The cannons sounded like ten thousand babies squalling as divots of earth danced wildly as they strafed the ground, flying directly over the soldiers. The bullets ripped through a hundred of them. It made a noise like a seaside spade hitting wet sand. *Plup-plup-plup!*

The panicked Spitfire pilots pulled up, their Rolls Royce Merlin engines screaming as they did so, and Junk opened another window directly in front of them, through which they disappeared.

Immediately Junk opened a third window to his left and three German Messerschmitt Bf 109s appeared. Like the Spitfires before them they were in mid-attack and their machine guns howled. Another hundred or more soldiers were taken out. Junk opened an exit window and the Messerschmitts were gone.

They were spat out over the skies of England in July 1940. The three German pilots were screaming questions at one another, but before they could get any answers they realized that there were three Spitfires directly behind them. The British opened fire and the Messerschmitts erupted into fireballs.

'Any of you chaps have any idea what just happened?' said the Spitfire commander.

'No idea whatsoever, sir,' came the reply.

'I think we should return to base, don't you? First round's on me.'

The three fighter planes banked to the right and headed for home.

Back on the plains of Cul Mallia, Foster and Ed's soldiers were picking themselves up. Their numbers had been greatly diminished. The remaining Pallatans in particular were raging. They were not used to losing fights and especially one that was so unfair. The Pallatan commander called to his men and directed them to fan out and move in on Junk, coming at him from two sides. They flanked him, getting closer and closer until, on their commander's signal, they charged, machetes held high.

Junk moved his hand and all the Pallatans to his left vanished. They reappeared half a second later on Junk's right and directly in front of their advancing comrades. Reacting on instinct, machetes sliced and chopped and the Pallatans managed to almost wipe themselves out.

Three of the Varangian Guard had used the time when Junk was busy despatching the Pallatans to edge around him. They sprang at him, bringing their battleaxes down on him. There was no time for Junk to move, but in the blink of an eye the Antricle's armoured shell covered his face just as it had done in the Room of Doors. The battleaxes bounced off. His armour was unmarked. The Varangians looked at one another and shrugged. They did what they knew best and set about hacking at armoured Junk with abandon.

Inside his shell, Junk was looking out through his tinted visor. He could see and feel the attack but it didn't hurt. The clanging assaults of the axes echoed inside his suit and he swayed a little.

Outside, the Varangians had stopped striking Junk with their axes and were now hurling themselves against his upright metalled figure, trying to knock him over, but it was if Junk was rooted to the ground. They just bounced off him. They kept going for a few minutes until they were utterly exhausted, gasping for breath and with sweat pouring off them. Suddenly Junk moved his hand in a circle and doorways opened up beneath the guards. They vanished from sight. The armour peeled back from Junk's head.

The other enemy soldiers were watching, wondering what had happened to the Varangians. Then they heard a distant screaming. It took them a moment to realize where it was coming from. The answer was directly above them. They looked up to see the Varangians plummeting to earth. They took out several others when they landed.

There was a lull then. The surviving soldiers, now numbering less than two hundred, looked at each other and at Junk. The siren sounded again from the palace. Suddenly half of the remaining Cavaliers and Roundheads threw down their pikes and other weapons and started to walk away. Away from Junk and away from the palace. They'd had enough. As they left, some of the Roman legionnaires decided to do the same. They threw down their weapons and set off after the seventeenth-century Englishmen.

Of the one thousand five hundred who had been there at the start, now there were about a hundred soldiers still standing their ground. Gaius Arrias took charge of them. He barked his orders in Latin, a language most of them didn't understand, but they fell into formation by following the legionnaires. Junk looked at them. He had to respect their determination, but it was time for this battle to end. He waved his hands in front of him and a hundred blue doorways appeared between him and the persistent soldiers. Cantibean troops in full and glorious orange-and-black battledress stepped through. Their armour sang out in unison as they stood to attention, forming a battle line. Their full-face war-masks sent a shiver of fear through the enemy. Their commanding officer was Jadris, Garvan's brother, clad in his black-and-gold armour. He barked out a command and the Cantibean soldiers fell into formation and raised their weapons: the vanguard with their armoured fists, the main guard with their broadswords, and the rearguard with their multi-barrelled crossbows. They were in perfect synchronization with one another, so well coordinated that it made them even more frightening. They were like one huge organism.

Junk expected the enemy soldiers to surrender or flee now but they didn't. Gaius Arrias ordered them to attack, and attack they did. They charged. Jadris sounded the counter-attack. The vanguard thundered forward, meeting the enemy full on. The armoured fists sent soldiers wheeling into the air and smashing to the floor.

The few warriors who made it through the frontline were met by the main guard with their four-bladed broadswords. No one made it through to the rearguard. The battle was over.

22

Foster and Ed looked down at their defeated troops.

'I think it's time to go,' said Ed. He dashed inside to grab their Antricle but it was no longer on the table where he had left it. He looked around, trying to figure out if in fact he'd put it somewhere else. He crossed to the safe. The concealed panel on the back was still open and the safe was empty. He stopped to think for a moment. He glanced out at the terrace and saw Foster. He realized then that someone was missing.

'Otravinicus,' he said to himself. A door to his left led to an anteroom. Ed tried the door. It was locked. He put his shoulder to it and forced it open. The door swung inwards and he staggered into the room. He was greeted by the sight of the doctor standing in the middle of the Antricle's projected map. Otravinicus looked at Ed.

'Wait,' said Ed.

Otravinicus had no intention of waiting. He stabbed his finger into the circle at the heart of the projection. The moment he touched it bright beams of light shot out and joined together to create a doorway of green light. It moved towards him at speed. Ed ran at him, racing the doorway. He hurled himself at the doctor, but he wasn't fast enough. The portal passed over Otravinicus and in a flash he and the Antricle were gone. Ed let out a bellow of rage. He turned and raced back out to the terrace.

'He's taken it!' he shouted. 'Otravinicus has taken the box.' Ed was shocked to see Foster aiming the long-barrelled rifle down at the battlefield. He had Junk in his sights.

'Did you hear what I said?' asked Ed.

'Shut up, Ed,' said Foster. He was trying to concentrate. The rifle sight zoomed in on Junk automatically. There was little that Foster had to do. It was a smart gun that required little skill from the shooter. At that moment Junk looked straight at Foster, who could see him magnified greatly in his sight. Junk pointed to the sky and it took Foster a moment to realize that Junk was pointing for Foster's benefit. He looked up and cried out, reeling backwards.

Emerging from a vast blue doorway in the sky directly above them was Jadris and Kyril's airship, the one that Junk and the others had first seen back in the snowy wastes of Ollamah. It descended and pivoted to bring it side-about. A dozen cannons pimpled the starboard wall. Foster reacted without thinking. He whipped the rifle up and fired at the airship. Once. The airship fired back, unleashing its horrifying firepower. Foster and Ed threw themselves to the ground as machine gunfire riddled the side of Versailles. A thousand rounds peppered the palace in a matter of seconds, blowing out windows and turning masonry to dust.

Down on the battlefield, Junk looked on in horror. 'NO!' A blue doorway appeared and he leaped through.

A second later he was inside the palace. In the room beyond the terrace. The airship had stopped firing and there was an eerie calm. The little that was left of the floor-to-ceiling velvet curtains fluttered in the wind. The parquet floor was littered with shards of glass, fragments of the brickwork and splinters of the wood from the window frames. Junk stepped carefully through the detritus. He found Ed first. Junk knew straight away he was dead. He was about to despair that his only lead to Ambeline had died in this room when he heard a groan. He shifted a large piece of the ceiling that had dropped down and found Foster. He sat him up and brushed some of the plaster from his face. He looked like he belonged in Versailles, but Versailles in the eighteenth century. His face was floury white and speckled with pimples of blood. It was clear he didn't have long left to live.

'You've lost,' said Junk. 'Tell me where my sister is. Come on, just tell me.'

Foster shook his head. 'I can't,' he said in a barely audible whisper.

'Please,' said Junk. He was almost in tears.

'I can't,' said Foster, 'because I don't know where she is.' Junk hung his head. His journey wasn't at an end. He'd thought he was almost done.

'You took her though?' said Junk. Foster considered his answer for a moment before nodding. 'Tell me why.'

'I knew,' said Foster. 'I knew . . .' He struggled to speak and Junk was worried he was about to expire. '. . . your mother.'

Junk frowned. 'What?' he said. That was the last thing he had expected him to say.

'We were going to be married,' said Foster.

'What are you talking about?' asked Junk. Was Foster playing some sort of game with him? How on earth could he have known his mother?

'In college,' said Foster. 'I loved her. Then one summer she goes travelling to Europe. Meets some Irish guy.' Junk knew he was now talking about his father. 'Writes me a letter saying how she's sorry, but she's in love and plans to live in Ireland now.' Foster coughed and vomited blood down his chin. Junk knew the story of how his parents had met. His mother, Janice, was travelling with her friend Esther, whose grandfather was from Galway. Esther dragged his mother to Ireland. Esther hated it and couldn't wait to get back to the States, but Janice loved it. Loved Ireland and fell in love with his father. She stayed. She married and they had Junk and later Ambeline. Foster continued: 'I jumped on the first plane over to talk some sense into her but it was no good, she was adamant. Tried to pretend she and I were nothing special. I understand. I understand a woman's mentality. How they think. This guy was clearly rich.'

Junk couldn't help but laugh. 'Really not,' he said.

Foster ignored him and carried on talking. 'So I figure all I've got to do is make something of myself and then I'll get her back. That's what she's doing. That's what she's telling me. She was telling me I had the potential to be great but I needed the incentive and that's what she gave me. I realized how much she truly loved me then.'

Junk had to laugh. Foster was utterly deluded.

He went on: 'I stuck around. Headed to London. One job led to another till I'm working for this finance company in Sussex and we go to Yorkshire for a team-building weekend and we find this pyramid box.'

'Yeah, I know the story,' said Junk.

Foster nodded and carried on. 'Once we've got that, then I go back to Ireland to see her, to get her back. I say I've done what you wanted me to. Made something of myself. Something incredible. But she still says no. It doesn't matter. She doesn't care. Says she's got a life there now. Kids. Loves her husband.' Foster waved his hand dismissively as if he didn't really believe that.

Junk thought back to the story of the Nine Emperors that Shaun had told him. He remembered him telling the story about Foster going to visit his great love only to be rejected and it was that rejection that brought them here.

'Tell me why you took my sister,' said Junk.

'To punish her,' said Foster, his bitterness plain to see.

'To punish Ambeline?' said Junk, horrified.

Foster shook his head. 'Janice. She broke my heart.' He shrugged. 'Let's see how she likes it.'

Junk stared down at this shattered, pathetic man and realized that he was the root cause of his suffering. There was a piece of jagged brick on the ground next to them and Junk's fingers curled around it. He wanted to pick it up and smash it into Foster's stupid, insensitive, psychotic face but he didn't. He stopped himself. There was more to find out.

'Got my man Tolfke to hire one of the shark scum. He got the girl, delivered her to Tolfke.' Junk looked around, wondering what had become of the man in red. Was that who he should be talking to? 'Tolfke brought her here.'

'Then what happened?' asked Junk. 'Did you hurt her?'

Foster made a noise in the back of his throat that might have been a laugh, a bitter one. 'She was like a little she-wolf, clawing, biting, screaming. I was terrified of her.'

'Yeah, big man. She was six years old.' Junk grabbed Foster by his front and pulled him towards him. 'Tell me what happened to her. Tell me what you did.'

'Nothing. Nothing happened,' said Foster. 'She ran away.'

'What?'

'I planned to send her back. I didn't want her. I just wanted to hurt Janice like she had hurt me, but the little brat was here less than a day and she got out. She vanished. I've got no idea what happened to her after that.'

Junk stared at him as he spoke. It seemed as if he was telling the truth. He really didn't know what had become of Ambeline. She could be anywhere. There was no guarantee that she was even still alive. That thought chilled Junk's heart. But at the same time it didn't mean she was dead either.

'You must have some idea about what happened to her,' asked Junk imploringly.

Foster shook his head. 'She was just gone.'

That was the last thing Foster said. Junk saw the life fade from his eyes. The Falcon Emperor was dead.

Junk considered that as he walked through the resplendent corridors of Versailles, glancing out at the manicured gardens. Seven of the Nine Emperors were dead. There was Shaun happy in his exile and Danny unhinged on his train, but the rest were all gone. And now his quest to find Ambeline had reached an impasse. When he had found out from Mestrowe that Ambeline was potentially still alive, that had given him a new goal, a new direction: to find the Nine Emperors. Which he had done, but now the trail had ended. Ambeline could be alive or dead, he had no way of knowing, but either way he had no first step on the road to finding her. She could be anywhere, and *anywhere* was big.

His head throbbed. Should he go home now? Take Mestrowe with him. Explain to his parents what had really happened. Why Ambeline had been taken.

Somewhere on the periphery of his consciousness he became aware of a rhythmic *squeak-squeak-squeak*. Junk turned a corner and stuttered to a stop. He looked around at the floors and the walls. Something was wrong. There was pockmarked grey-blue linoleum on the floor, and the walls were two-tone; grubby institutional cream at the top and diarrhoea brown at the bottom. This corridor didn't belong in Versailles.

He took a step back and looked along the length of the passageway he had just walked down. It had been broad with a floor of polished wood mosaic. There had been mirrors on one side, floor to towering ceiling. Royal-blue velvet curtains hung at the windows opposite, but not any more. Now it was the same dirty, restricting corridor as its neighbour.

Junk moved to the window and looked out. A few moments before he had glanced out at a topiary garden. There had been tall lovingly trimmed bushes peppering an immaculate lawn. Now he was looking out on a drab grey car park and a handful of cheap cars, saloons and hatchbacks mostly. Where it had been a bright, cloudless day, now it was drizzling needles of grimy rain that fell diagonally past the pane.

Something was wrong. Something had changed. Where was he? He looked down and saw that he wasn't wearing his Antricle armour any more. He was wearing a cheap, thin tracksuit. The legs were bruise purple with a yellow stripe running down the out-seam and the top was yellow with purple arms. The cuffs of the sleeves were frayed. He was wearing mismatched socks, one black, one blue with orange stripes, and a pair of faded green Crocs that squeaked on the lino as he walked. He looked at his hands. His fingernails had been bitten down till they bled. His skin was pale. Not tanned and weather-roughened as he had been for the last few years.

He became conscious of his breathing. It was getting louder and faster, working towards a panic attack. He didn't understand what this was. What was happening? Then he heard footsteps running towards him. He turned to his left and saw two burly men sprinting his way. His instinct was to move, but when he looked along the adjacent corridor there were three more men coming from that direction. They all wore a uniform of pale blue slacks and matching polo shirt. There was a symbol of a sun and an oak tree on the left breast pocket of each. Was this Pirestus? It didn't look like any part of Pirestus Junk had seen, and these men were most definitely not thirty metres tall or half made of metal.

The five men swarmed over him then, grabbing him roughly and forcing him to the ground, pushing his face into the floor that smelled of disinfectant.

'WHAT ARE YOU DOING? GET OFF ME!' he shouted. They didn't listen. His hands were wrenched behind his back and Junk felt a plastic cable tie being wrapped around his wrists. It was pulled tight. Too tight. He cried out. 'WHERE AM I?'

He felt hot breath in his ear and one of the men, the one who had tied his wrists, was leaning over him. 'You need to calm down now, Colin. You listening to me?' The man spoke with a thick Irish accent. His voice was calm and measured.

'Who are you?' said Junk. 'Where am I? What's happening?'

'It's OK. It's me. It's Jimmy. You're safe but you need to calm down. You listening to me? You're having an episode. A reaction to the new medication the doctor put you on.'

'Medication? What? What are you talking about? Where am I? What's going on?'

'You're fine. You're safe. You're in St Jude's. No one's going to hurt you. We're just going to give you a little shot and calm you down.'

The man, Jimmy, looked to one of his colleagues and nodded. The other man stepped forward holding a syringe, tapping the side of it to get rid of any air bubbles. He stabbed the needle into Junk's upper arm and depressed the plunger. It was all over in a second. Junk's body went limp and Jimmy climbed off.

Junk saw the men in pale blue standing over him. A swarm of bees or at least their shadows were starting to cloud his vision, blackness moving slowly in from the edges.

He heard Jimmy speaking: 'Bit of excitement for your first day there, son.'

'Is it always like this?' asked one of the other men.

'Nah, this one's usually fine,' said Jimmy. 'His name's Colin. Colin Doyle. Been with us for a while now.'

'What did he do?'

'Ah, it's a sad one,' said Jimmy. 'Killed his sister when he was twelve. Threw her off a cliff. Totally delusional, poor little bastard. Come on, let's get him back to the ward.'

Junk felt himself being lifted off the ground and carried. His vision was more dark than light now and he wanted to scream. He wanted to bellow and howl at the top of his lungs so he did. But no one heard him. The scream was just inside his head. And then everything went black.

TO BE CONCLUDED . . .

ACKNOWLEDGEMENTS

I would like to thank Roisin Heycock, Niamh Mulvey, Lauren Woosey and everyone at Quercus. A really outstanding team. A huge thanks to Talya Baker for once again showing me where semi-colons should actually go.

Thank you to Eugenie Furniss and Liane-Louise Smith at Furniss-Lawton for all their hard work on my behalf. And Lucinda Prain and Rob Kraitt at Casarotto-Ramsay for guiding the other half of my working life for me.

Thank you to Isabella Donnachie for sea lions and coffee mugs and Gracie for Jeff the whale.

And thank you to my awesome children, who make me very proud, Joseph, Grace and Gabriel, to the best dog in the world, Harper, and to my amazing, gorgeous wife, Lisa.

Watch out for the final instalment of

THE
LEAGUE
OF
SHARKS
TRILOGY

COMING SPRING 2015 . . .

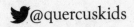